A Den Of Rhyme

A COLLECTION OF AWARD WINNING, OR NEW
SHORT STORIES, AND ONE-ACT PLAYS

CRAIG FARIS

BellaRosaBooks

A DEN OF RHYME
ISBN 978-1-62268-171-6

First printing: June 2022

Cover design by Meghan Bushbacker and Craig Faris.

10   9   8   7   6   5   4   3   2   1

DEDICATION

To my wife, Deena Faris who supported and encouraged me through the years of trying to market and publicizes my first novel. You are the best thing that ever happened to me.

And to my children, Katie Faris and Charlie Faris who gave me the inspiration to write these stories.

And to my friends, who read my work, encouraged, and believed that I had a talent for telling stories. Thanks for the reviews and kind words.

ACKNOWLEDGMENTS

This book would not have been possible without the support and assistance from the following:

To my publisher, *Rod Hunter* of Bella Rosa Books, who believed that theses short stories in a collection would make a great book along with a series of standalone short stories.

To my current and former editors: *Maureen Angell, Rod Hunter, Lona Gilmore, Ann Cox*, and the late *Toni Child* and *Susan Parrado*. You guys taught me how to write. Thanks for finding all of those missing words, fixing my horrible spelling, and correcting my atrocious grammar. I couldn't have done it without you.

To the original members of my South Carolina Writers Workshop (now Association) critique group:

Gwen Hunter, aka Faith Hunter, who first saw promise in my first novel, which thankfully remains unpublished, and rightly so. Your encouragement that I try shorter fiction is why this book is being published today. You still remain my inspiration and mentor.
Dawn Cook , aka *Kim Harrison,* you were the first of us to reach the dream and boy did you ever show the way with your Kim Harrison series, and multiple New York Times Bestsellers. Thank you, and Tim, again for your original writing desk and your encouragement throughout the years.

Misty Massey, for all of your great critiques and instructions on how to "show, don't tell. I still use those rules in every story."

Melissa Hinnant, wherever you are, thanks for all of those wonderful literary images I'll never forget.

Norman Froscher, thanks for sharing the use of your name in my first published novel.

To all the former and current members of the SCWA critique group: *Betty Beamguard, Grace Looper, Donna Wylie, Martha Robinson, Claire Iannini, Ed Green, Roxanne Hanna, Becca Dickinsion, Carol Taggart, Kim Boykin, Laura & Andy Lawless, Pat FitzGerald, Liz Bankhead, Pete Hildebrand, Kim Hyclak, Scott McBride, Steve Denison, Susan Bosscawen, Bill Childers,* and all of you who took the time to read many of these short story selections, thank you for those wonderful words of encouragement.

To my biggest fans, *Dianne Hutchins Hall,* the late *Susan Starnes Parado,* and *Mark Nunn,* who believed that I had a future in writing before anyone else did.

To *Brenda McClain.* Author of One Good Mama Bone, you are perhaps the most gifted author I've ever met. Thanks for remaining such a supportive friend. You're my Harper Lee.

To *PJ Woodside* who took my manuscript of *The Spectrum Conspiracy,* and made it come to life in her live action book trailer. Now we'll need another one for this book, and I couldn't ask for a better director.

To *Mr. Richard Curtis, Sulay Hernandez* and *Ted Tally,* for taking time to out of your busy schedule to read my work, and for going out of your way to offer references, reviews, and recommendations.

To all of you who have permitted me to bring my characters to life by allowing the use of parts of your name. You know who you are, just read the stories.

To the following York Technical College graphic design students who allow us to include their designs on the facing pages of each short story. They are:
   Christiaan Volstead, for **A Legacy in Secret**.
   Kayla Porter, for **Last Run to Broad River**.
   Ethan Hoover, for **Dawn's Last Gleaming**.

Shade Thomas, for **The Ground Before Zero**.
Julia Graham, for **Silent Assault**.
Christiaan Volstead, for **Big Daze**.
Alaina Preslar, for **A Pretty Good Year**.
Mia J. Macy, for **Souls of the Abyss**.
Stephen Simpson, for **Echoes From the Ether**.
Michaela Krug, for **Grand Slam**.
Jillian Pauline, for the **Guatemala Header & Billboard Design**.
Meghan Bushbacker, for **The Guatemalan Antidote**.
Stanley Todd Robertson, for **Cinders in the Attic**.
Meghan Bushbacker, for **Den of Rhyme Short Story**.
Meghan Bushbacker, for **A Den of Rhyme Story Collection's Full Cover**.

Finally, to my family, who continued to love me, despite the long hours, the countless disappointments and setbacks. I love you all.

TABLE OF CONTENTS

A DEN OF RHYME

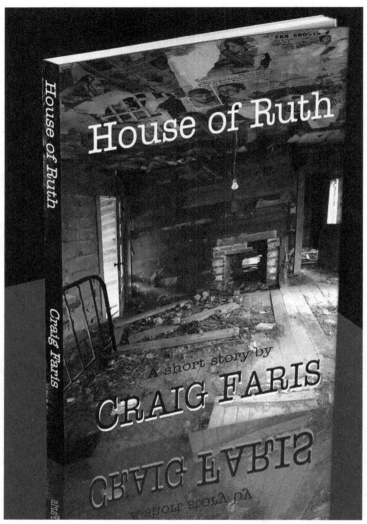

Cover design by Craig Faris.

House of Ruth – Synopsis

In 1972, three teenagers find a cryptic message on a crumbling newspaper article glued to the ceiling of an old abandoned house. Deciphering it reveals the story of the 1949 shooting of an all-star first-baseman, and leads them to a long forgotten secret. Their discovery forces them to confront their own fears, emotions and prejudices, leaving them with the last thing they ever expected.

HOUSE OF RUTH

Lucy was born on the right side of the tracks, I on the left, but I was still smitten as the three of us ran down that railroad bed in 1972, crossties beneath our feet, and how their varying heights commanded hypnotic concentration. My buddy Dan, who was used to running, led Lucy and me by about ten paces. The hot September sun and the high humidity of South Carolina's piedmont did little to quell our excitement as we neared the site of the old abandoned crossing.

A paper mill, built in the late '50s, replaced the houses and farms that had once occupied the left side of the tracks. On the right side, countless acres of trees and kudzu vines had returned those farms to a wilderness.

"Hold up," I called out to Dan. "This is it."

The three of us slowed to a walk, gulped in air, and wiped the sweat from our faces with our shirttails. I caught a glimpse of Lucy's bra and smiled at Dan. It was amazing how a brief sight of white material could send the testosterone surging through our veins. Lucy either didn't notice or didn't care. She was one of us.

"So, where is it?" Dan said. He was incredibly smart and athletic, playing on the varsity teams for baseball, basketball, and football, but his hair was never neat. Maybe he had some of Einstein's genes.

I unfolded an old aerial photograph taken in the 1950s from my back pocket, and nodded toward a fence post barely visible under the dense growth. "The old road bed follows that fence line to the right," I said. "She's about three hundred yards into the woods." I pointed to a small, white rectangle in the photo. "That's the roof of the house. The barn is gone."

"My dad said all of those houses were either moved or burned back in '57," Lucy said.

"This one survived. I saw it yesterday."

Dan looked at the vines and shook his head. "We'll need a weed cutter."

"Aw, it's not that bad. Come on."

We were seventeen—young, bored, and eager for the adventure.

The sunlight faded under the thick canopy of undergrowth as we forged our way through a twisted mass of honeysuckle, kudzu vines, and briers taller than we were.

Lucy's shoulder-length, brown hair got tangled in a brier, and I stopped to help her free it. "I can't believe my parents lived down this road," she said. "I was only a baby when they moved."

Lucy was our "girl next door" even though she lived about a mile from my home. She was pretty, the youngest of three sisters, and a tomboy. She could hit a softball farther than most of the men on our church league, and she ran like an antelope. It was all I could do to keep up with her and several of my cuts and scrapes were owed to the fact that her rear was far more interesting to watch than the crossties my toes encountered.

We followed the old roadbed away from the railway, the thicket soon giving way to non-native plants that had once occupied a front yard. The yard was now only an overgrown clearing with a wall of vines at one end.

"That's it," I announced. Except for a rusted tin roof, the wall of kudzu completely covered the aging structure.

Lucy furrowed her brow. "We're going in there?"

"We didn't come all this way for nothing." Dan led us around the left side of the house where the briers were thinner. There, the side porch had collapsed level with the ground and a back door stood ajar. With cautious apprehension, we crept across the rotted porch and stepped inside.

A quarter inch of gray dust covered the floors and counters in the kitchen. Despite years of neglect, the tin roof had kept the main structure dry and the floor seemed sturdy. Vines covering the windows shaded most of the sunlight and every windowpane had long since fallen from their rotted sashes. Down a hallway, we entered an empty room, its walls and ceilings covered with brown, peeling newspapers.

"Some wallpaper," Lucy said. "This is downright creepy."

"They used newspapers as insulation in winter," I explained. "See, they kept adding layer upon layer over the years."

Dan, who grew up in California, had never seen anything like it. An old fireplace stood against the interior wall, and Dan ventured through a small closet doorway that opened into another room. "Hey, guys, I think I found the bridal suite."

We followed his voice through the closet and found him staring up at a ceiling covered in decaying newspapers. Beside him, in the center of the room, was a broken cast-iron bed frame, its rusted springs standing against one wall. A bare, dusty light bulb dangled from a twisted wire over the foot of the bed, and Lucy clicked the switch as if expecting it to glow to life.

"Look at this." Dan began reading aloud from a newspaper headline glued to the ceiling directly over the bed. "PHILLIES FIRST-BASEMAN SHOT BY DERANGED FAN." A photo of an attractive brunette behind prison bars accompanied the article.

"Leave it to you to find the sports page," Lucy said.

"This sounds strangely familiar." Dan read the story aloud. "Ruth Ann Steinhagen, 19, invited first-baseman Eddie Waitkus to her room at Chicago's Edgewater Beach Hotel with a note saying she had a big surprise for him. Waitkus entered the room, where Steinhagen shot him pointblank in the chest with a .22 caliber rifle. Saying that if she couldn't have him, no one would, Steinhagen called an ambulance and held Waitkus's bloody hand until the police arrived. A former Chicago Cub, Waitkus, age 30, played in the 1948 All Star Game before being traded to the Philadelphia Phillies in December."

Dan, who played first base on our varsity team, looked at us, "I've read about this somewhere."

"That's horrible," Lucy said. "Did he live?"

"I don't know. The rest of the article has disintegrated."

At our feet, the floor was littered with scraps of newspaper that had turned brown and crumbled to dust, any missing pieces of the article crushed beneath our shoes.

"Maybe we can find that article in a library," I said. "What's the date?"

"Looks like June 15, 1949 or '47. I'm not sure which."

"What are those circles, squares, and triangles for?" Lucy was pointing to pencil marks scribbled on the page.

Neither Dan nor I had noticed the faint symbols drawn around various letters in the article. Dan and Lucy studied them closely as I examined the surrounding papers on the ceiling. None had similar marks.

"I think a girl did these," Lucy said. "See how she looped the ends of her circles like I do?"

"*Right!*" I immediately regretted my sarcasm when she glared at me.

"This is some sort of code," Dan said. "Anyone have a pencil?"

I rummaged through the kitchen cabinets, finding a broken grease pencil, while Lucy found a faded clothing receipt in a closet to write on. The light was quickly fading as Dan jotted down the symbols and letters.

"It's getting kind of late, guys." Lucy's voice was edgy. "Maybe we should come back when we have more time."

Exiting the house, we retraced our trail back to the railroad by the last rays of sunlight. All the way home, we speculated about the article and the symbols.

"Maybe Ruth broke out of prison and was hiding there," Lucy suggested.

"More likely just some kid who was a fan of Waitkus," Dan said.

Before heading to our respective homes, Lucy and I promised to ask around, while Dan tackled the code. That night, I showed my parents the aerial photograph and told them about the old house and newspaper article we had found.

"Do you remember who lived there in the early '50s?" I asked.

Mom was putting dinner on the table. "I'm pretty sure that Mrs. Ratterree used to rent out that house after she moved to town."

"Did anyone named Steinhagen ever live there?" It was a stupid question. An escapee would surely use an alias.

"I have no idea. There was a lady who did washing and ironing. I think she had a teenage daughter with long, brown hair."

I brightened. "Do you remember her name?"

"It's been twenty years, son."

After supper, Lucy called to confirm that the house wasn't on their former property. Other than that, she hadn't learned anything. We chatted a while about the mystery and school until I ran out of ideas to keep her on the phone. It was nice having a girl call me even though she was just "one of the guys." I finished my homework and called Dan before I went to bed.

"Each symbol spells out a different word," Dan explained as if code breaking was an everyday task. "It's really simple, but the letters are scrambled and whoever did this apparently couldn't spell."

"How do you know?"

"Because the first word was only three letters. The other two don't make sense."

"What did it say?"

"Big," he said.

I went to sleep trying to picture how the baseball player must have felt when he saw Steinhagen's rifle pointing at his chest. The story had filled my mind with all kinds of questions, but not a single answer. Obviously, she was crazy and why would anyone choose that particular article to write a coded message? Maybe Lucy was right and Ruth did escape. After much tossing and turning, Dan's call woke me at 7 a.m.

"I think I've got it," he said. "First I have to look up something in the library. I'll explain at lunch."

The minutes and hours at school seemed to creep by until; finally, the lunch bell rang. Lucy and I met in the hall and raced to the cafeteria where Dan was waiting.

"She spelled the second word SIRPRIZE with an 'i' and a 'z'!" he said.

"She?" Lucy nudged me with her elbow. "I see someone agrees with my loopy circles."

"I knew this story sounded familiar," Dan said, "then I remembered this baseball novel I once read called *The Natural*." He held up a copy of the book. "It was written in 1952 by Bernard Malamud, and the fore-word said it was based on the Waitkus shooting."

"Did it say what happen to Ruth?" Lucy asked.

"No. Look, I don't know who lived there, but whoever it was took a keen interest in this story." He tapped his index finger on the book. "That article is like a treasure map."

"Treasure?" I said. "How?"

"Because of the *third word*; actually, it was two misspelled words. That's why it took me so long to decipher it."

"Well, what was it?" we asked, cold chills rising.

"Big Surprise," Dan said. "Root Cellar!"

Returning to the house took us twice as long due to the shovels, picks, and flashlights we had to carry. It was nearly 7 p.m. by the time we arrived, and the house seemed even darker and creepier. Before go-ing inside, Dan got on his knees and shined his flashlight under the crawl space.

"There's a ladder going down into an open pit," he said. "It's near the fireplace."

A breeze caused the shreds of newspaper to cast eerie shadows in our flashlight beams as we entered, and the air had turned unseasonably cool. We found a trapdoor in the floor of the closet between the two bedrooms, and it took two of us to pry it loose while Lucy held the flashlight. The rusted hinges squealed in protest as the door unveiled a net of spider webs that covered the opening and inky blackness beyond. Dan brushed them aside and tested his weight on the ladder's top rung.

"Come on, guys," he said. "It's just a hole."

"Just a hole," I kept repeating until my foot found the dirt floor ten feet down. A large hole, that's all it was, dug into the red clay and littered with dried cornhusks, rusted farm tools, and moldy, broken furniture. Above us, spider webs hung from every floor joist—an ideal hatchery for the Brown Recluse, the Black Widow, and whatever else might crawl, or slither into a cool cellar on a hot day.

I held the ladder as Lucy descended into my arms. She turned, looked into my eyes, and rewarded me with a hug and a quick kiss on the lips—our first.

We took a step forward and a small rabbit shot out from behind an old bucket causing our heart rates to leap as it ran up a mat of dead vines and out of the cellar. We each took a deep breath and tried to hide our anxiety with grins since it wasn't cool to show fear.

Everything was covered with dust and leaves, and we searched for ten minutes before finding an old trunk half-buried under junk in one corner. Clearing it off, we nervously pointed three flashlight beams on the lid as Dan used his shovel to break the lock.

Reaching for the hasp, we had no idea if the trunk would make us all fabulously wealthy, or subject us to decades of sleepless nights. Despite these misgivings, we slowly, carefully opened a lid into the past.

Forty-one years after reading that headline glued to the ceiling over Ruth's bed, I was looking at the exact spot where it had once been. The newspapers had vanished to dust, but incredibly, after sixty years of neglect, the house was still standing, eerie as ever, the trapdoor still open. No way was I venturing down that ladder in its current state.

I thought of Lucy and how that first kiss was also our last. It was just a kiss, and, as a friend, I think she sensed my fear and knew exactly how to calm it. It certainly worked, but there were other reasons. Her family was well educated; mine where mill workers, and even in the '70s there was a social prejudice that frowned on such unions. Still, looking into that hole, I wish I had listened to my heart instead of my parents, since I have never forgotten our brief moment together at the foot of that ladder.

In my hand was a newspaper obituary Dan sent which answered some lingering questions from our night in the root cellar. Now a Ph.D. and living in Illinois, Dan wrote that his wife taught in Chicago near the site of the old Edgewater Beach Hotel. The hotel was long gone, but his research revealed that Eddie Waitkus survived Ruth Steinhagen's attack. He helped the Phillies win the pennant in 1950, while Steinhagen spent three years in a mental institution. Waitkus recovered but was never the same. His marriage failed, and he spent his latter years looking over his shoulder while drowning his anxiety with alcohol. He died of cancer on September 16, 1972, the *same day* we found the root cellar.

To my surprise, Ruth Steinhagen's obituary revealed that after her release, she lived a reclusive life another sixty years with her sister in

Chicago, mere blocks from her crime scene. She even autographed several copies of Bernard Malamud's book, *The Natural,* which became quite valuable. She died on December 29, 2012, so the only part of Ruth Steinhagen that ever entered this house was her photo on her story glued to the ceiling. But that newspaper article became an inspiration for another unstable girl sleeping in the bed beneath it.

I don't know what we expected to find in that trunk, but it wasn't someone's bones or a treasure. What we found was a diary from 1950, and a moldy, moth-eaten uniform from a minor-league baseball team called the Durham Rams. The diary's pages revealed the sad story of Ruth Burns—a poor, uneducated girl, whose abusive mother and obsessive love for a baseball player nearly led her to suicide.

Burns wrote that she had attended a Rams baseball game while spending the previous summer with her cousin in Raleigh. It had only taken a smile from the pitcher, Tommy Sands, to captivate her heart, and throughout the following year she schemed of ways to win him over. The opportunity finally presented itself on a summer trip to Myrtle Beach, which coincided with a Rams game in the area. Following Steinhagen's example, Burns lured Tommy Sands to her motel room with the words "Big Surprise" scribbled across a partially nude photo of herself. Her plans for Tommy, however, were interrupted when her mother burst into the room. Tommy fled with only his socks, leaving Ruth with just her fragile sanity, the treasured uniform, and his baseball card.

That night in the root cellar, Lucy had sat on a bucket reading the pages of Ruth's diary under the fading light of our flashlight beams. She couldn't understand why Ruth would leave her precious trunk buried in a cellar and the cryptic message on her ceiling. None of us understood until the last page. Like Steinhagen, Ruth wanted the one thing she couldn't have, but decades of prejudice made that impossible. She had to flee, and her trunk had to disappear because it contained the evidence of her crime.

I can only imagine Ruth Burns standing here in her bedroom with all her bags packed, staring up at this ceiling from the middle of her broken, iron bed frame with bruises on her face and tears in her eyes. The cryptic message might have been a cry for help, a message to Tommy, or maybe she just wanted someone to know the truth—to know she existed.

We found Tommy's baseball card with her last entry in the diary. It said, "I'M PREGNANT."

It seems like nothing now. But this was 1950. It was the Deep South. And the Durham Rams were in a Negro league.

House of Ruth has won eight literary awards, including Fourth
Place, (out of 11,800 entries) in the 80th Annual Writers Di-
gest International Writers Competition. In 2007, it received an
Honorable Mention, (28th place out of 19,500 entries) in the
76th Annual Writers Digest International Writers Competition.
It was also a four-time finalist in the William Faulkner/
William Wisdom Pirates Alley short story competition in
2010, 2011, 2012, and a 2014 Shortlist Finalist. In 2014 it
placed second in the York County Arts Council's Literary
Competition.

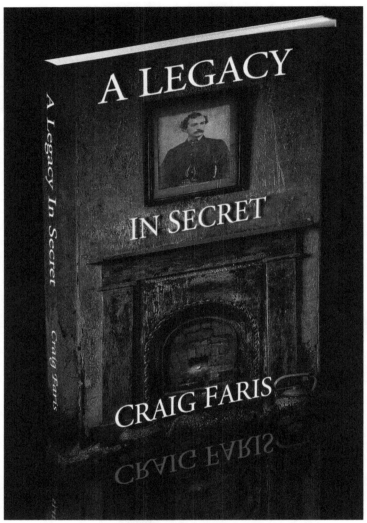

Cover design by Christiaan Voldstad.

A Legacy in Secret – Synopsis

In 1974, seventeen-year-old Jane Connor learns that she is heir to a family legacy that has been passed down from generation to generation, and that her family was tied directly to one of the most shocking crimes ever committed in the United States. Now she must decide if she should honor the wishes of her great, great grandmother, or cash in on what could be a priceless artifact.

A Legacy In Secret
Fiction

1974

Seventeen-year-old Jane Connor parked her father's Oldsmobile in the driveway and walked to the front door, a canvas bag at her side. She rang the doorbell twice as she waited for her elderly grandmother to answer, and was greeted with a warm hug. A scent of stale cigarettes hung in the room as she was led to a couch in the parlor.

"Can I get you a Coke®, Jane?" Grandma Toni asked, already heading toward the ancient kitchen.

"Thanks." There was no refusing. Her grandmother had invested heavily in Coca-Cola® and cigarette stocks, and it was rumored she had made a killing.

Grandma Toni returned with two glasses of cola and Jane placed hers on the rickety coffee table in front of her. Her grandmother eased into a threadbare recliner, its tan cover now brown from years of smoke. Toni lit a cigarette, put it to her lips and washed the smoke down with a swig of cola. The nicotine and caffeine were making their own killing.

"Mom says you're trying to quit," Jane said.

"Your mother says a lot, but I'm nearly eighty, and at this point it isn't going to make any difference. So what brings you here on this fine Saturday?"

"Actually, I was wondering about my middle name."

Grandma Toni raised an eyebrow and reached for an overflowing ashtray.

"No one else in our family has the name Surratt, and Mom said I needed to talk with you about that."

"I see. Well, Surratt was the maiden name of my grandmother, Anna, who died in 1904. Why the sudden interest in your genealogy?"

"We've been studying the Civil War in history class, and yesterday I found this picture." Jane retrieved a thick book from her bag, opened it on the coffee table between them, and slid the book towards her grandmother. "She looks just like me, and the caption says 'Mary Elizabeth

Surratt.' So, I was wondering if we're related."

Toni adjusted her glasses and examined the photo. "Yes, the resemblance is uncanny. I had forgotten how much she looked like you."

"But you said your grandmother's name was Anna, not Mary."

"My dear, Anna was Mary's daughter."

Jane's eyes widened. "What? You mean I'm like the great, great, great granddaughter of a murderess? She helped kill Abraham Lincoln, for God sake!"

"Jane," Toni said, her voice calm, "Mary didn't kill anyone. John Wilkes Booth and his conspirators stayed at her boardinghouse. Where's the crime in that?"

"But our teacher said she helped Booth escape. There was this Mr. Lloyd who testified at her trial. He said she took Booth's rifles to some town called Surrattsville, but we can't find it on any atlas."

"The town was renamed after the assassination. It's now called Clinton, Maryland. Jane, you have to realize that the country had just fought a bitter war, the president was assassinated, and Booth was killed while being captured. The government wasn't interested in justice. They wanted vengeance."

"How do you know she was innocent?"

Toni smiled and exhaled a ring of smoke. "Because Grandma Anna told me. She lived in the boardinghouse with Booth. Actually, I think she was in love with him."

"This is so weird! It's like over a hundred years ago, yet you actually spoke with an eyewitness?"

"Many times. I was only ten when Grandma Anna died, but I remember our conversations like it was yesterday. She told me many secrets."

"Were those her . . . legacy?" Jane asked.

Toni crushed out the cigarette. "Where did you hear that?"

"Last night I overheard Daddy say, 'she'll fill her head with that cock -in-bull story about the legacy.'"

"Your mother runs her mouth," Toni said curtly. "She always did. I knew she couldn't keep it from your father. I was right not to entrust the story with her, much less the locket."

Jane leaned forward. "What locket?"

Toni sighed. "I suppose you're old enough, but if I tell you this, you must promise me three things."

"Of course."

"No." Toni lowered her voice. "This is *serious*, Jane. Will you give me your solemn vow that you will follow these instructions to the letter?"

"I will," she said. "You have my word."

"Your word is your greatest bond. Remember that." Toni lit another cigarette. "First: The legacy can *only* be entrusted to your daughter or your son's daughter. Anna knew that only a woman would fully understand, and it's been passed down from daughter to granddaughter and so on." Toni sipped her cola. "Second: You must not disclose the contents of the locket to anyone until at least one-hundred years after Anna's death. That would be October, 2004. Understand?"

Jane nodded. "Why?"

"That was Anna's last request." Toni took another drag and exhaled. "Third: You may *not* use the locket or the legacy for personal gain. As a relic, it would now be priceless. It can either be donated to a museum or destroyed. Those are your only options. Will you swear to carry out her instructions exactly as I've indicated?"

"I will." Jane closed her eyes. "So help me God."

Grandma Toni reached for her Bible and opened it to her family tree. "This is difficult to remember, so I'll start at the beginning."

"She was born Mary Elizabeth Jenkins in 1823, and at only seventeen, she married twenty-seven-year-old John H. Surratt. They had three children, Issac, who never married, your great Grandmother Anna, and John Surratt Jr. In 1852, the Surratt's bought 287 acres thirteen miles southeast of Washington City. They built a two-story tavern, and the area became known as Surrattsville. They were successful, and in 1853 John expanded by buying a boardinghouse in Washington for $4000. An enormous sum at that time," Toni said.

"Then the war came, and in August of 1862, Mary's husband, John, took ill and died. Mary tried desperately to pick up the pieces, but was left deep in debt. In October of 1864, Mary rented the tavern to John Lloyd, a former policeman, and moved her family to the boardinghouse in Washington. To make money, she rented every spare room.

During the war, Mary's son, John Jr., became a Confederate spy. In January of 1865, John introduced Mary and Anna to the stage actor John Wilkes Booth. He was charming, attractive, and single, with devout Southern opinions. Anna was only twenty years old and both Anna and Mary found him captivating. Booth became a frequent visitor to the boardinghouse and brought others with him. From later testimony we learned that Booth, John Jr., and the others had designed a plot to kidnap Lincoln and hold him for ransom to negotiate better terms for the South.

On April 11, Mary traveled to Surrattsville with one of her boarders and on the way met John Lloyd, who had leased her tavern. Lloyd later testified that Mary said, "The shooting irons will be needed soon." On April 14, she again traveled to Surrattsville to deliver a package containing Booth's field glasses, but Mary never knew what was in the package. She was just doing Booth a favor. That night, Lincoln was assassinated, and on April 17, Mary was arrested and charged with conspiracy to aid the assassins. At her trial, Mary said she knew nothing of Booth's plans and that her trips were only to collect the money Lloyd and others owed her. Lloyd's testimony was enough to convict her, and on July 7, 1865, Mary Surratt stood on the gallows with three other conspirators. When the floor fell away, she became the first woman to be executed in the United States."

"She was only forty-two," Toni said.

"Why did Lloyd lie about her involvement?" Jane asked.

"Lloyd had been arrested himself. The prosecution needed a witness, and Lloyd's testimony was his ticket out of prison. The law back then stated that if a witness testified against a fellow conspirator, he couldn't be prosecuted. Plus, no one ever expected them to execute a woman. With Mary in prison, Lloyd could avoid his $500 lease payments for years. That's a pretty big motive."

"That bastard!" Jane said. "Why would they accept the word of Lloyd, who gave Booth the firearms and was clearly involved in the assassination, over a woman who simply owned the boardinghouse?"

"Because it was a ploy by the prosecutor to lure Mary's son, John Surratt Jr. back to stand trial after he had fled to Canada. You see, John Jr. was involved in the plot to *kidnap* Lincoln, but when that failed, he wouldn't go along with Booth's assassination plans. John Jr. knew that if he returned he would be hanged, but he never expected them to actually hang his mother."

"What happened to him?" Jane said.

"He fled Canada and a year later was arrested in Alexandra, Egypt by American officials. He was returned to stand trial in 1867. But since the prosecution had no evidence that John Jr. was involved in the killing, it ended in a mistrial and he was released."

"What about the locket?" Jane asked.

"The day before Mary was hanged; Anna went to the White House to plea for mercy. President Johnson refused. That night, Anna was allowed to say a few parting words to her mother. Mary told her about a locket hidden within the fireplace hearth and that its contents must never be revealed. Several days later, Anna discovered the gold locket, underneath a loose brick where Mary had indicated. It was inscribed with the initials J.W.B. Anna read the letter inside, but because of her grief for Mary, she couldn't bring herself to destroy it. It remained hidden there until the 1950s when the building fell into disrepair. When I read that the boardinghouse might be torn down, I retrieved it myself."

"You have it?" Jane asked.

"My attorney has it. When I die, it's your responsibility to protect her legacy."

Jane nodded.

"That's enough for now," Toni said. "I'm tired and we'll have plenty of time to discuss this later."

2004

They never did. Within a month, Toni died of a stroke, a cigarette still clutched between her lips. She was buried in Mount Olive Cemetery only a hundred yards from Mary Surratt and Anna's headstones. At the reading of the will, Jane received a manila envelope containing Toni's Bible and the locket. Honoring Anna's request, she kept it hidden for thirty years. On the evening of October 24, 2004, a glass of wine in hand, Jane reread Mary's legacy one last time.

April 13, 1865

Dearest Mary,

I received your note of April 11th and can only concur that Dr. Mudd, being an honorable man, would have no reason to mislead you in this issue. I accept full responsibility for my actions in February and any blame is mine alone. I can only offer the feeble excuse of excess of drink and your beguiling beauty in the candlelight.

Fearing that my actions would only bring ruin and shame upon your family, I have endeavored to dissuade Anna's affections toward me, and to distance myself from you, less temptation overcome me again.

Yet, this news has renewed my faith that the hand of Providence is guiding me forward, and God makes no mistakes.

If you are willing to accept me, take the package to Surrattsville tomorrow and await my arrival. If you decline, I shall know your answer.

Our cause is just, the opportunity is at hand, but if perchance I do not survive to look upon you again, please name the child Edwin Brutus after my brother, or Elizabeth for your mother.

Rest assured that I shall fulfill my obligations to God, country and you. Should they prove successful, we shall be united as husband, wife and child in our new country.

My invitation awaits only your blessing. Until that moment,

I am yours,
J. Wilkes Booth

Grandma Toni was right. The letter was priceless, but Jane had given her word. The gold locket would be donated to the Surrattsville Museum in Clinton, Maryland. Booth's letter would not. She put down her wine, held a corner of the paper to a lighted match, and watched blue flames consume Mary's greatest secret.

That night, after one-hundred-thirty-nine years, they could all rest in peace.

Cover design by Kayla Porter and Craig Faris.

Last Run to Broad River - Synopsis

On a foggy early morning in 1980, Len Durant Broome stepped aboard a consist of four diesel locomotives at the head of a one hundred and twelve car freight and pulp wood train, weighing over 14,000 tons. He was a month away from retirement, but this would be the last run he would ever make.

LAST RUN TO BROAD RIVER
Based on a True Story

September, 1980

The impact was deafening. The front windows and side doors exploded as pulpwood logs came crashing through, filling the cab of the GP40 locomotive with wood, shards of broken glass, and bark. Len Durant Broome took a deep breath and opened his eyes. A heavy log lay across his back, and his right shoulder ached from hitting the bulkhead. His heart was pounding, his hands clammy, and his forehead dripped beads of sweat. The sound of the splintering logs, the grinding steel, and the memory of a quick muffled scream echoed through his head. Dust filled the cab, burning his eyes with the overwhelming smell of pine rosin. Incredibly, the engines had not derailed. The vibration told him the diesel engines were still running wide-open and something, probably logs, was bumping along the cross ties beneath the traction motors.

L.D. was a big man, with soft broad cheeks usually covered in a day's growth of stubble. He wore overalls, a plaid shirt, and an old NASCAR jacket. Lying under him was his brakeman, Vic 'Shade Tree' Goodman. Vic was thirty-eight years his junior, and L.D. had tried to shield the younger man by covering him with his body.

"You alright?" L.D. asked.

"Will be when you get your lard-ass off of me," Goodman said.

L.D. shifted his weight, pushing the log off his back. There wasn't room to even stand. Goodman squeezed out from under him and surveyed the demolished cab. "Jeez, we didn't derail?"

"Not yet, but from the sound of those engines we're still at Run 8."

"Wide open? What the hell are we waiting for? Shut them down!"

L.D. pointed to a mangled pile of metal on the right side of the cab. "That's what's left of the control stand."

Goodman's eyes grew wide. "What about the emergency brakes?"

L.D. again nodded at the pile. "The controls are gone."

What little color there was in Goodman's face vanished. "We're on a runaway?" His voice breaking on the last syllable.

L.D. hated explaining the obvious. "There's fourteen thousand tons of train behind us, Shade Tree, and we're at Run 8. It's four miles down-hill to the Broad River and by the time we round the curve at the bridge she'll be running at over ninety. You figure it out."

"But the bridge . . . it should handle it, right?"

"The maximum rating on the bridge is fifty. If we even make it to the bridge, we'll shake it apart before we're halfway across and it's a hundred-twenty-foot drop into the river."

"You're scaring me, Head," Goodman said.

"Nothing like a little fear to bring out a man's faith, is there?"

"There must be something we can do?"

"I suppose you could jump out that window." L.D. nodded toward the opening in the left side of the cab. "Probably break every damn bone in your body, but you won't drown."

"Let's do it. Sounds better than going off a bridge."

L.D. shook his head. "I've been out that window once. Wasn't something I care to ever do again, so I think I'll take my chances riding this one down."

The radio on his belt crackled and L.D. put it to his ear.

"What did we hit, Head?" came the voice of his conductor.

"Cut yourselves loose, boys. We just hit a pulpwood truck at Carlisle. Brakes are gone; engines," he hesitated, "engines are wide open. Looks like I'm making the last run to Broad River."

"Don't do it, Head. You can jump!"

L.D. switched it off. They couldn't possibly understand what it was like to jump from a train at this speed.

Goodman pushed his way up through the tangled web of pulpwood and crawled toward the rear door. He turned and looked back at L.D. "I'm not going to die like this."

L.D. sat up and put his back against the bulkhead. This wasn't how he had pictured it, either. He thought of his wife. She would be sitting at the kitchen table about now, dressed in her robe, sipping her first cup of coffee. It was still dark when he had signed in at the train depot in Ab-beville. Two hours that now seemed a lifetime.

"You coming?" Goodman asked.

"Take care, Shade Tree. Tell my wife . . . Well, she'll know."

Early that morning L.D. had looked over the track bulletins of the day's run as he ambled into the freight agent's office. Derrell Caldwell had a phone receiver to each ear, yet she managed a friendly smile and nodded at the coffee maker across the room. "Help yourself, Head," she mouthed.

He filled his coffee thermos and smiled at the moniker. Every crewman had one. Nicknames like "Sheep-head," "Screamer," "Much Butt," and "Half Ass." All lightheartedly assigned, but well deserved. Everyone assumed that "Head" stood for 'Head Strong,' but only L.D. knew the real meaning. His nickname had stuck for forty-three years, and this year would be his last. Two more months and he would retire.

Derrell put a hand over one of the receivers. "What a morning. Fog is as thick as pea soup, and half the crews are running late."

Only Derrell could keep track of three conversations at once. "You've got a hundred and twelve cars, Head. Shade Tree's already aboard. Much Butt and Half Ass are running the check."

L.D. nodded, stuffed the thermos into his leather satchel, and headed out the door. The fog was so thick he could barely make out the side of the train only twenty yards away. He stepped off the platform and crossed the tracks of the main line. On the siding were four one hundred-thirty-four-ton engines, lashed together into a consist; multiple locomotives controlled by the lead engine.

He climbed aboard the lead unit and walked sixty feet to the engine cab. The idling twelve-cylinder engine inside rattled the enclosure doors and a strong odor of diesel exhaust filled the air. He entered the cab and greeted his brakeman. "Mornin', Shade Tree."

"Mornin', Head," Goodman replied. Goodman was twenty-five, blonde, with a muscular build.

L.D. settled into his seat on the right side of the cab, inserted the reverser in its receptacle, and tested the train-line air brakes. He picked up the radio. "How we lookin', Half Ass?"

"Good set and release," crackled the voice over the radio.

"Clear block," reported Much Butt, the conductor.

Goodman checked his watch and searched through the fog for the block signal down the track. "I can barely see the green, Head."

L.D. moved the reverser to *Forward*, and brakes to *Off*. It took a full fifteen seconds for the brakes on the rear cars over a mile behind him to release. He moved the throttle to Run 1, the lowest speed. The four diesel engines revved up and he feathered the brakes to keep the slack from running out too fast in a domino effect down the length of the train.

"Can't see a damn thing," Goodman reported. "You ever hit anything in the fog?"

L.D. shrugged. "Fog or no fog, someone's always going to drive around a gate. Fog just makes them bigger idiots."

"What's the worse thing?"

"I had a friend who hit a gravel truck once. He jumped against the forward bulkhead, but the gravel buried him. He suffocated before they could dig him out. I saw one hit a gasoline truck once. You cross one of those, kiss your ass goodbye."

"I guess so."

L.D. sighed. "You get used to hitting cars and trucks, but never people. Sometimes they stand right in the middle of the tracks and dare you. Body parts scattered over a mile and they shut the whole line down to collect them. But the worst are kids, playing out on a trestle, or just too damn young to know better. You never get over hitting a child. It's awful!"

Goodman grimaced. "Sorry I asked."

"Station cleared," crackled the voice of Much Butt over the radio.

L.D. moved the throttle to Run 6, and they passed small towns, crossed creeks, and pulled hills. Running a train was not so much watching the dials; it was feeling what was behind you, and looking out for what was ahead. In recent years the one-hundred-foot rail sections were being replaced by welded rails that were much smoother, but you had to watch out for *sun kinks* on hot days that caused the rails to expand enough to push them off the bed, thus creating a massive derailment.

Just past the Tyger River, L.D. shoved the throttle to Run 8, making the four engines run wide open for the long climb through the Sumter National Forest. The fog was beginning to lift as they crested the hill and they picked up speed on the long downhill stretch into the little hamlet of Carlisle, South Carolina. L.D. could make out the King Street concrete overpass and the trestle just beyond.

At an intersection, twelve hundred feet down the tracks, a Tatum pulpwood truck started across, just as the crossing arms began to close.

Goodman saw it first. "Truck!" he yelled, but at seventy miles per hour, they were closing at a hundred and two feet per second.

It took a moment for L.D. to see the dark shape in the fog. "Damn it to hell!" he said, "Not today." He grabbed the air-horn cord, gave it two quick blasts, and held it down.

"Back up, you fool!" Goodman said.

"Too late! Hit the floor; against the bulkhead." L.D. shoved the emergency brake handle into *Stop*, glanced at the truck for a split second, then threw himself on top of Goodman.

L.D. could still see the expression on the truck driver's face, a mixture of determination and fear. *Why did they always try to beat it?*

The cab door opened and Goodman stepped back inside.

"I thought you jumped, Shade Tree."

"Too many damn stumps and rocks, besides I have a better idea."

"I'm listening."

"Can we shut down the engines by shorting out the electrical panel?"

"That's not the problem. It's the fourteen thousand tons of train pushing us."

"The train's gone," Goodman said. "Must have broken loose when we hit. Only the four engines are left."

A smile formed on L.D.'s face. "Well, help me up, Shade Tree. We've got about a minute before we hit the bridge."

They pulled away the logs in front of the main buss panel and pried open the door. To their surprise the main breaker was still intact. L.D. flipped the switch, shutting down all four engines of the consist.

"Thank you, God," Goodman prayed.

"We're not out of the woods yet," L.D. said. "Still don't have any brakes."

They rounded the curve at eighty miles per hour and started across the bridge. They could feel it swaying beneath them, but without the added weight of the train, it held. The engines began to slow as they rolled up the long hill toward Leeds.

L.D. gathered his grip satchel and coffee mug from under a log on the floor and took one last look around the cab. "Come on, Shade Tree," he said. "Once it stops we have to keep it from rolling back to the river." They stood on the catwalk and waited for the engines to slow to about five miles per hour. L.D. stepped down from the train and walked along beside the forty-inch wheels as they slowed. The moment the wheels came to a complete stop, he picked up a piece of gravel, no bigger than his thumb, and placed it behind the wheel. It didn't roll.

Goodman's jaw slackened. "Good Lord! You stopped five hundred and thirty-five tons with a pebble?"

L.D. smiled broadly. "Sometimes you have to put your faith in the little things." He handed Goodman the radio. "Better call Derrell and get a salvage crew out here."

Goodman made the call. A few minutes later he said, "Derrell says your wife is on the other line. Do you have a message for her?"

"Yeah," L.D. said. "Tell her I've just retired. That's the last run I'll ever make to the Broad River."

Last Run to Broad River, won a Honorable Mention in the 2001 *Horizons*, Anthology Collection.

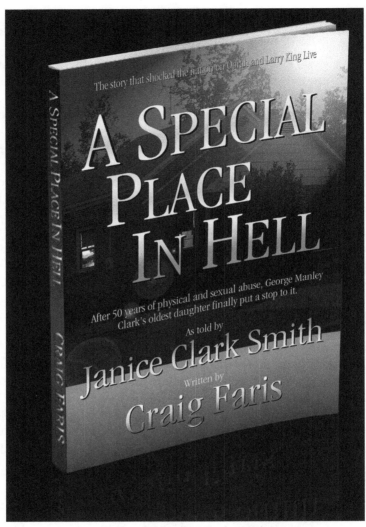

Cover design by Craig Faris.

A Special Place in Hell - Synopsis

A forty-eight-year-old grandmother is at last pushed over the brink by the physical abuse inflicted upon her mother, her siblings and her grandchildren. In a brave act of defiance, she finally puts a stop to the monster of Pottery Road. This man she calls Daddy.

A Special Place In Hell
The Janice Clark Smith Story
Non Fiction

We all thought he was harmless. Everyone knew Manley Clark drank too much and couldn't keep a job, but he would go out of his way to help a neighbor when sober. "He's just drunk," we would say when he wasn't. Growing up in Catawba, South Carolina, I could see the ramshackle home of Manley and Martha Clark every time I walked out the front door. We played with their eight kids, until Donna died of leukemia, and Manley seemed nice enough, but other times he would stumble through our yard, a brown paper bag in hand, and yell, "I've seen your Momma butt naked!"

I'm sure it was just talk, because if nothing else, Manley was smart enough to know if the truth ever came out, he would suffer the same fate he inflicted upon so many of his kids' pets—dropped from the Catawba River Bridge, cinder blocks tied to the feet.

But none of us knew it then. It wasn't until 2003 when their eldest daughter, Janice Clark Smith, finally admitted that a depraved monster had roamed the streets of our quiet town. Years later, she told me what happened that night. Only then did I learn the extent of the terror that was endured daily on Pottery Road.

Janice

On the night of December 11, 2003, I stumbled out of my Ford Explorer, a bottle of wine in one hand, a revolver in the other, and a somewhat blurry vision of what I needed to do. I'd spent the entire day sipping wine and thinking about Momma's words earlier that morning. "Has anyone checked on Manley?" I left a note to my husband, Jerry, and my daughter, Alicia, "We're finally going to have peace in this family," I said before driving to Momma's house.

Momma was seventy then and suffered from a rare form of stomach cancer. The doctors only gave her two months to live, so we had to remove Momma from her home because Manley was so abusive when drunk. Still, Momma was concerned that he might be so inebriated that he could be sitting in his own urine and feces, too drunk to even find the toilet.

Momma missed being home, but now was far too feeble to defend herself. Even when Manley was sober, he would drag her off the couch and yell, "Get up you bitch and fix me some dinner!" If she didn't, or couldn't, well, Manley knew where the bruises wouldn't show.

It was cold that night, forty degrees and falling with a slight breeze. The moonlight filtering through high clouds gave me just enough light to walk to Momma's home from where I hid the Explorer.

The bottle of wine was my ticket into her home, because I knew Manley would say, "Did you bring me something to drink?" Without it, he would simply punch me in the face and throw me out the door. In my coat pocket was a 32-caliber revolver that Jerry had bought for me. I had never fired it. I wasn't even sure it was loaded, but it was always best to have a back-up plan when dealing with Manley.

I could see Momma's old house silhouetted against the moonlit sky and recited a prayer, "Lord, if you don't want me to do this, let the door be locked."

The old house had never been much more than a shack, even though Momma had done everything she could to make it comfortable. She even paid to have the exterior bricked and the interior remodeled, but the roofline still sagged in the center. Those improvements only masked the decay that lay within.

As I stood before the new front porch, a disturbing memory came to mind. When I was only fifteen, a boy from school asked me out on my first date. I got off the school bus that evening and found Manley passed out on the floor of the old wooden porch, directly in front of the door. When my date arrived, I took him in through the side porch to introduce him to Momma. By the time we left, Manley had roused enough to yell out, "Yeah, take her and fuck her. She needs a big 'ole dick!" I was horrified, and since my date had been given permission, of course he tried.

Walking to the eastern side of the house, I saw a light in Momma's bedroom. I climbed the four steps to the side porch, placed my hand on the doorknob, closed my eyes and repeated the let-the-door-be-locked prayer. The knob turned, and the kitchen door swung open with a groan.

Instantly, I knew he was home. An odor filled my senses, one that we all had become very accustomed to. Variations in the smell indicated what "mood" Manley was in. Beer meant he was probably mellowing out in front of the television or lying in bed. Wine meant he would be confrontational, and it was best just to leave. But that was never as bad as the awful smell of liquor, which meant Manley was ready for a fight with my brothers, or his idea of *lovin' up* on us girls.

The kitchen lights were off, lit only by a lamp from the room across the hall. That's where Manley usually sat in his easy chair, drank his wine or beer, smoked his cigarettes and, ignoring the trashcans, tossed the empty cans, bottles, dirty socks, shoes, newspapers, his filthy clothes and cigarette butts onto the floor. Power tools and thousands of cigarette burn marks covered the vinyl flooring around his chair. The television he kept tuned to old John Wayne Westerns, or those "weird" TV preachers, was casting its bluish glow onto the wood paneled walls.

I switched on the kitchen light and placed the revolver on the kitchen counter behind Momma's portable radio. I put the "peace offering" wine bottle on the counter beside the sink, which was clean and smelled of bleach. When sober, Manley was a neatness freak, yet when drunk would not even bother to aim his urine stream at the toilet bowl.

The kitchen table was covered with spice bottles, along with a half-empty bag of hotdog buns, and an empty, gallon jug of Carlo Rossi red wine. Manley had obviously fixed himself hotdogs, washed the dishes, and drank the entire gallon of wine. The bottle confirmed the odor that somewhere within the house, Manley was probably sick, pissed off and in need of more wine.

I fully expected to find him passed out in his easy chair, but when I reached the hallway and looked into the den, the chair was empty and the television's volume muted. I glanced down the hall at the bathroom, hoping he had slipped on the vinyl floor, cracked his head on the sink, and drowned in the toilet. However, the bathroom door stood open with no sign of Manley sprawled on the floor.

Momma kept a small table in the den stocked with cleaning supplies that she used when Manley was on a drunk. She was only five-foot-three, but she would wrestle Manley out of his easy chair, drag him to the bathroom, get him into the tub and turn the hose on him. Once when she left to answer the phone, Momma discovered that he had passed out in the tub, his head beneath water. I never understood why she didn't simply turn around, fix herself a cup of coffee, and let the hand of Providence deliver us all from bondage.

At the far end of the hall was the living room, its door to the front porch directly ahead of me, and a brick fireplace to my left. I switched on the light, and the beige carpet Momma had worked so hard to provide, still looked new. One of Momma's blue and brown plaid sofas still had her pillows, blankets and stuffed animals where she had slept during her illness. For three days it had been empty. Now she wanted to come home, but couldn't.

Years earlier, when my younger sister Donna was suffering from leukemia, Momma decided to treat Donna and Shari to a rare trip to the beauty parlor for Easter. That night, she lined us up in our Sunday dresses on a couch in this room, but Manley would have none of it. He hated makeup and hairdos, and was so outraged when he saw that Martha had cut her hair, he shaved Donna's and my youngest sister Shari's heads with a dull pocketknife. Donna died from leukemia later that year.

At the right, was Momma's bedroom. Since I had eliminated every other room, I was sure that here I would find Manley, dead or alive.

I prayed, "Lord, please let him be passed out," and for good reason. For a drunk in his seventies, Manley was surprisingly strong—dangerously so. At a recent family gathering, I saw him curl a fifty-pound barbell with one arm.

The bedroom was cluttered with boxes stacked against yellow wall paneling, and the same beige carpet as the living room. Against the north wall, a large mirror reflected my image just outside the doorway, and directly beside it, just out of sight, was the foot of the bed.

I eased into the room, and from behind the open door I saw the thick patchwork quilt that Momma kept on the bed. Everything about the bed looked perfectly normal with the exception of its lone occupant. There, under the covers, were two lumps that I knew were the feet of the monster of Pottery Road.

George Manley Clark lay under the covers dressed in a white T-shirt stained with red wine across his chest. His gray hair was close-cropped and the pillow on which his head rested had dark purple stains where he had apparently spit up wine.

I crept closer, leaning over the bed, wondering if he was asleep or dead. His eyes blinked open. I jerked back as a shuttering chill crawled up my spine. He raised his head off the pillow and gave me the same devilish smirk that I had seen so often, daring me to speak, yet knowing I was too terrified.

"Are . . . you sick?" I said, my voice trembling with fear.

"Hell yeah, I'm sick! I'm out of wine!" he said. "Did you bring me something to drink?"

I took a breath, feeling my courage return. "Yes, I brought you some wine."

Manley swung his legs off the bed and struggled up. Wearing stained blue boxer shorts, he followed me out the bedroom door and down the hallway.

I paused at the kitchen doorway, watching him sit in the recliner in his den, and light up a cigarette. Manley never helped himself when there was someone else to serve him. He'd been drunk for a week when we removed Momma from the home. At some point over the past three days, he had sobered up enough to drive to Wal-Mart to buy food and wine, and then emptied the jug. He was now clear-headed enough to walk to the den, but it wouldn't take much to return him to that state.

No matter, I thought as I broke the seal on the peace-offering. *He won't get drunk from this.* I fixed his wine the same way I had for years, an ounce or two poured into the bottom of a paper cup and filled to the top with water. Manley switched the television to a wild-haired preacher crawling around on a floor covered in newspapers, praying for the lost souls in the articles. I never understood how he could watch shows filled with compassion, forgiveness and love, yet beat the hell out of his own family at the slightest infraction. It didn't make sense. How could his mind receive the message, but never make the eighteen-inch journey to his heart?

Near the television was a can of kerosene he used to light the old Seigler oil heater. It reminded me of a plan my youngest sister had once suggested. Manley was always passing out with a lit cigarette clutched between his fingers. Why not slide the can of kerosene under his hand, make sure the doors were locked so he couldn't be rescued by the neighbors, then wait for the phone call announcing his tragic loss?

Manley handed the empty cup back to me and smoked his cigarette. I refilled it in the kitchen and when I returned with the drink, I squatted down on my knees in front of his recliner.

"We need to talk about Momma," I said.

"Where the hell is she?" Manley said, clutching his cigarette between his middle and index fingers forming a fist.

"Why are you doing this to Momma? She's spent her whole life taking care of you, cleaning up after you and raising the kids. Now that she's sick with cancer, why can't you help her, just once in your life?"

Manley took another drink and glared down at me. "She's just lying around. She ain't that sick."

"She's dying! She's over at Michelle's and can't even get off the couch. I'm begging you. Please stop drinking and let her come home. Please! She misses home so much, and she's worried about you."

The two ounces of wine only made him more confrontational. "Oh, so she's over there with her bitches!" His voice was now angry. Just the mention of the children or grandchildren could send him into a jealous tirade. "She's always there for you sons-of-bitches, but never does a damn thing when I'm sick. She needs to be here, taking care of this house instead of running off to those bitches." Setting his wine cup on a chair, Manley started to stand.

I knew what was coming—the yelling, the cursing, and then he would use me as a punching bag. I got up first and headed to the kitchen counter where my 32-caliber revolver was hidden. When I turned, Manley was leaning against the den's doorframe, steadying himself with a drag from his cigarette.

I was surprised at my confidence now that I had a weapon. Manley used to put pistols into our little hands, point the barrel at his own chest and dare us to pull the trigger. Then with his smugness, he called us cowards when we couldn't.

"So, you got yourself a gun," Manley snorted. "You know how to use it?"

"Yes, I do," I said, and pulled the trigger. It only made a click. I looked at the revolver and pulled the trigger again with the same result. Manley just stood there as if hoping that I would finally put an end to his cycle of drinking, fighting, and waking up on vomit-covered floors.

I cocked the revolver a third time. Still, there was only the sound of the click, and I realized that I was powerless against him.

"What's wrong with this thing?" I said, squeezing the trigger again. It bucked in my hand as the bullet left the barrel and tore a hole in Manley's T-shirt near his heart.

Manley staggered and fell into the hallway onto his back. A small trickle of blood ran from his mouth down his cheek. He raised his head off the floor, fire in his eyes. The voice that I heard wasn't his. It was the "devil's voice" we had heard many so times when Manley used to burst into our bedroom and whisper into our tiny ears.

"Well, you've done it now!" he said, and coughed. Blood poured from his mouth and mingled with the wine stains on his white T-shirt. I stepped forward, looked down into his eyes and said, "Yes, you bastard, I finally did it." I aimed the revolver at his left nipple and pulled the trigger again.

His eyes never closed, but the hate in them vanished as if the devil had finally abandoned his useless body. I knew he was dead, but I wasn't willing to risk a miraculous recovery. So, I shot him again, right through the heart.

I grabbed the wine bottle and looked at Manley's unblinking eyes—his cigarette still clutched in his fingers.

The monster of Pottery Road was finally dead—this man I had called Daddy.

Epilogue

Janice turned herself in the next day, and it wasn't long before the horrors of Manley's abuse leaked out. Martha testified that Manley terrorized all of them for fifty years and had once held a loaded shotgun to her head, daring his kids to shed a tear. He forced his kids to watch as he shot their favorite pets, and her sister's confessed that he sexually abused them and used them as entertainment for his drinking buddies.

Oprah Winfrey interviewed Janice twice, and a national outcry arose that she shouldn't be prosecuted. Clearly, Janice had mitigating circumstances, and seeing Manley drag her dying mother into the kitchen was what set her off. The prosecutor reduced the charge, and Janice pled guilty to voluntary manslaughter. She served seventeen months in prison and was paroled at her first hearing. Both the judge and prosecutor testified on her behalf at her last hearing.

In subsequent interviews with Oprah Winfrey and Larry King, Janice always maintained that she was wrong to have killed her father despite the abuse they suffered.

Her mother, Martha, died a few months after her release and chose to be buried between Manley and Donna. After a long illness, Janice also lost her husband, Jerry, who had been her rock of support throughout her ordeal.

"I did what I did," she said, "and now they are both gone."

After her final release from parole, I asked Janice where she thought her father was now.

"I hope he's in heaven," she said.

That was the Janice I knew, taking all of that abuse, yet still kind and forgiving.

But we all know where Manley is. There's a place for monsters that beat and sexually abuse their wives, children and grandchildren. A place with a river called Styx, where the souls of the wicked cry out for mercy and reap the harvest they have sown.

It's a *special* place.

A Special Place in Hell, won the 3rd Place prize for
Nonfiction in the 2011 Carrie McCray Literary Award.

Cover design by Ethan Hoover and Craig Faris.

DAWN'S LAST GLEAMING – Synopsis

In the summer of 1941, three-year-old Kato Nagai Stevens traveled to Japan with her native Japanese mother to visit her grandparents. Their plan was to stay six months, but when war broke out between Japan and the United States on December 8, 1941, the little girl and her mother were trapped in her grandparents hometown. Now, four years later, with the war nearing a close, seven-year-old Kato is looking forward to the day when her father, an American pilot, will come to rescue them.

Dawn's Last Gleaming
Fiction

Cheryl Stevens entered her mother's home using a key she hadn't utilized since her college years. The big house was cold and silent now. Her father having passed away years before, and yesterday her mother finally succumbed to the tumors she had fought all her life.

The house was now Cheryl's; presented to her in her mother's will along with a package. The lawyer said only that the package contained a book her mother wanted her to have in the hope that it would help explain things.

"I doubt that," Cheryl had said. Their mutual resentment had created far too great a rift for mere words to resolve. They had not spoken since her father's funeral, and even then her mother would not tell her why she bore such anger in her heart. It was never directed at Cheryl or her father, but they suffered as victims of her rage nonetheless.

Cheryl had her suspicions. Her grandmother, who was Japanese, had married her American grandfather in 1938, but her mother, Kato Nagai Stevens, was born and raised as an American citizen. All Cheryl knew was that her grandmother had died sometime during the war when Kato was only seven.

With most of her mother's anger directed at the government, especially the military, Cheryl had always suspected Kato and her grandmother had been among the thousands of Japanese-Americans who were locked away in internment camps for the duration of the war. She was convinced of it. That explained the resentment, but not why her mother refused to speak of the war or any of her childhood memories. They were like a blank page and Cheryl had always wondered what terrible experience could have created such rage in a seven-year-old child.

Cheryl climbed into her old bed, the sheets stiff and bearing a slight musty odor. She pulled the blanket up around her, reached into her bag and removed the small package painstakingly wrapped in linen cloth. She untied a ribbon securing the cover and cautiously opened a tattered hardbound book inscribed with Kato's name in faded gold leaf. On the inside cover, written in her mother's hand, was a title, *Dawn's Last*

Gleaming, Memories of a Nisei Survivor. She turned to a well-worn page; its corners creased down into makeshift bookmarks, and began reading the passage.

AUGUST 6, 1945: I awoke from a strange dream this morning. Father was standing by my bed kissing me on the forehead, just as he had that day on the docks when I was only three years old. He kept whispering something in my ear, but it wasn't what he had whispered then. This time he said, "Don't look at the light, sweetheart. Turn away from the edge of darkness and come with me." Then I saw my mother. She was smiling and telling me to go with him. She kept reassuring me that it was only for a little while, but when I looked back, I knew I would never see her again. The familiar scent of steaming rice, and my mother's voice was what awoke me from the dream.

"Kato," mother said in her broken English. "Time to get up now. Come eat your breakfast."

It was then that I realized it was only a dream, but it seemed so hauntingly real.

Mother was at her place in the kitchen, preparing the food, while humming the tune to "Sakura." I sat up, wiping the sleep from my eyes and touched the photo of my father that I kept hidden in my pillow. He looked so brave in his American pilot's uniform. Soon the war would be over and he would come to take us back home. Our home in America was but a vague memory now. I remembered my room; the swing set in the backyard, but little else. I was only three when we left and our visit to my grandparents had lasted four years longer than expected.

"Kato," mother repeated, this time in her native Japanese, "come on. We don't have much time." Mother insisted on speaking English, lest I forget it, so this slip into Japanese meant she was serious.

"Coming, Mama-san," I called.

"No, Kato. Call me Mother."

"Yes, Mother."

I was still very tired since we had spent most of the night at the air-raid shelter, but once again our town had been spared from the bombing. How I wished the war would end. Mother had told me that if we prayed hard enough, Jesus would answer my prayer. I had prayed everyday. I even prayed in the Buddhist temple while my grandparents lit their prayer candles, but it wasn't directed at their God. Their God, with his fat belly and bronze smile seemed like a storybook character when compared to the thin, suffering Jesus. Of course, I never said these things in front of my grandparents, as it would be considered disrespectful.

I slipped on my wooden sandals, collected the tattered American doll my papa had given me, and followed the sound of my mother's voice into the kitchen.

"Where are Sato-san and Mito-san?" I asked, looking around the room for my grandparents.

"They got up early and took a pushcart into the Mitaki Hills to find firewood. It's a beautiful day."

The morning air blowing though the open windows was cool and the sky was perfectly clear. I could see why they had wanted to get out for a walk.

"Why didn't they wake me? I love to gather firewood."

"You know the rules, Kato. Our job is to clear the streets."

Although our city had so far not been attacked, we were told it was only a matter of time. We were on the western side of Japan and we hoped this might spare us, but since the defeat at Okinawa, the American fire-bombing raids were getting closer. With that possibility looming, the Army ordered everyone to help demolish old buildings to create fire prevention lanes. Since we lived only two kilometers from the center of town, we had to do our part as well.

A little after 8:00 a.m., Mother and I went into the garden to gather some food for lunch. She picked vegetables from the vines, but I mostly looked up at the deep blue sky. After a while I heard the distant sounds of a plane and spotted its reflection very high towards the north of the city. Mother was picking peas and I asked her if it was an American plane; the type my father flew. She looked up, but since it was just one plane, she said it probably wasn't.

I could see the sun reflecting off of its shiny surface, and somehow I knew my father was aboard.

I saw a shiny object falling from the plane, and a parachute open above it. I pulled on mother's skirt and pointed upward, "Papa-san! Papa-san!"

"Kato," Mother said, "it's Papa, not Papa-san!"

"Ok, but look, Papa has jumped from the plane. He's coming to get us."

I pulled harder on Mother's skirt and implored her to look; please look. In that moment I had convinced myself that it was indeed my American father who was parachuting into the city. Our prayers had been answered. The war was over and Father was coming to tell us. Mother finally gave in, gazed up at the tiny object, and blocked my view for only a second.

In that moment an intense flash overwhelmed us. It was so bright that I could see my mother's ribs through her dress-covered flesh. To this day when I close my eyes I can still see the purple outline of her ribs. I remembered my dream where Father told me to turn away from the light. I heard Mother cry, "Kato!" and suddenly I was lying flat on my back in the garden. Mother was on top of me and I couldn't move.

Her weight was intense, and my body sank into the soft earth of the garden. I called out to Mother but she didn't respond. With my free hand I managed to dig out the dirt beside me and after what seemed hours, crawled out. As I got up, I felt dizzy. The once beautiful clear morning had turned as dark as a moonlit night. Black smoke poured from everywhere. The vile smell of burned hair and flesh filled the air and it hurt my lungs to breathe.

Our home had been pulverized into a million shards of wood and glass. A section of one wall covered my mother's body and this is why she had felt so heavy. I reached for her hand and to my astonishment it moved. She was alive! I tried to lift the wall, but it was far too heavy for my small body to budge. I pulled on her arm and felt her skin slip, sliding off into my hand as easily as the skin of a roasted tomato. A wet thread of viscous liquid streamed from the blistered peelings back to her blackened fingernails. I held the fragile pieces in disbelief, too stunned by the sight to utter a word.

Even in her agony, Mother thought only of me. "It's all right, Kato," she kept saying from within her tomb. "As long as you're alive, everything will be all right."

Cheryl closed the book, shutting her mother's memories like the lid of her casket. Tears streamed from her eyes. The bomb had claimed one last victim and had she known her mother's secret, it would have changed everything.

She carefully re-wrapped the memoir in its linen shroud and returned it to the bag. She could tell by the wear on the last page that Kato had always stopped at this point, preferring to freeze the hands of time at precisely 8:15 a.m. She pictured her mother as a child; still gazing at the clear blue sky with the faint flicker of answered prayer. The Americans had come. This was the moment her mother had always remembered; that fleeting second of innocence, preserved like a marble plaque, for all of the burned children of Hiroshima.

Dawn's Last Gleaming, won Best of Issue in the 2000 South Carolina Writers Workshop's *Horizons*, Anthology Collection. An excerpt from *Dawn's Last Gleaming* also appeared in part in this author's novel, *The Spectrum Conspiracy*, published in 2013 by Bella Rosa Books.

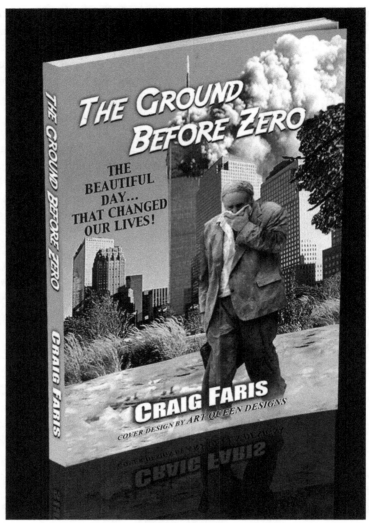

Cover design by Shade Thomas.

The Ground Before Zero – Synopsis

On a beautiful clear day in September 2001, Steven Mobley stepped aboard an elevator in tower II of the World Trade center with the cute blonde that had been flirting with him for weeks. Five years later, he is summoned to an arbitration hearing in the case of Delia Moore verses the New York Port Authority. He has no idea why he has been summoned since he hardly knew her, or even if Delia is the same girl. He doesn't even know if she survived, but on this day, he will finally relive the events of that day.

THE GROUND BEFORE ZERO
Fiction

May 2006

My wife, Beth, was driving as we neared the entrance of the Manhattan Bridge upper roadway that crossed the East River. Just prior to reaching the first bridge pylon I caught my first clear view of lower Manhattan's financial district where only five years earlier had stood the twin towers of the World Trade Centers. Once again, my mind drifted back to that crystal clear September morning. I pictured myself standing before my desk on the eighty-fifth floor of the South Tower, looking out toward the Southeast at the shape of a jet airliner, its left wing tipped down in a slow arch as it began its final approach directly towards our building. Seeing it come right at us, growing larger and larger, and then that terrible ripping sound, explosion, and searing heat of the fireball.

"Why you?" Beth said, snapping me out of my trance. "Did you even know this person?"

"No, not really," I said glancing down at the summons lying in my lap. Other than basic details, for years I had remained virtually silent on what happened that morning in the South Tower. But now I needed to picture it again in my mind, since my account would surely be required if I needed to testify.

Our relationship had improved greatly since both Beth and I realized how close we came to losing each other. But now, due to this summons to appear before an arbitration hearing, all of those terrible memories came flooding back. Beth knew that I didn't like to talk about it, and for the most part, she understood.

9/11/2001

The alarm woke me from my dream at the worst possible moment. I rolled against my wife's back and reached for the snooze button. The clock displayed 5:01 a.m. I was already running late and needed to leave the house in twenty-six minutes, to catch my train. It was Tuesday, not even the middle of the week yet.

Beth murmured something.

"I'm late," I said. "Go back to sleep."

My wife of eight years was dressed in flannel pajamas from neck to ankle. I couldn't remember the last time I'd seen her completely naked, but as a full-time mother of two, most days we were just too tired for romance.

"Be sure to kiss the kids before leaving," she said.

"Okay," I replied from the bathroom door.

"Steve," she added, "it's important to them."

"Okay!" I closed the door and switched on the light. The shower was cold, but it had the desired effect of clearing my head. I tried to remember the dream, where I had been sitting at a bar with that pretty blonde from work. I couldn't remember her name, but our knees had been touching when she had leaned over to whisper in my ear *Let's get a room*. That's when the alarm had gone off.

Just my luck, I thought. Stepping from the shower, I toweled myself in front of the mirror, and examined my body. A slight bulge around my waist, but I still looked pretty good for forty-four. It took less than ten minutes to get into my work clothes; a starched white shirt and blue suit. In the kitchen, I threw a piece of frozen strudel into the toaster, put a cup of day-old coffee into the microwave oven and checked my watch. It was 5:20.

A quick peek inside my briefcase confirmed that my laptop was still inside. I poured the coffee into an insulated cup, clamped the strudel between my teeth, grabbed my briefcase, and was out the door. My new Lexus was already backing out of our garage when I remembered the kids, and their forgotten kiss; another broken promise to Beth. *At least she's asleep*, I thought. *I'll give them an extra kiss tonight.*

I made the train at Bellarose Terrace station for the ride in from Long Island and switched to the Path Train in New York, which stopped directly beneath our office in the south tower of the World Trade Center.

Up the escalator to the main concourse, I waited for an elevator. At the forty-third floor the clear morning light streamed through the windows and reflected off the polished marble floors. While waiting to switch elevators, I spotted the blonde from my dream and she smiled at me. She was dressed in a red blouse, and a dark blue, pleated skirt. We both worked on the eighty-fifth floor, she for an investment firm and I at a financial law firm. She often stopped by my office with legal documents requiring a notary seal. Lately, it was nearly every day.

I returned the smile and let my mind drift back to the dream, our knees touching under the bar, my hand on her thigh. I opened my eyes, and she was standing beside me.

"Good morning, Mr. Mobley," she said.

"Good morning, Miss uh—"

"Moore," she interrupted. "Delia Moore. I'm with KB&W's loan underwriting."

"Uh, yes," I said as if I didn't already know. "Beautiful morning, isn't it?"

"It's called *severe clear* in the airline industry," she said. "My dad is a pilot with United. He says it's the kind of morning that makes you glad you're alive."

The elevator opened and we stepped into the rear of the car. The passengers packed in and I felt her body pressed against mine.

"Sorry," she said.

"That's okay," I replied with a smile. *Press a little harder*, I thought as I breathed in the scent of her perfume.

My cell phone vibrated in my pocket. It was Beth. No doubt fully awake and pissed. "Hello."

"Steve!" she said. "Did you forget to kiss the kids *again?*"

"Uh, well—"

"You did, didn't you? Since you forgot mine!" Her voice was angry. "Is a kiss goodbye too damn much to ask?"

"I was running late, Beth. I'm sorry."

"You've got *that* right!" The line went dead.

"Trouble?" Delia said.

"Yep! Perpetual trouble."

"Some girls don't realize what they have," she said, and I felt her hand caress the small of my back.

May 2006

We exited the parking garage onto Essex Street and Beth asked, "Would you like to talk about it before we go in?"

Since I was about to be questioned at the hearing, now seemed as good as any. "Okay."

"Where were you when it hit?" Beth asked.

"I was in the South Tower," I said. "I remember the elevator doors opening on the eighty-fifth floor and everyone spread out toward their respective offices and cubicles. There was this one lady I chatted with on the elevator. I think she worked in the investment firm on the north side of our floor."

"What was her name?" she asked.

"I think it might have been Delia something. Their company used our notary services."

"What did you talk about?"

"Oddly enough, the weather," I said. "She made a comment about it being *severe clear*. It's what pilots called super clear weather."

"Did she survive?"

"I don't know."

"What happened next?" Beth asked.

"I was talking with someone in my office when there was a distant boom. It vibrated the windows in our building. Everyone got up and looked around. Then, I saw a flash and a huge fireball erupted from the North Tower about ten stories above our floor. Burning debris flew past our windows. The air was full of paper, some on fire, swirling around like a ticker-tape parade. Smoke poured from a gaping hole. My supervisor was in that building and I called his cell phone. There was no answer."

"You must have been terrified," she said.

"Everyone thought it was an accident. A small plane," I said. "But it was so clear out. I couldn't imagine how a small plane could cause that huge fire ball. We debated on what to do and most of our employees started down the three staircases. We opted to use the elevator."

"Who was with you?"

"The company president, the CEO, and the human resources director joined a few of us on the seventy-eighth floor and we proceeded down to the main lobby. There, we encountered a security guard."

"So, this was before the second plane hit?" she said.

"Right. The guard insisted that it was a small plane that hit the North Tower, probably the result of the pilot having a heart attack. He was just guessing but assured us that the accident was confined to the North Tower and that our building was secure. He asked that we please return to our offices because of debris falling in the courtyard outside."

"He sent you back up?"

"Yes. I can't imagine how many lives he cost by saying that. But, at that time it seemed plausible, so I went back up to get my briefcase and laptop."

"All of you?" she asked.

I thought for a second before responding. "I think so. Maybe not everyone. I remember the CEO joked that it was time to move to a new building."

"So, if you suspected that it was a bigger plane, why the hell did you go back up?" Beth asked.

"To get my stuff. That's why I was on the eighty-fifth floor when you called."

"Oh, God," she said. "That was so stupid! I was scared to death. I couldn't remember if you were in the North Tower or the South. I was so thankful that you were in the South Tower, and okay. And then the TV showed that other plane circling in from New Jersey."

"I had just closed my phone when I saw the reflection of the other plane across the Hudson Bay. It was coming right at us."

"No, Steve, don't you remember? I had just said that there were reports of planes being hijacked, and that's when you saw it coming at the tower. You said you loved me, and seconds later the line went dead."

"I guess I dropped my phone when I crawled under my desk. I curled into a ball and thought about you and the kids left with no kiss."

She hugged me and I drew a sigh of relief.

September 11, 2001

My office was against the windows on the southwest side of the South Tower, looking down on Battery Park and the Statue of Liberty. My email indicated that my supervisor was attending a meeting at the Windows on the World restaurant in the North Tower and would return at 10:00 a.m. Then I checked my phone for messages. The latest was from Delia.

"Hi," her message said. "I was just wondering if you had plans for lunch."

There was a Bible on top of my desk, and suddenly the dust on its cover caught my attention. I kept it there as a reminder that I was a deacon in our church, but it was more of a prop since it was never opened. Beyond it, was a desk clock that read 7:59. I called her back and left a voice mail. "Miss Moore, this is Steven Mobley. If you get a second, could you come by my office, please?"

At 8:03, Delia appeared at my door. "Mr. Mobley?"

"Yes," I said. "Would you mind closing the door?" She did, and then she said in a low voice, "I want to apologize for intruding into your conversation this morning. It was inappropriate—"

"No, that's fine, and I appreciate your concern. You mentioned lunch. Well, I have a question."

May 2006
New York Court of Mediation
Moore versus the New York Port Authority

Steve, Delia had said, *I'm ready when you are . . .*

"Mr. Mobley, are you ready to continue?" the lawyer asked.

I blinked from my trance. I had just returned from a bathroom break and focused on the attorneys across the table from me. "Yes, I am."

"Now in the case of the estate of Ms. Delia Moore versus the NYPA, you have testified that Miss Moore came aboard the elevator when you and the aforementioned company executives boarded it on the seventy-eighth floor. Is that correct?"

"Yes, sir. That is correct."

"Did she say why she chose to take that elevator when the rest of her colleagues at KB&W Investments exited using the stairs?"

"No. I can only assume that it was because this was the express elevator that went down to the plaza level. It was the quickest way down, and at that time, all of us were unaware that both buildings were targeted in the attack."

"Did you have a conversation with Mrs. Moore earlier that morning?"

I hesitated and glanced at Beth before answering. "Uh, yes, her company had some documents that needed a notary seal. She was at my desk when the first plane struck the other building."

"What time was that?"

"Uh, I think it was shortly after 8 a.m."

"You mean 8:46?"

"Oh, that's right. It must have been shortly before that."

I smiled at Beth across the room. She now knew that I had neglected to mention my conversation with Delia at my desk and that she was aboard the elevator.

"How well did you know Delia Moore?" Beth asked, her voice calm when we were alone in the hallway.

"I told you. Her company used our notaries to seal their legal papers."

"Then why would they call *you* to testify about her?"

"I don't know. I guess because she came to our offices."

"Why didn't you mention that she had talked with you that morning?"

"I talked with a lot of people that morning. Most of them didn't make it, but I failed to mention them, too. I didn't even know her last name until—"

My eyes began to well up with tears. "It's hard to remember that day. All those friends and colleagues were gone in just an instant."

Beth took my hand. "It's okay, Steve. At least you came back to me."

May 2006
New York Court of Mediation
Moore versus the New York Port Authority
Afternoon Session

"Mr. Mobley, you said the security guard specifically told you and the others to return upstairs to your offices?" The attorney representing Delia's estate asked.

"Yes," I said.

"Why?"

"He said there was debris falling from the North Tower and it was too dangerous to exit the building."

"Would you have left the site if he had not instructed you to do so?"

"I'm sure we all would have," I said.

"No more questions," he said to the arbitrator.

The plaintiff's attorney stood and asked the arbitrator for a follow-up. It was granted.

"Mr. Mobley, how well did you know Miss Moore?"

"The company she worked for was on the same floor as ours. She would regularly come by to have my notary seal on legal documents."

"So, your relationship was strictly professional?"

"Yes."

The attorney put on a pair of rubber gloves, opened a plastic bag, and placed a dark burgundy-stained, badly scorched object on the table in front of me. "Do you recognize this?"

It was very difficult to tell what it was. "No, I do not," I said.

He handed me a pair of the gloves, which I put on. Would you please open the cover of the book and read the first page?"

I did and, despite the dark burgundy stains, I saw my name printed on the first page. It was the Bible that I had kept on my desk. "Oh, my

Lord! This was on my desk," I said. "How did it survive?"

"It was inside the remains of a human torso found on the south side of the South Tower.

"My God!" I said. My hands recoiled as I realized that the burgundy stains were blood soaked into the pages.

"DNA samples identified the victim as Ms. Delia Moore and, given its location, it looks as if she may have fallen or jumped from the South Tower while holding it. Do you have any idea how it might have ended up in her possession?"

"No, I do not." I said. "The last time I saw it, it was on my desk on the eighty-fifth floor of the South Tower."

"You were not with her?"

"No!"

"Did you give it to her before she fell? Or, was she pushed?"

"Of course not! I barely knew her and I never saw her again after leaving the building. I can only assume that she grabbed it for spiritual comfort and fell or jumped to avoid the flames."

"Why don't you tell us exactly how you left the building that day?" the Arbitrator said.

My Testimony

It was basically the same story I had told Beth in the car that morning.

"When I returned to my desk on the eighty-fifth floor, I closed my laptop, and my cell phone rang. It was Beth, my wife. She said, "Thank God, Steve, you're okay." I told her it was only a small plane and that I was fine.

Then, she interrupted and said, "No, it wasn't! The news just reported that commercial jets have been hijacked. Get out of there! Now!" I heard some people in the next office yelling, "Oh my God!" Then I looked across the Hudson Bay and saw a large airliner arching its way toward our tower. Beth screamed into the phone. I was motionless as I watched it come; it seemed to be headed right at us. I told Beth I loved her and dropped the phone.

There was no place to go, so I dove under my desk and curled into a ball. The explosion threw my desk, with me under it, across the room and pinned me against a wall. An intense wave of heat passed through the room, but under my desk, I was shielded from the flash. The black smoke was so thick I couldn't see my hand in front of my face. Some of the windows in my office had blown out, so a lot of the smoke was being sucked out of those. Wreckage was piled up around me; ceiling panels, sheetrock, twisted metal studs, wires hanging everywhere and heaps of splintered wood furniture still on fire.

I crawled out from under the desk, but the floor was too hot to touch. I saw areas of the carpet steaming as it melted. I tried to make my way toward the staircases but with all the wires, wrecked walls, and smoke it was nearly impossible. After climbing over a fallen wall, I saw a mangled piece of a wing that was on fire. I climbed and crawled my way around it and spotted a light through the smoke. It turned out to be a crack in the sheetrock of one of the staircases. I could hear voices yelling in the stairway beyond it. I kicked at the three layers of sheetrock until I could squeeze my way through.

Once inside the stairway, I saw a man and a woman climbing toward the roof. She said it was better to go up, because there was too much fire in the staircase below to get past. I figured the roof doors were probably locked, so I broke off a big piece of sheetrock and used it as a shield as I made my way down past the inferno. After I got below the sky lobby, I was able to run down the stairs until I reached the main lobby. Bodies, paper, and wreckage littered the courtyard, but I didn't care. I ran out the south side and kept running toward Battery Park.

After the collapse of the towers, I began to walk home and was finally able to call Beth once I was in Brooklyn."

The Arbitrator suggested that we take a break.

The Same Day, Fifteen Minutes Later

"That's a pretty interesting story, Mr. Mobley," the Port Authority attorney said. "Where, exactly, was your office in the South Tower?"

"It was in the southwest end of the eighty-fifth floor."

"You said you saw a section of a mangled wing in that end of the building?"

"Yes. It looked like part of a plane, near staircase A," I replied.

The lawyer held up a photograph of the damage, showing an outline of where the plane struck. "As you can see, the angle of the impact clearly shows the wings at the time of impact were at a thirty-eight-degree downward tilt toward port or the left side of the jet. The left wing entered the building approximately at the seventy-seventh floor, the fuselage at the eighty-first, and the right wing entered at the southeast corner at about the eighty-fifth floor. That was the opposite end of the building from where you were located. Can you explain how the left wing might have ended up in a section of the building eight floors above where it struck?"

I studied the photo. He was right. "Then it must not have been a wing. I said the object was a mangled piece of metal and I just assumed it was a wing."

"You also said that the windows in your office were blown out?"

"Some of them," I said. "It was difficult to see with all of the smoke."

The attorney held up the photo with the floors labeled. "Do you see any windows broken out near your office?"

"I can't really tell," I said. "Something was sucking the smoke out."

"You said you had to kick your way through three layers of sheet-rock to reach a stairway, that you spoke to a couple going up those stairs, who advised you not to go down, and that you had to climb over a wall," the attorney said. "Do you realize that parts of your story almost exactly mirror well-documented accounts that the other South Tower survivors have written about?"

"Ugh," I shook my head. "I'm sure many of the survivors had similar experiences."

"Shall I cite the exact passages you used? After all, there were only *fifteen* survivors who made it down from above the impact zone. Yours seems to indicate a sixteenth."

"I never testified before the 9-11 commission," I said, "so they didn't know."

"Did you burn your hands crawling across the hot floor or while holding that piece of sheetrock in the stairway as a fire shield?"

"I assume so, I don't remember."

"You can't remember any burns? Were your clothes burned, or your hair singed?"

"I'm not sure. I was covered from head to toe with dust."

"You dropped your phone on the eighty-fifth floor yet you called your wife from Brooklyn. How?"

"I guess it was still in my pocket."

"Mr. Mobley. Why did Miss Moore use her credit card to reserve a room at The Marriott World Trade Center at 8:25 on the morning of September 11, 2001? Were you having an affair with Delia Moore?"

I closed my eyes and remembered Delia saying, *Steve, what the hell was that?* She had just emerged from the bathroom and was completely naked. My lies, all of them, were falling apart.

"Mr. Mobley?"

"No," I said, my eyes closed. "But that was only because we were in-terrupted by the jet hitting the North Tower."

The Same Day

"What really happened, Mr. Mobley?" the Port Authority attorney asked.

"We didn't even know each other that well, but I could tell Delia liked me because we had been flirting for a while. I had been neglecting my wife and my kids for far too long. That morning, my wife, Beth, simply asked me to kiss the kids goodbye, but, of course, I forgot. I saw Delia in the elevator on the way up and she overheard our conversation when Beth called and blessed me out for forgetting, again.

When I got upstairs, I was angry, not only at myself, but with Beth for pointing it out. That was the *first*, and *only time* I had even considered having an affair. I wanted to strike back, so when I got an email from Delia asking if I would like to have lunch and talk, I suggested we go have a drink at the lounge at the Marriott."

"What about your boss?" the attorney asked.

"He was at a meeting at the Windows on the World restaurant until 10 a.m. So, we took the express elevator down. We were alone and kissed in the elevator. We didn't even make it to the bar. Delia got us a room on the first floor. I got undressed while she was in the bathroom and climbed into the bed. She said, "I'm ready when you are," and when she came out of the bathroom we heard a huge boom and saw pieces of metal falling into the courtyard outside. She turned on the TV and that's when we realized what had happened."

"Did you leave the hotel together?"

"Yes. We got dressed and rushed back into the South Tower. She had only taken her wallet to the Marriott, so she wanted to go back upstairs to get her pocketbook. The security guard assured us that the South Tower was secure and when the elevator arrived he told those aboard to please go back to their offices.

Delia and I were just about to step into the elevator when I got the second call from Beth. I told Delia that I would see her upstairs in a few minutes.

I walked out the south side of the tower and answered Beth's call. She told me about the hijackings and then she screamed that there was another plane. I looked up just in time to see Flight 175 plow into our tower. By then, I knew that Delia was already on the eight-fifth floor and I could only hope that the jet had hit much higher."

I ran across Liberty Street into another building to avoid the wreckage falling all around us. From then on, the firemen wouldn't let anyone go near the Towers. I watched from a window and began to see people falling from the South Tower. It was the most horrible thing I've ever witnessed. At one point, I thought I saw a figure falling, turning red and blue as it tumbled downward. I couldn't watch, because I knew Delia was dressed in a red blouse and a blue skirt that day. So, I left and started walking toward Battery Park where we were all engulfed in the dust cloud of the South Tower collapse."

I looked at Beth. "I want to apologize to my wife and my children, for continuing this ruse all of these years, and to the family of the late Delia Moore, for not coming forward with the truth sooner. That's all I know, and it is all true."

Aftermath
Today

Beth filed for divorce the following week. She said she could never trust anything I ever said again. I don't blame her. I told the worst kind of lie, just to protect that one indiscretion and to make myself look less like the coward I was. I gave her full custody of the kids and they moved to New Hampshire the following year. We talk every now and then when I see my children on holidays. She has moved on, but I can't seem to get beyond that lie that I wove so tightly around me. I feel as if I am buried under all that steel and rubble that destroyed so many lives.

I want so badly to fix it, to go back to that day, to kiss my wife and kids that morning, to hold my head high as I blow the dust off that Bible, and finally begin reading its bloodstained pages.

But I can't. No one can ever return to the ground before zero.

The Ground Before Zero won the 3rd Place Award in the
2020 York County Arts Council's Literary Competition

Cover design by Julia Graham.

Silent Assault – Synopsis

For US Army Air Corps, flight Officer Oliver Carmichael Faris Sr. and his co-pilot, John R. Jackson, this mission was supposed to be a piece of cake. It certainly couldn't be nearly as bad as what they experienced on the night of June 6th,1944, the D-Day landing. This time they would be landing in daylight, and southern France has many vast open fields in which to land their US made WACO combat glider. But sometimes things just don't turn out like they are supposed to.

SILENT ASSAULT

*Based on a memoir of Oliver C. Faris, Sr. originally
compiled by Oliver C. Faris, Jr. in the 1960s*

The phone call telling me of my father's death was not unexpected. I
was in my car, about a mile from my parents' home when I got the call
from my older brother, Michael. "Daddy is gone," is all he said.

At least my father was home when he died and not in some cold
hospital. His last days had been spent in his own bed surrounded by the
people he loved. His body had been racked with bone cancer for many
months and the last few days had been the worst. He lay in the bed, his
mouth agape; unable to move or even swallow the water we gave him on
a sponge. It was a terrible time, half wishing for a miracle, half wishing
for it to just be over. I felt guilty for wanting the latter, but I knew this
was no way to live.

As I pressed the end key on my cell phone, I noted the time. It was
10:15 on the morning of November 18, 1991. It wasn't a date I cared to
remember as I wished I could put it as far from me as possible. There
were so many questions that remained unanswered. So many things I
still needed to tell my father. That's when the tears came. That's when I
realized that I would never again look into his eyes, never hear him
speak my name, never again be able to give him a hug on his birthday
and whisper, "I love you, Dad."

The house where my father died was less than a mile from the spot
where he was born. He was the third child of Mattie Bell Simpson and
James Craig Faris, Sr. He came into the world in breach position on Friday,
March 13, 1918 in the front bedroom of his parents' farmhouse in a tiny
South Carolina hamlet called Catawba Junction. His mother named him
Oliver because she liked the name and Carmichael after the new preacher
who had just been hired at their church. Only later did she realize that the
preacher's first name was also Oliver. Because of this, his brothers
teased him about the name and called him "Rev" the rest of his life.

I knew little about his early years. Only that he grew up milking cows,
feeding the chickens, and every day before breakfast he would walk three
miles to read the river level gauge for his father who served as the local

weatherman. My grandfather ran a grocery store and never had enough time to spend with his own children. That was probably why Dad spent so much time with us. He loved to fish, but not with a rod and reel. All he needed was a cane pole, a can of red worms, and a clear stream. Fishing was Dad's one great passion and he would take us along whenever he could. I soon learned that whether the fish were biting or not, the fishing would continue all day, eventually making me detest the sport.

Dad was only fifteen when my grandfather died. Oliver had to quit school to help support his mother, Mattie Belle, and his younger brother, Joe. It couldn't have come at a worse time. The year 1933 was in the depths of the great depression and jobs were hard to come by. A job was not something you walked away from, he always said. After weeks of waiting outside one of the local textile mills, he finally was hired. Except for a leave of absence during the war, he kept the same job his entire life.

As I pulled into the driveway of my parents' home, I thought about my father's war stories. Most World War II veterans wanted to forget the war, but not Oliver Faris. He had been a glider pilot and loved to talk about how he had crash-landed seven times, five of them behind German lines. It was almost as if the war had been the defining years in his life. My brother had helped him write his war memoirs in the form of a manuscript, and throughout his life he had dreamed of someday having them published. For years, I had listened to him retell the same old tired stories but had never bothered to sit down and actually read his manuscripts. As I walked into the house, I was overcome with a desire to do so. Perhaps through them, I might once again hear his voice.

His body was still lying on his deathbed when I entered the room. Catawba was twenty miles from the county coroner's office and it would take them a while to arrive.

"Where did you put them, Dad?" I said as I touched his limp fingers. They were still warm. They had once been strong hands; hands that had never struck any of us in anger. His eyes were still open, and despite my attempts to close them, they remained that way.

"Where did he put what?" my mother asked as she came to the doorway behind me.

I turned and gave her a long hug. She was holding up well, but she always had been strongest in times of crisis. Her tears would come later.

"Where did he put what, son?" she repeated.

"His war stories," I explained. "I just feel like he would want me to have them, now that he's—" I found that couldn't say the word.

"It's all right," she said. He fought a brave fight and now he's finally at rest. I'm glad you and Mike could be here with him to the last. He loved both of you so much."

I thought about the last words I ever heard him say. "I had two fine boys," he had murmured only a week before. I sat on the edge of my father's bed and let the tears flow.

My mother sat beside me and put my head on her shoulder. She was being strong so I might grieve. "I know he would have wanted you to have his stories," she said, "but I have no idea where they are. There is nothing we can do until the coroner arrives, so why don't you go upstairs and poke around his old file cabinet. I bet they're somewhere in there."

I counted the twenty-one steps it took to reach the second floor. I could've walked those stairs blindfolded as I had every morning in my youth; my eyes still asleep and remembering to duck under the door-frame on the 15th stair when I had outgrown its clearance. It's odd what you remember at a time like that.

Through the upstairs windows I could see cars pulling into the drive as neighbors and family members began stopping by to offer their con-dolences and plates of food. I had been to enough wakes to know that within the hour the house would be full of people and the smells of fried chicken and mashed potatoes. Mourning food.

I began searching through the drawers of my father's file cabinet but all I found were copies of mimeographed newspapers called *The Catawba Gazette* that my brother had published his last year of high school. They were interesting, but not what I was looking for.

I was just about to give up when I remembered my father's old army trunks. I opened the small door leading into the attic and knocked away the cobwebs. The space was dark as I felt my way along the edge of planks that had been loosely laid over the ceiling joist to form a floor. The cord to the bare light bulb was where I remembered, and I gave it a yank. A forty-watt bulb manufactured before I was born flickered to life and filled the attic with a yellow glow. Before me stood two wooden trunks, their tops covered in a layer of dust. I could barely read the faded stenciled letters on the top. F/O O. C. Faris, 75th Squadron, 435th Troop Carrier Group. I unlatched the stiff clasps and slowly lifted the lid.

Inside was an object that would have struck terror in any unsuspect-ing visitor: an unexploded German hand grenade. It was about a foot long with a wooden handle to make it easier to throw. My father had told me the GIs called them "potato mashers" and once they were dis-armed they were excellent for mashing potatoes in a helmet. I remem-bered him showing it to me years before, and how he had unscrewed the handle and dumped out the explosive to disarm it. I removed the grenade and set it aside. The trunk was filled with old copies of *Stars and*

Stripes newspapers, German helmets, and other mementos of the war, but no memoirs.

When I opened the second trunk my luck changed. Folded neatly on top was one of his olive-green Flight Officer's uniforms. Attached above the left breast pocket were the silver wings with a "G" stamped in the center: the unique insignia of the U.S. Army Air Corps Glider Pilots. I touched the uniform and remembered my father trying it on for size when I was a young boy. He never outgrew his uniforms and he proudly wore them when he returned to France for the 25th anniversary of the invasion of Normandy in 1969.

I continued to dig through the trunk and stopped to read the headlines of the *Stars and Stripes*. Deeper, there were boxes containing snapshots, apparently taken from dead German solders, that gave a glimpse of their comrades and loved ones. A stack of German helmets contained sewing kits, razor blades, and a box of chocolates that had melted and been nibbled on by generations of rodents. Still there were no signs of the manuscript, but near the bottom of the trunk I found a vital clue. A photograph, taken of my father in France during the 25th D-day reunion, showed him holding a leather satchel. It was only then that I remembered him taking it with him every time he attended a war-related event. I found the satchel lying beside the doorway to the attic where it probably would have gone unnoticed had I not found the photo.

Downstairs I could hear voices, and realized the house was filling up with people. I wanted privacy and there was no place more private than where I was. I blew the dust from the lid of one of the trunks and sat with the satchel in my lap. The dried leather strap cracked as I unclasped it from the side and opened a gateway of memories recorded in double-spaced type on yellowed sheets of paper.

He flew in a time before the invention of the helicopter, when the only way to get heavy equipment behind enemy lines was to load it aboard a crate with wings. I felt as if I were sitting there in 1944, right beside him in the cockpit of a combat glider, as we were literally being dragged through flack and machine gun fire, and dumped into the middle of a ditch surrounded by Germans.

Operation "Dragoon"
August 15, 1944 3:00 a.m.

This mission is supposed to be a piece of cake. Nothing compared to the hell we experienced on D-day. That night we flew right over Omaha

Beach into the heaviest fighting the Third Reich could possibly throw at us. Even worse, our glider landed less than two hundred yards from German headquarters in Normandy, France. This time will be different since we're taking off from an airfield on the Italian coast, and landing in daylight near the Argens River valley in the coastal area of Southern France. This part of France is sparsely defended with vast open fields in which to land. Besides, the Germans are nearly defeated. You can see it in their eyes. They've lost the will to fight and are reduced to using old men and children. Even Hitler's own people tried to kill him a month ago.

My mother named me Oliver Carmichael Faris, after a preacher, twenty-six years ago in South Carolina. Jackson is from someplace called Terrell, Texas, so at least we have similar accents. In each of our pockets is an envelope with our home address on the front, and a note on the back that says, "If killed, please see that this gets to my mother." Inside is a final message of love and affection, not unlike the ones stuffed into the pockets of thousands of GIs on every mission; nothing special. It would either be tossed away at the end of this mission or cherished for decades as the last memento of a fallen son. I thought about my mother rocking in her swing on her front porch the day I left, and I prayed it would not be the latter.

At six foot and nearly 200 pounds, I'm bigger than most of the pilots. I have fair skin and dark hair, and was pretty popular with the girls back home. I learned to fly in 1938, when a local theater owner, Bob Bryant took me up in his Piper Cub. I became such a fanatic about flying that he agreed to give me flying lessons. I love flying almost as much as I love fishing, and spent two summers barnstorming before joining the Army Air Corps in 1942. It was the perfect experience for my eventual entry into the glider program—one part pilot, two parts daredevil. The best part is, unlike the infantry troops aboard, we get to go back to England after every mission to train for the next mission.

"There's the ELCO signal light, off the coast of Corsica" the co-pilot John R. Jackson says. He's only a co-pilot in the academic sense; he's in the right seat, I'm in the left, but truthfully, this bird is pretty easy to fly since it is controlled only by a stick. There are very few gauges, the most important of which is the altimeter which is invaluable in fog and rain. We take turns controlling the helm, or "stick," while the other pilot follows our location on a map. The fact that I'm in the "traditional" pilot's seat is meaningless. We are both flight officers in the 535th group of the United States Army Air Corps, and this is our second mission together.

This bird is called a WACO CG-4A cargo glider. Her wingspan is eighty-four feet and fully loaded she weighs 7,500 pounds. The troops in the back call it a "Flying Coffin," because a coffin maker was one of the sixteen building contractors in the states, but we know better. We call it "the dope on a rope."

It's hardly your traditional sailplane. Behind us are four troops of the 101st Airborne Division and a Jeep. I take a nervous breath and remember the announcement I had made on our first mission two months earlier on D-day. "Here we go, boys," I had said. "We'll set her down in a nice French meadow for ya. It'll be a piece of cake." Actually, it couldn't have been worse, so this time I make no promises.

While airborne, we are joined by other aircraft and gliders from other squadrons, all headed out over the Ligurian Sea, just north of the island of Corsica, toward our landing site in southern France.

At least this time we'll be landing in daylight as opposed to the pitch black we had to deal with two months ago. I find comfort in thinking back to that first mission, as nothing could possibly be as bad as our landing was in Normandy on D-day.

Operation "Elmira"
The Evening Assault on Normandy
June 6, 1941 6:00 p.m.

On a landing strip located outside Welford Park, England, our years of training in the states and on fields in England had finally come down to that moment. Jackson and I looked out of the Plexiglas-enclosed cockpit where fifty-two aircraft were lined up beside each other as though prepared for a parade. The C-47s, our British-made HORSA gliders, were staggered in a straight row ahead with their corresponding C-47 tow planes at a 45-degree angle to each side. Many of the C-47s already had gaping holes in their skins from anti-aircraft fire they had encountered on their earlier paratrooper raid into Normandy. Strips of tape were placed over the holes and the planes were once again deemed ready for battle. Rumor was that the anti-aircraft fire had been far worse than expected. Most of the inland gun emplacements had been unfazed by the Allied bombardment from the sea, allowing the Germans to throw up a lead gauntlet for the C-47s to fly through. It had taken a heavy mechanical toll on the planes, but by some miracle all twenty-six C-47s in their squadron had returned safely, though some of them had wings and tail sections barely attached. On the first wave, they had the element of surprise. This time the Germans would be waiting for us.

Our group commander was Col. Frank J. MacNees, a man we all admired greatly. He insisted on flying the lead C-47 tow plane into battle instead of commanding from the rear. His plane was already in position, at the end of the runway, testing its engines and slowly playing out its towlines. Within moments, his aircraft, with glider in tow, was roaring down the runway, leaving a cloud of exhaust fumes as the second row pulled into position for takeoff. As each plane and glider lifted from the ground, they circled the field in a continuous line, like some bizarre children's game of pulling ribbons through the air.

We were several rows back, in Glider Number 13, aboard a British-made HORSA cargo glider, named after a fifth century German mercenary. HORSAs were much bigger; twenty feet longer than the American-made WACO CG-4As we had trained in back in the states. They were so big they could carry three jeeps and up to twenty-eight men. Some gliders were even bigger and could carry a mini bulldozer, or even a small tank. Constructed completely of plywood covered in canvas, they could carry twice the payload of the WACOs, and on the inside they looked like a giant gun barrel.

I peered through the blue haze of smoke as the group in front of us took to the air. We watched as the ground crew double-checked two ends of a Y-shaped towrope hooked to our wings. Dust swirled around them as our C-47 tow plane slowly pulled away. The plane followed a signal jeep on the left-hand side of the runway trailing a 350-foot length of rope, the same length of the towropes. Once the plane pulled up even with the jeep, its pilots knew that all of the slack was out of our towlines.

When we were training back in Texas, one general had suggested that the tow plane try taking off at full speed and simply jerk the WACO gliders into flight. We were the first two pilots to try it and it worked fine on an empty glider, albeit nearly snapping our heads off. However, on the first try with a fully loaded glider, the rope completely jerked the frame of the cockpit off it, thankfully leaving those pilots still in their seats attached to the glider. On the second try, the towrope snapped at the glider end, and recoiled toward the plane, but on the final try, the tow rope broke where it was attached to the plane, and the recoil snapped back right through the cockpit, and knocked both pilots out cold. From then on, snatching a glider into flight was only used to retrieve empty, undamaged gliders, using a tail-hook and a rope stretched between two tall poles. Thankfully, I never was asked to pilot one of those.

"There's the signal," Jackson said. With our towrope tightened, and the C-47 cleared for take off, with a lurch, Glider 13 began to roll. The pilot of the plane gunned his engines, and we were off. We were lighter than the C-47, so at eighty-five knots we lifted off while our tow plane was still gaining speed on the runway. He eventually increased altitude and we began a slow arc around the field as twenty-six of our comrades took to the air one by one. Once our squadron was airborne, and were joined by other squadrons, we all headed south toward the English Channel.

The six members of the 101st Airborne Division behind us were called Glider Infantry and, unlike the pilots, they were not volunteers. Had they parachuted into Normandy they would have gotten hazard pay, but these guys got nothing. They sat on a row of benches lining each side of the plywood walls. The canvas skin of the HORSA was so thin many of the men would simply stick a finger through the side to get some fresh air or make their own window. Behind them was the cargo—22 rounds of 105mm artillery shells, cases of ammo, a Jeep, and several Jerry cans full of gas. Fully loaded, our HORSA glider weighed over 15,000 pounds, and the only engine onboard was in the Jeep.

As we neared the English Channel, as far as I could see, to the front, sides, above, and below, were planes and gliders packed so closely together it seemed that one could almost walk across the sky from wing-tip-to-wingtip. Three thousand feet above us were C-47s returning on the same narrow ten-mile-wide path. It was critical that the planes stick to this path as allied warships had been instructed to shoot down any aircraft outside of it. Invasion stripes had been hastily painted on every allied aircraft, but these were probably invisible to the warships after dark.

We later heard that Air Chief Marshal, Sir Tafford Leigh-Mallory, had convinced Eisenhower that to fly gliders on D-day in daylight over German-held territory would result in losing at least seventy-five percent of them. Eisenhower had reluctantly agreed even though many of our glider pilots had no training whatsoever in nighttime formation flying, much less landing in tiny French fields, surrounded by hedgerows, in the middle of a raging battle.

Portable lighthouses had also been set up along the route to aid navigation and each had been given a code name. Our squadron had taken off from an area code-named "Austin" and they converged with other squadrons at a point called "Elko." The route then took us southwest over the English Channel. About halfway across the channel, we found a floating lighthouse, mounted on a barge called "Gallup," where the entire armada turned ninety-degrees east.

All the planes and gliders flew in standard double-column formations with 300 feet between columns. Below us, in the channel, was an unbelievable sight, literally hundreds of ships, of every size and shape, as far as our eyes could see, all heading toward the Normandy beaches.

Jackson seemed oblivious to it all. He hadn't said much since liftoff, not that anyone could hear him if he did. Between the drone of the tow plane's engines, the wind whistling through the canopy, and the creaking of the plywood superstructure, it was a wonder we could hear ourselves think.

We were flying into battle for the first time, with almost no control over our flight path, and all I could do was think about the letter I had received from my mom the previous week. Times were hard at home. Everything was rationed, and her only income was the checks I sent her, the few odd sewing jobs she had on the side, and the little bit of money that my older brother, Jimmy, earned at the local textile mill. Jimmy was 4-F, unfit for service because of an old back injury, but he loved the attention of being a young single man in a country filled with lonely women. My mother suspected that at any moment he would run off and get married. To top it off, my youngest brother, Joe, who was in the Navy was training for the invasion of Japan. If both Joe and I were killed, there was no telling what might become of our mother.

My years of training seemed a distant memory, and try as I might, I couldn't think of a single thing that had prepared me for this moment. We were being dragged into battle with cases of high explosives, gallons of accelerator, and a quarter-ton Jeep chained to a plywood floor. If it broke free of its restraints during the landing it would crush us all like a boulder on wheels. "What in heaven's name am I doing here?" I said to myself. To make matters worse, in a few minutes the Germans would be shooting at us.

8:30 p.m.

The evening sky still had shades of blue in the west as the air armada approached the Normandy coast. From "Gallop" we had flown east until we had reached a point over the channel, code-named "Spokane," where we had taken an abrupt right turn toward the Normandy coastline. The section of beach we flew over was called UTAH and had been captured earlier in the day by the Americans. It was now lined with landing craft and men moving inland. In the distance we could see the first bursts of flack and tracer rounds of the anti-aircraft fire about a mile or so inland. Within moments it looked like the entire area was a fountain of white streaks. My heart began to pound at the sight, and I had trouble breathing.

"We're dropping down to 500 feet," I said, watching the altimeter and yelling over the wind noise, "below the flack."

"Just wonderful!" Jackson said as he put on his helmet. "That puts us within machine gun range!"

The tracer bullets were getting thicker and we were headed straight for them. It was a chilling thought to realize that for every tracer there were four lead slugs. We began to smell gunpowder as we passed through the first layer. Bullets hit the glider, slashing up through the floorboards and smashing holes in the plastic cockpit canopy as they exited. One bullet hit the Jeep, busting its left headlight. I glanced back at the troops. There were splinters of wood and dust flying around from the bullet holes. Some of the men had taken off their helmets and were sitting on them. Someone kept repeating, "Hail Mary, Mother of grace" and another screamed "Oh, Lord" with every bump.

A huge explosion blasted to the right of the glider sending pieces of shrapnel flying through our cockpit. One piece sheered off the end of Jackson's boot.

"Hot damn-it!" Jackson yelled.

"Are you okay?" I asked.

"Just great!" Jackson complained as he examined the boot. "Just missed my big toe. That was the only pair that fit!"

I shook my head in astonishment. Jackson was more concerned about his boots than his foot. "Is that all?"

Jackson shrugged. "I've got news for you, buddy. It might have missed my foot, but you try walking back to England with your big toe hanging out."

Another bullet crashed through the floor between my legs, just missing my right thigh. I wished I shared Jackson's optimism.

The tracers and bullets kept coming, and big puffs of blinding orange from the flack, followed by black smoke. It was unbelievable how many long streams of tracer rounds there were. Even though the sun had set, through the canopy we could make out the long gray shadows of trees outlining hedgerows and fields below.

The glider was still being pelted, and less than a mile ahead we began to see the lights of the Normandy town of Ste. Mère-Eglise. Past the town, almost no tracer fire was visible. Jackson commented that in the distance was the green-lit "W" that marked our landing zone, just to the south.

A light in the cabin glowed red. "Not yet! You sorry-ass bastard!" Jackson yelled in the direction of the tow plane. "We're nowhere near our landing zone. He's dumping us."

I looked up to see the light change to green, which meant we had to release our end of the towrope. Jackson slammed his helmet into the floor amid a torrent of curses and fumbled through the fading light for an aerial photograph showing the landing zone. He found the picture but couldn't see what was on it.

"What's the damn point of giving us this without a flashlight?" He tossed the photo over one shoulder and it flew against the helmet of one of the troops. The man was too frozen in terror to bother removing it.

"If we don't drop our end of the towrope, the plane will drop his," I said, "and the last thing we need is 350 feet of rope dangling from our nose." We couldn't communicate with the tow plane's pilot, so we really had no choice. Jackson grabbed the rope release and pulled. Once the rope was released, we only had about fifteen to twenty seconds before we would hit the treetops.

"Take over," I said. I had flown the final leg and it was now Jackson's turn to land it.

A hush filled the cabin as the glider banked to its left. In the darkness, we silently floated above the treetops, with the gunfire following the sound of the plane.

The immediate problem was that we were so heavy we were dropping like a rock. This was bad considering we were flying only 500 feet off the ground to begin with. We flew over a big château, and I spotted a light through a hole in the roof. The Germans were running out its front door like fire ants protecting their nest. A front lawn stretched out in front of the building with tall trees that lined both sides. We came in low, and brushed the top of a tree.

"This is it," Jackson yelled. "No room to come around. Full flaps. I'm setting her down on their front lawn."

Won't the Germans be thrilled! I thought. "You better pancake it." I could already see there was no way we were going to stop in time to avoid the trees at the far end of the lawn. "Holy mother!"

Jackson plowed the glider hard into the ground, hoping to knock out the landing gear, but one of the wheels held. We both jammed on the brakes.

"All right now," I kept repeating, but the trees kept coming. I looked up and caught a glimpse of a wing passing over our heads, not ten feet above us. Another glider was trying to land in the same field.

Jackson yelled something about his helmet. I was focused on the tree directly in front of me and put out a hand as it blasted through the canopy; my face and shoulder brushed the bark as it passed to my left. I leaned to avoid the next one, but a tree slammed into my leg just below the right knee. Pain shot through it as I pivoted around and between two smaller trees.

Everything in the rear slid forward as we slowed, piling up on us. The grinding of wood and metal was thunderous. It seemed that the rear of the glider would never stop coming. I could just picture artillery shells, broken bones, and Jeep parts all pulverized together. I felt like I was trapped inside a house that had just been dropped on its side from a hundred feet and now someone was bulldozing its remains into the woods.

It all came to a screeching halt and then there was silence. We were completely buried under wreckage.

"Are we dead?" I asked. No one answered.

Within moments, bullets started tearing through the wreckage around us.

"What the hell are they shooting at us for?" I asked. "We're dead!"

"Faris, you all right?" Jackson murmured. We had been shoved together. I couldn't see him, but could feel him moving.

The roar of another plane just over the treetops muffled my reply. I tried to move, but both legs were completely numb and the skin on my left hand felt shredded. I kept trying to free my legs, but they were pinned. At least neither of my legs seemed broken. "A few cuts," I said. "I think I'll live. How about you?"

"Yeah. Tree hit me in the hip," Jackson replied. "Hurts like hell. You reckon we can dig out from under this?"

Suddenly machine gun fire sounded like it was only yards away. "I'm not staying here," I said, then thought about the troops in the rear. "You guys back there?"

Wreckage moved only inches from my face. I could make out the shape of a helmet.

"We'll ease her down into a nice French meadow, boys," one of the solders mocked in a southern accent. "It'll be a piece of cake." He spit out something. "Right! Where in the *HELL* did you guys learn to fly?"

Southern France
August 15, 1944

"Oliver!" Jackson says, snapping me from my trance, the metal framing of a WACO CG4-A in front of me instead of the wrecked cockpit of a HORSA glider.

"What?" I say, looking around. We're in a circling pattern.

"We have the green light, buddy. Take over!"

It takes me a moment to realize that we are over the Argens Valley in southern France. We start picking up some ground fire, but it's nothing like Normandy. I pull the rope release and bank the glider to the left. It's shortly after nine in the morning, but in the valley a layer of fog, or perhaps smoke, blankets the ground. I can't tell if the landing zone is already filled with gliders or not, so I scan through the haze for neighboring fields in which to take her down. They all look like vineyards with short posts. Not good.

"There's a spot," Jackson points.

Through the haze, a perfect field appears and lies directly ahead of us. It borders what must be a creek between us and the landing zone filled with gliders.

"All right!" I say. "Finally, we get the chance to land this bird the way we're supposed to, just like we practiced back home."

"Suits me!" Jackson says. "Better than landing in a tree."

We drop to fifty feet, and gray rows of the field confirm that it's not a vineyard. "Piece of cake," I mutter to myself.

At thirty feet we begin to notice a darker pattern to the rows. I can't tell, but perhaps the field has recently been plowed. "Jackson, what is that?"

"I'm not sure." He peers out his side window. When he looks back at me the blood seems to have drained from his face.

"What is it?"

Jackson can hardly say the words and we're only twenty feet off the ground.

"It's corn," he says. "Stalks of corn!"

"Oh, damn! Not again!"

We hit the cornstalks at seventy-five miles per hour. They wrap around the wings and landing gear like a giant spider's web. We might as well have thrown out a ship's anchor. The glider comes to rest in what seems less than twenty yards. Unfortunately, everything not bolted down, including us and the troops in the back, goes a bit further.

Since then, I haven't cared much for corn.

Oliver Faris was this author's father. He was 26 years old at that time.

Silent Assault, won the 1999 Carrie McCray Literary Award for Best Short Story (State-wide juried competition). This was the author's second short story, and the first installment of a three part trilogy.

Cover design by Christiaan Volstead and Craig Faris.

Big Daze – Synopsis

On the night of June 6, 1944, Army Air Corps Flight Officer Oliver Faris,was lying in the ditch of a hedgerow in Normandy, France which was less than 100 yards from German headquarters for this sector. He, along with his fellow pilot, John R. Jackson, and eight infantrymen, were surrounded by 15,000 German troops. Their combat glider was a total wreck, the Jeep was hopelessly buried in the wreckage, and even the plants in the ditch were attacking them. But the good news was, they were all alive, at least for the time being.

BIG DAZE

Based on a memoir by Oliver C. Faris, Sr.
Second of three stories

1995

There was a chill in the morning air as I watched the backhoe carefully position itself between two granite headstones and lower its stabilizers in front of my father's grave. I glanced at the workmen standing beside me, but no one said a word. My mother sat in her car out by the edge of the cemetery and I could see her dabbing her eyes with a tissue.

Most people only have to bury their father once, but this was the second time for me. At my mother's request, his grave was being exhumed and moved about thirty yards to a new plot. The old family plot was simply getting too crowded. I'm not sure who originally purchased it, but since the burial of my grandfather's grandfather in 1885, the family tree had sprung so many forks that half the names were cousins I'd never heard of.

Mom wanted to be buried next to Oliver, my father and her husband of forty-three years. But she also wanted to be buried next to John, my stepfather. Therein lay the problem. There wasn't room for all three. I took the liberty of suggesting a far easier solution: simply dig his grave deeper, then put her casket and John's on top of his. That way they could all be together.

Mom just gave me a weird look and went ahead with the exhumation.

It only took a few scoops to uncover the vault and I was surprised at how shallow Oliver's grave had been. It reminded me of a story he had once told me about burying the dead on D-Day during World War II.

"It was June," he had said, "so you had to get the bodies underground as quickly as possible. The problem was, we were trapped in these hedgerows and the only soft ground was out in the open fields, right where the German snipers could pick you off. So, we used our bayonets to cut the roots and dig out shallow depressions between the hedgerows. We wrapped the bodies in parachutes, rolled them in, and covered them with leaves and whatever dirt we could find."

I can only imagine how scared my father must have been after crash-landing his combat glider into the front lawn of German headquarters in Normandy. "We were surrounded by thousands of Germans," he had said, "but apparently they took one look at our glider's wreckage and assumed we were all dead. I came really close to occupying one of those shallow graves," he added, "but in the middle of all of that fighting I met *Big Daze* and it changed me."

WASP NEST
JUNE 6 - 7, 1944
Ste. Mère-Eglise, France
Around 11:00 p.m.

Flight Officer Oliver Faris was struggling to free himself from the wreckage when tracer bullets started coming through the glider from all directions. A bullet whizzed by his head and this was all the medicine he needed to get his legs moving. He put both hands under his left thigh and yanked it free. With a tremendous heave he managed to free the right. Sensation began coming back to his numb legs and it wasn't good. His right foot ached and he feared it might be broken.

The area around Ste. Mère-Eglise, like most of Normandy, was made up of small rectangular fields divided by hedgerows with trees, thickets, and shrubs. They had been told that the trees in the hedgerows were no higher that fifteen feet, but clearly these trees were fifty to sixty feet tall. The hedgerows had either drainage ditches or sunken roads running down the center of the trees. The Germans used hedgerows to their advantage by setting up machine gun nests that could sweep the surrounding fields. Glider 13 of the 75th squadron had come to rest imbedded in a hedgerow overlooking a low leaf-covered ditch. They were near the corner of a field, and on the far end, up a rise, was the château they had passed over. Most of the machine gun fire seemed to be coming from around there.

German anti-aircraft guns were sending up enough tracer fire to sporadically light the field, and Oliver noticed the tail section of another glider about thirty yards to his left. He assumed this was the other glider that had passed over them moments before. The remains of his glider were now an unrecognizable pile of tangled wreckage. It appeared the only way out was through the hole in the Plexiglas canopy left by the trees.

He kicked at the Plexiglas with his good leg. The whole plywood floor of the cockpit broke loose, and rolled end over end into the ditch, taking Oliver and Jackson, who were still belted into their seats, with it. The infantrymen tumbled out on top of them. In an exasperated tone, one of them said, "First we land in a tree, and now we somersault into a ditch. You fellows have any other surprises up your sleeves?"

"Yeah," Jackson said in a low voice. "Now the Germans show up and blow your head off for talking too damn much! So shut up, and give us a hand with these seat belts before they come looking for us!"

The noise had apparently attracted attention and tracer fire started coming from five directions. The men dove for cover and helped to free Jackson and Oliver from their seat restraints. Branches and small debris rained around them cut by bullets whizzing through the trees. The scent of cordite and smoke burned their eyes and nostrils. They could hear the muffled sounds of German voices, so they hunkered down as low as possible in the ditch and did a head count. Despite the landing, everyone seemed to be healthy enough to fight. .

Oliver reached for his sidearm. It was gone. His rifle, which had been right beside him in the glider, was also missing. So was Jackson's. Jackson began digging through the cockpit wreckage searching for his M-1 rifle. He eventually found both rifles, but they were smashed into several pieces. "Just great!" he said, and threw the broken stocks down the ditch. The infantrymen couldn't account for many of their weapons, either, and it was nearly impossible to dig though the wreckage in total darkness. Out of the eight men's weapons, they were only able to find three M-1 rifles and two pistols. Oliver and Jackson had only one weapon apiece, their bayonets.

Jackson did manage to find his helmet, but he complained that it didn't fit tight enough. Oliver pointed to his own naked head and said, "At least *you* have one."

The ditch provided good cover and after a few minutes the enemy tracers were again aimed skyward toward planes and gliders. In the relative safety of this lull, Oliver again tested his foot. He reached down to rub it, and instantly let out a muffled cry of pain. Instinctively, he jerked his hand back, the noise prompting additional gun fire.

"You hit?" Jackson asked, unable to see what happened.

"Something stung me," Oliver replied, sucking on the wound. "I must have put my hand in a wasp or yellow jacket nest."

"Wasps don't fly at night," Jackson said. "That's the stinging weed we heard about. I think one got me on my big toe when I fell out."

"It's called a nettle," one of the infantrymen said, his face and body shadowed in the darkness. He was on his belly beside them with the silhouette of his rifle pointed toward the château.

"A what?" Jackson said.

"Stinging nettles. The stems are covered with thousands of tiny sharp hairs; only these are more like needles. They're like pressure-loaded hypodermic syringes. When you touch the stem, it shoots a caustic solution of formic acid under your skin. Swells up and hurts like hell, just like a bee sting."

"Yeah, tell me about it!" Oliver said.

"What are you, a doctor or something?" Jackson asked.

"Something like that," he replied, tapping his helmet. It had a medics cross on it, barely visible in the darkness.

"What do I do about it, doc?" Oliver asked.

The medic shrugged. "Stay away from 'em."

"We know that!" Jackson said. "How can you treat it?"

"Usually with the juice of dock, or mint," the medic replied.

"Right!" Jackson said. "We'll just head out into that field and tell the Germans we're looking for mint juice!"

The medic didn't seem amused. "I've heard the juice of the nettle itself helps."

"I ain't touching those things again." Oliver said.

"Well, if you can find some cool mud, you could try rubbing that on it."

"Mud? Great!" Oliver said. "We're completely surrounded by Germans, my hands are torn all to hell, and now we have souped-up plants shooting at us. How in the hell did we get in this mess?"

"You guys landed us here, that's how," one of the other infantrymen said.

Jackson countered. "We were supposed to land at a pre-lit landing zone with twenty-six other gliders. It was that damn tow plane pilot who dumped us here!"

"You mean we're separated from the rest of the squadron?" the medic asked.

"You guys pipe down," Oliver cautioned. "We're not totally alone. There's another glider around here somewhere."

"How do you know?" one of the infantrymen asked.

"It almost landed on top of us. I saw the tail section of a glider about thirty yards down this hedgerow on the left. Those guys are probably just as scared as we are."

"That might be our tail section," the medic said. "It broke off when we hit."

"It did?" Jackson and Oliver said in unison. They had no idea.

"Why do you think we're still alive?" the medic said. "The Jeep stayed with it. That's the only thing that saved us."

"Then if we can salvage the Jeep," Oliver said, "it could be our ticket out of here."

"Who's in charge of your group?" Jackson asked the infantrymen.

"I am." One of the shadowed men crawled forward. They couldn't see his face, but he sounded like the one who had mocked them earlier.

"What's your name, soldier?" Oliver asked.

"Just call me Sarge," he said. "Everyone else does!"

"Okay, Sarge," Jackson said. "Why don't you take a couple of men and see if you can check out that glider?"

A shell exploded in the orchard filling the sky with light for an instant.

"Why don't you?" Sarge replied sarcastically.

Jackson scowled. "All right, but you'll have to give me your rifle. All we have left are bayonets."

Sarge hesitated. "That's not my fault and I'm not about to give up my rifle."

"Looks like you're elected, then," Jackson said.

"Who put you in charge? You might have been hot shots in the air, but we're on the ground now."

"We're flight officers," Jackson said. "As long as you're in the wreckage of this glider, we're still in command."

"Look," Oliver reasoned, "if we don't hook up with the crew of the other glider before daylight, the krauts will come looking for us. Right now, we need to join forces with someone and get some firepower up here."

Sarge didn't argue that point. "Corporal, you and your buddy come with me." The three men crawled down the ditch toward the broken tail section. While they were gone, the Germans started sending up white flares which lit up the surrounding fields like it was daylight. Directly across from where Glider 13 had landed, there appeared to be some kind of orchard. At the far end, less than a hundred yards away, they spotted a machine gun emplacement. The Germans who occupied it were facing the opposite direction and would have been easy targets if any of the remaining infantrymen had a rifle. The primary mission was to salvage the Jeep, look for rifles, and any ammunition, so they kept down and crawled.

Within fifteen minutes all the flares had died down and the scouting crew returned. Sarge, still shrouded in darkness, reported. "The tail section is ours. The Jeep looks okay, but the front wheels busted through the floor of the glider when she landed. We'll have to wait until daylight to get it out."

"Where's the other glider?" the medic asked.

"No idea."

"They probably landed in the trees and bought it," the Corporal answered.

Tracer bullets buzzed over them, slamming into the walls of the ditch with chilling little "Hmp" sounds.

"Maybe they're the ones shooting at us," Sarge added.

"Keep your voices down," Oliver cautioned in a whisper. "Every time you talk it draws more fire."

"We spotted a machine gun nest not a hundred yards out in that field," Sarge said.

Without weapons, they knew they would be sitting ducks if the Germans came looking for them, so they hugged the ground every time a shell burst would light up the sky. As he lay there, Oliver began to realize what they were facing. With their maps and weapons buried under tons of wreckage, they had no idea where they had landed. Worse, they were right in the middle of thousands of Germans; eight men, with a busted Jeep, three rifles, and two pistols. Jackson sure picked a hell of a place to land. This wasn't any French meadow; it was hell.

Muffled voices in German had kept them all hunkered down as low as possible for hours, and sporadic light from anti-aircraft fire silhouetted the château at the far corner of the field. Most of the initial gunfire had come from there but had since died down.

It began to rain, and Oliver was tired of lying in a wet ditch with his foot getting stiffer by the minute. He was scared and ready to move to any place with better cover. "I'm going to crawl down this ditch and see if any other gliders landed near us," he whispered.

"Are you, crazy?" Jackson replied. "The Germans have rifles. All you have is a busted foot."

"Beats staying here just waiting for them to come find us."

"Look at that wreckage," Jackson said. "They think we're dead. So, whatever you do, don't give them a reason to think otherwise. Oh, and don't forget your cricket."

"Don't have it," Oliver said. The cricket was a clicker that produced a cricket sound when pressed to notify friendly troops that they were Americans. Oliver either forgot his, or it fell out of his pocket when they rolled into the ditch.

"Then use the password," Jackson said.

Oliver agreed and crawled down the ditch. The leaves smelled of mildew, and every few minutes he would run into another stinging nettle. It was all he could do not to yell out every time he got nailed on the hand or face. The bare underbrush soon gave way to vines that provided a thick canopy of cover. Despite the broken foot, he decided it was easier to walk than crawl. He stuck his bayonet down in his boot to help his ankle support the weight.

Oliver crept along slowly and crouched with each shell burst. He had traveled about a hundred yards when he heard muffled foreign voices. If he was killed or captured, the Germans would follow the ditch and discover the others. He decided it was time to retreat and silently crept back down the ditch.

In the flash of an exploding shell, Oliver saw something move. He dropped to the ground and froze in complete terror. The vines, just in front of him, moved upward and dropped. He held his breath and listened. In the silence, he heard heavy breathing.

Again, the tangle of vines was lifted, shaken, and dropped. Oliver instinctively reached for his pistol, finding only the empty holster. Instead, he reached for the bayonet inside his boot. With his free hand he dug into the mud and smeared some on his face for camouflage. The vines were again lifted, pulled, and dropped. Someone had obviously heard him and was trying to loosen the matting of vines to spot him. Each time, the vines were lifted as if with the end of a rifle, and with each thrust they were moving closer. In the flash of a shell he saw a mottled-brown shape and remembered that German paratroopers wore brown and white camouflage uniforms.

He stayed perfectly still, but his pursuer kept at it. Each time the vines were lifted closer, he became more vulnerable. He had to do something.

Oliver decided that the next time the vines dropped he would make his move. At that point, the paratrooper's rifle should be pointing at the ground. He would have to ignore the vines and lunge forward, embedding the bayonet before the man could react. He slowly moved to a crouched position and put the bayonet behind him so it wouldn't glint in the light of a shell blast. His heart pounded. He remembered his training in hand-to-hand combat. Within a few seconds one of them most likely would be dead. He thought of his mother and said a silent prayer.

The vines moved. Oliver took a deep breath as they dropped. He closed his eyes and surged forward, vines entangling his head. He opened his eyes, drew back the bayonet, and saw his assailant step back. He was huge. Oliver stepped forward, ready to thrust the bayonet, just as an explosion lit the scene. Staring back were strange brown eyes, large eyes. He shook his head in disbelief. It was a cow. A brown Swiss cow! In the midst of all the shelling and bullets, she was grazing on the vines.

Tears burst from Oliver's eyes as the cow let out a soothing "moo." He started shaking with laughter and dropped to his knees. He had never seen a more beautiful face.

• • •

"In the middle of all of these flying bullets, she was simply being a cow," my father had explained. "She had a dazed look on her face. Not scared, just confused. In that moment all my fear seemed to vanish. She didn't care about bullets. She was just grazing, like cows do. I realized then that no matter what I did, no matter how carefully I tried, I wouldn't live one second more or less than the good Lord intended."

I smiled at that memory as the workmen shoveled the last clumps of dirt onto my father's new grave. By the time he returned from the war, Oliver had crash-landed seven times, and the broken foot was his worst injury. For the next forty years, he raised beef cattle on a farm with his younger brother, Joe. He never seemed to worry about tomorrow. He just enjoyed raising his children and working the farm.

They're all gone now, and his younger brother occupies the grave that once held my dad.

I remember he always had this one cow that he treated specially. I guess her face reminded him of something from his past. That's probably why he named her *Big Daze*.

Big Daze was previously published in the
2005 Catfish Stew Anthology Collection

Cover design by Alaina Preslar and Craig Faris.

A Pretty Good Year - Synopsis

In this, the third installment of my father's World War II story, we pick up as he rejoins his fellow solders in the hedgerow, dodges more bullets, and makes an interesting and unexpected discovery.

A PRETTY GOOD YEAR

A story based on the memoir of Oliver C. Faris, Sr.
The third story of a three-story trilogy

The guys back at the glider would never believe it, Oliver Faris thought. Especially Jackson. If he had a helmet, he would have milked the cow just to prove his story. He had a sudden urge to take the cow with him, down in the ditch and out of harm's way. But to do so he would have to find a larger opening in the vines. If spotted, they might both end up dead. He had already scared her enough, and she had managed to survive thus far without his help. She had a dazed look on her face, like she couldn't understand why her world had been invaded. "Big Daze," he said, rubbing the cow on the forehead, "you be careful, girl. With any luck we'll both make it out of here in one piece."

He made his way back through the vines and into the ditch. He worried about the cow as one might worry about an innocent child in the middle of a busy street. He made a vow right then that if he ever got home he would buy a herd of cows and raise them on his mother's farm.

He passed the glider's tail section, but there was still too much light from distant explosions to risk checking it out. The shelling seemed to be targeted further inland. Things were calming down and he hoped he might get a few minutes of sleep before dawn. He was almost back to the place where he had started walking, when he stepped on a stick and heard a pop. He dropped to a crouch. A small branch landed near him and he realized that the pop was actually a gunshot, directed at him. He heard voices but couldn't tell if they were English or German. He was still too far from the wrecked glider for it to be his own men. He considered the possibility that the Germans had overrun their position and either killed or captured the others.

"Dodgers," he heard a voice whisper. It was Jackson's voice, and he was giving the first half of the password.

Oliver drew a blank. He wasn't much of a baseball fan and couldn't remember which answer went with the question. Unsure, he tried to keep his voice low and replied, "It's me!"

Jackson and the other men emerged only a few yards away. They had crawled up the ditch toward him, away from the wreck. "Keep down!" Jackson said. "There's a German patrol headed this way and we had to move."

"Then why did you shoot at me?" Oliver whispered.

"Wasn't us," Jackson whispered, motioning toward the field. "Them. You made enough noise to wake the dead. We figured you got captured."

"Shut up," Sarge whispered, motioning that the Germans were approaching the glider remains.

Oliver peered through the dense hedge and could see the shadowed shapes of the patrol approaching. The men huddled against the lip of the ditch and drew the few weapons they had. It would be foolish to attack them unless it was absolutely necessary.

"Guck mal dir diese Körper." they heard from near the wreckage. "Nein, niemand hätte das überleben können."

Oliver could see dark shapes moving around the glider. "Any of you guys know any German?" he whispered.

One of the infantrymen moved closer and whispered, "Something about bodies." "They doubt anyone could've survived."

"Suchen Sie nach amerikanischen Zigaretten," one of the Germans said.

"Zu dunkel und zu viel Wrackteile."

"They're looking for American cigarettes," the infantryman whispered, "but it's too dark in the wreckage."

Sarge put a finger to his lips and pointed to the German patrol as they passed within a few feet of them. They headed toward the tail section. One of them had dropped a lit cigarette butt which glowed through the damp grass and gave off the acrid odor of foreign tobacco.

"Was ist mit diesen Geräuschen in der Hecke?"

The translator readied his rifle. "They heard noises in the hedgerow," he whispered. "Get ready."

"Diese dummen französischen Kühe sind überall." The Germans laughed.

Oliver watched as the patrol reached the broken tail section. Two of them stood guard, their rifles drawn as the others went inside. He realized how close he had come to being trapped had he gone to it. They made a few inaudible comments and noises while in the glider.

"Keine Zigaretten," one of the Germans said as they emerged. "Die müssen alle tot sein. Sie verließen ihren Kübelwagen.Wir werden die Zigaretten morgen finden, wenn es wieder hell ist."

"Looks like they're leaving," Jackson whispered. And the rest of the troops relaxed.

"They figure we're dead because we left the Jeep. A Kubelwagen is their version of ours." the translator explained. "They're coming back in the morning to look for cigarettes."

"Could be a trick to lure us out," Sarge added. "Stay put."

"Why the hell didn't you give me the password?" Jackson whispered to Oliver.

"I couldn't remember if it was New York or Brooklyn," Oliver admitted.

"Brooklyn Dodgers, you idiot. Everybody knows that!"

"Right."

They lay in the wet ditch for a long time expecting the patrol to return. The earth smelled musty and there was the constant fear of putting their faces in the dreaded nettles. After a while it was clear the patrol was gone, so they relaxed and sat up.

"Where did you learn German?" Jackson asked the translator.

"I can't say I did," the infantryman said. "I grew up in a neighborhood with German immigrants and picked up a few words here and there. When I joined the army, I bought a dictionary to brush up on it. I figured it would be helpful."

"What was that thing they were laughing about?" Oliver asked.

"Something about cows. They said the stupid French cows were everywhere and it might be one of them making the noise in the hedges."

Oliver laughed. "They're right. I came within an inch of bayoneting a heifer on the way back. Scared the hell out of me."

"A cow?" Jackson laughed. "You attacked a cow?"

"It was dark. She was lifting and dropping the vines. I thought it was a German paratrooper. I leapt out of the vines with my bayonet, but it was just a cow grazing. How was I to know?"

"You thought a cow was a paratrooper?" Sarge said with a laugh. "And they let these guys fly aircraft. No wonder we landed in a tree!"

At around 2:00 a.m. Sarge led the scouting crew from the other end of the hedgerow away from the château to see if they could find survivors of the other gliders. They returned from their search a half hour later. They reported they had found the second glider crew and all were alive, but both pilots had broken legs and couldn't be moved. The remaining crewmembers had refused to leave their comrades.

One of the returning men was a paratrooper they had picked up along the way. He had dropped into the orchard the night before and was separated from the rest of his squadron. He had played a cat-and-mouse game of hiding from the Germans all day in the hedges.

"Private Andreas, sir," the paratrooper reported. "I dropped with the 505th 82nd Airborne last night."

"Any idea where we are?" Oliver asked.

"I climbed a tree yesterday and could see the church tower of Ste. Mère Eglise about a mile to the west," Andreas said. "I saw a parachute hanging on the tower. Our men were supposed to drop there but they overshot the drop zone and are scattered all over the place."

"That means that Landing Zone W should be a couple of miles south of here," Oliver said to Jackson. "Our men are supposed to converge at Ste. Mère Eglise."

"You guys picked one hell of a place to land," Andreas added. "Did you see a big château when you flew in?"

"See it? We landed on its front lawn," Jackson replied.

"Well, didn't they tell you that's the German headquarters for this entire area?"

"Oh, that's just wonderful!" Jackson said.

"There's been fighting around it all day," Andreas continued, "but I couldn't seem to hook up with any of our guys, until now. Boy, was I ever glad to see you. Where's the rest of your group?"

"Looks like we're it," Oliver said. "We don't know how many gliders landed near us. The tow plane cut us loose before we reached the landing zone. The good news is that we all made it. The bad news is that we only have three rifles between us."

"Rifles? There're plenty of those around," Andreas said bitterly. "Our men were slaughtered when we landed. They won't need them."

The big shells from the ships offshore were getting closer and were now being answered by German artillery from further inland. Each time a shell came over it was like the fluttering sound of a released window shade. The shorter the sound, the closer the shells hit and the more terror they inflicted. It didn't take long for the shells to start bursting in the fields around them and there were some close calls. At least the shelling shut down most of the machine gun fire. It was beginning to rain and the men were worried that the ditch would fill with water and force them out into the open.

Oliver was tired of lying in a wet ditch and his foot was still aching. He was ready to move again. Jackson was still complaining about his helmet and adjusting the wayward straps when Oliver asked, "Weren't there a couple of cases of ammunition and small arms in the glider?"

"I think so," Jackson replied, "but it's buried under tons of wreckage now. We'll never find them in the dark."

"Maybe it's in the tail section."

"Could be," Jackson said. "The 105mm shells were under the wings. They may have stored the ammo in the back of the Jeep."

"I'm going to check it out," Oliver said.

"In all this shelling? What are you, crazy?"

"Beats staying here and at least that end of the glider is dry. You want to come?"

Jackson shook his head. "Hell no! That glider is a mighty big target, buddy, and don't forget the Germans said they would search there for cigarettes. Plus, there's a German command post at the far end of the field. If you go, just remember to give us the signal when you come back. Okay?"

Oliver agreed and inched back down the ditch. The leaves were soaked, the ground muddy. Despite the shelling, Oliver decided it was easier to walk than crawl. His foot ached but his bayonet inside his boot helped support his weight.

He crept along in a crouched position and dropped with each shell burst. At an opening in the vines, he spotted the glider's tail section. It was not imbedded in the hedgerow as expected but was several yards out in the field. To get to it he would have to cross over open terrain now lit by the shelling. That would be too risky, and there was no guarantee that he would find any weapons or ammo inside. It was better to just go back to the others where at least there were four armed troopers now.

The first light of dawn was greeted with a sense of relief as well as apprehension. As the field was illuminated, they were able to see the damage the landing had inflicted on their glider. The American WACO gliders had a steel frame that held together much better in crash landings. HORSAs, like Glider 13, were bigger and heavier than the WACOs, but were made entirely of a plywood frame, and canvas. Judging from the skid marks, it appeared the tail section had broken off on impact. The front third of the glider, containing the pilots and infantry, had careened across the field into three trees. The third tree stopped the cockpit cold and the rest of the glider had telescoped into it. The wings were bent forward, the ends touching the ground like they were praying. The remains were almost unrecognizable, and it was no wonder the Germans had thought they were dead. It was an absolute miracle any of them had come out of it alive.

The morning light revealed the suspected orchard, and the Germans who had occupied the machine gun nest within it, had vanished. As soon as it was light enough, Jackson and Oliver began digging through the front end of the glider's wreckage looking for weapons. They found three crates of ammunition, but no pistols or rifles. One of the boxes containing hand grenades had burst open and one of the grenades had its pin barely attached. Had it gone off, the resulting explosion would've killed all of them.

Jackson was looking for his missing pistol when he found a helmet with his name in it. He examined the one on his head, the one he had repeatedly adjusted and complained about being too loose all night. "Well, I'll be damned," he said, handing it to Oliver. "No wonder it didn't fit."

Oliver took the helmet and saw O. C. Faris written on the headband. He put it on and gave Jackson a scowl. "Now it doesn't fit either of us."

All morning, C-47s were parachuting supplies around the area, but they always seemed to land just over the next hedgerow and beyond reach. American fighters swarmed over the area like bees, and they could sense the growing panic in the German defenders. At one point an American fighter circled and strafed something just beyond a hill and the smoke from it stretched out over a quarter-mile.

"Must be a convoy," Jackson said.

"I just hope it's the Germans moving out of the château and not reinforcements moving in," Oliver commented. "We better get the Jeep unloaded before that patrol comes back."

With the orchard machine gun nest abandoned, Sarge and his men made their way to the tail section and began the task of freeing the Jeep. One man kept watch, and soon they were walking with apparent confidence in and around the outside of the wreckage.

Oliver and Jackson continued digging through the remains of the forward section and began uncovering the crates which held the 105mm artillery shells. Each shell was about a foot long and about five inches in diameter. With ten shells in each crate, it took both men to drag them out.

They had just pulled the first crate out of the wreckage when they heard a sound that sent a chill of terror through both of them: bullets punching holes in the wreckage. The sound of the gun followed. It was like a burp followed by a staccato of burps. Jackson and Oliver immediately hit the ground as thousands of bullets riddled through the glider and the trees around them. They could see Sarge and his men taking cover behind the tail section. Sarge motioned in the direction of the château, to indicate where the bullets had come from. All of his men had dove for cover and appeared to be okay, at least for the moment.

The intense fire continued to riddle the tail section and Oliver half expected to see the gas cans in the Jeep explode. He forgot about those when he realized that he and Jackson had taken cover behind a crate of artillery shells.

The bullets continued to pop the earth around them followed by the burp sound. "What is that?" Oliver asked.

"Burp gun," Jackson said, hugging the earth. "We had a training film on it. Remember?"

"Must have slept through that one," Oliver replied, bullets tearing through the glider just inches above his head.

"It's an MG-42," Jackson explained. "The GIs call it a burp gun."

"No wonder. Jeez, you can't even hear the rounds."

"The film said it fires eighteen hundred rounds a minute; thirty rounds a second. But that's also its Achilles heel. When his barrel gets too hot, he'll have to change it. That's when we move."

Within a few seconds, the burp gun stopped, and Oliver and Jackson sprang up and ran to the cover of the ditch. They met up with Sarge and his men who had already crawled to safety.

"We've got to take out that machine gun or we're all dead," Sarge said. "Here's the plan. We'll break up into groups of three with a rifle-man in each group. With Andreas's weapons, we have four M-1s and four pistols. That leaves only two unarmed men. They'll carry the am-munition." He turned to Oliver and Jackson. "Since you two are such valuable pilots, you get the honor." He handed each of them a box of ammunition clips. "You scouted that ditch last night," he said to Oliver. "Did you see anything besides cows?"

Oliver described the fork at the end of the hedgerow. "The château is off to the left," he said. "I went right about fifty yards, heard German voices, and turned back."

"All right, so we have krauts on both ends of the ditch. Private, your group will return to the glider tail section and try to draw the enemy fire from there. Corporal, your group will go right at the fork and try to work your way around the flank. I'll take Andreas and the pilots and we'll go left." He nodded at Oliver. "You think you can keep up with that foot?"

"I can walk," Oliver said.

"Private, give us five minutes to get into position, then open up on them. As soon as he changes barrels, we'll hit 'em from the flank with grenades."

The vines provided good cover as the two groups made their way silently up the ditch. Through the undergrowth they could see the machine gun nest, surrounded by sandbags on a terrace below the front of the château. Neither of the groups had good position and the vines were so thick it would be impossible to lob grenades through them. They moved forward to look for an opening and were just about at the fork of the ditch when all hell broke loose.

They heard the sickening "burp" as bullets cut through the hedges like a lawn mower. They huddled in the ditch as bullets flew over their heads and ricocheted in all directions. After about a minute of intense fire, there were explosions and the machine guns fell silent. To their astonishment, they heard the unmistakable sound of M-1 rifles and American voices. Through the underbrush they saw three Americans standing over the smoking remains of the burp gun nest.

Sarge shouted a warning. "GIs from the 101st, coming out." The glider men emerged from the ditch with a collective sigh of relief. They made their way out of the vines and walked over to meet the GIs. Other than the machine gun nest, the lawn in front of the château appeared to be abandoned. Sarge talked to the three men for a minute as they sat on the sandbags around the dead Germans and shared a cigarette.

"Who's in charge?" Oliver asked.

"Captain's over there," one of the GIs said. He pointed to a group of men standing under some trees that bordered the far end of the field.

"We'll wait here," Sarge said; his men were already sharing stories with the Americans. "I don't care much for captains."

Jackson and Oliver walked across the field, jumped a small creek, and crossed over a barbed wire fence to meet up with the patrol leader who was busy studying a map.

"Flight Officer O. C. Faris, sir," Oliver reported. He started to salute but remembered this was forbidden in the field of combat. "This is Flight Officer J. R. Jackson. We're glider pilots with the 435th troop carrier group, sir."

The captain didn't identify himself. "Is that your glider?" He nodded toward the far end of the field.

"Yes, sir," Oliver said. "We were too low and came in the wrong way. Skidded on the wet grass and hit pretty hard."

"We figured you were dead," the captain said. "I was wondering who the Germans were shooting at. You guys did an excellent job of drawing the enemy fire toward that hedgerow. It allowed our men to sneak up behind them."

Oliver and Jackson looked at each other and gave the captain a smile like that had been their plan all along. "Yes, sir," Jackson said.

Just then a machine gun opened up on them from behind the châ-teau and the whole group hit the ground. The entire patrol of perhaps twenty Americans returned fire.

"I'm getting tired of being shot at," Jackson said as they lay sprawled in the dirt.

"Better get used to it, son," the captain said. "This whole area is cov-ered with snipers."

"Those krauts let us walk right across that field," Oliver said. "They could have picked us off like sitting ducks."

"No sense in getting one when you can get a whole group," Jackson said. "Around here it pays to spread out."

"Corporal!" the captain ordered, "take three men and go get them."

"Hold on, sir," Oliver cautioned. "We've heard that's German head-quarters for this entire area. They probably have a lot more than just one machine gun up there."

The corporal and his men ignored the warning and left. "Don't worry, son," the captain said. "They'll get 'em."

Within five minutes, the firing stopped, and the men got to their feet. The corporal came back with three young prisoners in tow. The Germans couldn't have been over fifteen, but the determination in their eyes made them far more dangerous than regular soldiers.

Oliver couldn't believe how quickly the corporal had captured them. These guys knew what they were doing.

"Do you have any cases of ammunition in your glider?" the captain asked.

"Yes, sir," Oliver said. "We have a couple of cases of M-1 ammo, twenty rounds of 105mm artillery shells, and a Jeep, if there is anything left of it."

"We could use some rifle ammunition if you can spare it."

"Yes, sir, and we need rifles," Jackson said. "Do you have a medic in your group, sir?"

"He was killed," the captain replied. He looked down at Oliver's hands. "You need something for that?"

"No, sir. It's not for us," Oliver replied. "One of the gliders landed in the woods and both pilots have broken legs."

"There's a field hospital about three miles south of here," the cap-tain said. "We'll radio for a medic to pick up your friends. Where are you guys headed?"

"Our orders are to make our way back to the coast as soon as possi-ble, sir," Oliver said. "The men we flew in with have orders to take both Jeeps from the gliders and join up with their group commander in Ste.

Mère-Eglise."

"Well, you're welcome to come with us, but we're headed inland," the captain said.

"Thank you, sir, but we'll stay with the injured pilots until the ambulance arrives," Jackson said.

"Corporal," the captain commanded, "go with these men and radio the position of the injured pilots to the field hospital. Take a couple of men to bring back a case of ammo."

Oliver, Jackson, and the three GIs took the most direct route to the remains of Glider 13, straight across the field in front of the château. The château now had white flags hanging out of every window.

Jackson and the corporal were walking on either side of Oliver who was chatting about how they crash landed into three trees. The two privates followed along behind them. They were about 100 yards from the glider when the corporal offered Oliver a cigarette.

"Don't smoke," Oliver said.

Jackson accepted and was just leaning across him for a light when Oliver felt something whiz by his head. A half-second later, he heard the crack of a distant rifle.

"Sniper!" one of the privates yelled. "Hit the deck." The bullet had passed between his legs and struck the earth behind him. The men all dived into the tall grass, but it was too thin to offer any cover.

"Where did it come from?" Jackson yelled.

"Ahead of us," one of the privates said.

"There's no cover," the corporal yelled. "Keep your heads down."

Jackson and Oliver kept their heads buried in their helmets. They heard M-1 rifles firing from the hedgerow, and within a few seconds American voices were calling out "clear" to each other. Sarge emerged from the trees and yelled, "We got 'em. You guys okay?"

The corporal got to his feet and gave Sarge a thumbs-up.

Oliver and Jackson eased up and brushed the dirt from their uniforms.

"That's the third time we've been shot at today," Oliver commented.

"That time he was shooting at you, buddy, not me," Jackson said.

"Me? Why me?"

"You were walking in the middle," the Jackson said. "If you walk in the middle, the Germans assume you're an officer, especially since you don't have a rifle."

Oliver looked at Jackson. "Now you tell me."

"It was in the briefing," Jackson said. "Some of us actually listened."

They reached Sarge and his men standing around the base of the glider. Some of the men were looking up in the trees.

Oliver expected to see a dead German on the ground, but there was no body. "Where is he?" he asked.

"Up there," one of the men said. "He's dead."

"Where?"

Sarge pointed to a clump of leaves about fifty feet directly above the glider's wreckage. "He's hung up in that poplar tree," Sarge said. "He's camouflaged pretty good."

Oliver couldn't spot the sniper, but he immediately realized that the tree was the same one that the nose of their glider had wrapped around. "He's in that tree?"

"Yep."

"You're kidding. That's the one we hit."

"Climb up and see for yourself," Sarge said. "He must have been up there all night watching us."

"Boy, he sure picked the wrong spot," Jackson chuckled. "Can you imagine what the top of that tree must have felt like when we crashed seven tons of glider into it?"

Everyone began to laugh. "No wonder he didn't shoot at us," one of the men commented. "It probably took him all night to clean the poop out of his pants."

Oliver still couldn't make out the body. "How are we going to get him down?"

"He'll come down in a few weeks," Sarge said, "once the vultures start on him."

A few of the men grimaced.

"That ain't right," Oliver said. "Even they deserve a decent burial."

"He tried to put a bullet through your head, Oliver," Jackson said. "I'm not breaking my neck to get him down."

Oliver seriously considered attempting the climb, but his first priority was to lead the corporal to the location of the injured pilots. Besides, his foot was swollen badly, and it was all he could do to walk, much less climb a tree.

Sarge's men returned to the task of freeing the Jeep, while Jackson and the paratrooper, Andreas, went off to search for rifles. Oliver led the corporal down the hedgerow to where the second glider had crashed and they radioed their position to the field hospital. The corporal left and Oliver sat with the injured pilots, chatting about where they were from and if their injuries would give them a ticket home. The consensus of opinion was that unless they actually lost one of their legs, they probably would be back in the cockpit within two months.

After about an hour, Oliver heard a vehicle approaching and took cover. It was the Jeep from Glider 13 with Jackson and Sarge's men piled aboard.

Jackson got out with two rifles and handed one to Oliver. It was no more that two feet long, and at first, he thought it was a Thomson submachine gun. He let out a sigh because Tommy Guns ate ammo and the 75-caliber bullet clips were heavy as hell. But on closer inspection he realized that this was the paratrooper version of an M-1 carbine with a folding metal stock. The carbine was the GI's equivalent to the German assault rifle. It fired a lightweight 30-caliber shell and each clip held thirty rounds, far superior to the eight rounds in the standard M-1 Guran. The folding metal stock allowed it to be held like a machine pistol. It would be perfect to store between their seats on the next glider mission.

Sarge helped the men unload the Jeep from the second glider and soon they were ready to leave. There were a lot of handshakes and pats on the back as the men climbed aboard. Sarge lingered behind for a moment.

"Well, flyboys, I guess this is it. You can catch a lift with the ambulance when they pick up these fellows." He glanced down at Oliver's rifle. "You know how to use that?"

"I went through basic," Oliver said. "I'll manage."

"Well, I just hope you can shoot better than you can fly. That was one hell of a landing, but I guess you boys managed to keep us in one piece." Sarge extended his hand.

Oliver shook it and saw Sarge smile for the first time.

"Don't get me wrong," Sarge added. "It will be a cold day in hell before I step foot in one of your gliders again."

"We'll see you in London," Jackson said as he shook his hand. "Piccadilly Circus."

"Yeah," Sarge said, "you boys save me a seat in that burlesque theater."

"The Windmill?" Jackson said.

"Right! Sit down front?"

"We'll be there," Oliver said.

Sarge climbed into the Jeep, touched his finger to his helmet in a mock salute, and they sped off in a cloud of dust.

Jackson and Oliver settled into the ditch alongside the injured pilots as they waited for the ambulance to arrive. The men were obviously in pain but refused to take any morphine for fear they wouldn't be able to defend themselves if the Germans overran their position. The only way Jackson and Oliver could help was to keep talking and give them something else to think about.

"What group did you say you're with?" Jackson asked.

"The 436th out of Membury," one of the pilots replied. "We were part of the second echelon of Operation Elmira. First serial."

"You guys were just ahead of us. We were in the second serial," Oliver said.

"Our tow plane took a direct hit and we had to cut loose," the pilot continued. "I think some of the planes behind us saw what happened and got the hell out of there. Gliders were dropping like flies around us."

Jackson looked at Oliver. "That's probably why our tow pilot dumped us," Jackson said.

The distant sounds of small-arms fire seemed to be fading. The battles were moving further inland, so Oliver removed a cleaning kit from his leg pocket and was studying how to best take apart the carbine. He had never been trained on this weapon.

"You guys get into London much?" the other pilot asked.

"Used to," Jackson said. "Not lately."

"Same for us. We rehearsed landings until we were blue in the face. Never so much as a scratch, until now."

"Well, you'll get to spend the rest of the war in a clean hospital with nurses leaning over you," Oliver said. "Makes me wish I'd busted my leg."

The pilots smiled. "I heard you mention Piccadilly Circus and that burlesque theater that never closes."

"Yeah, The Windmill," Jackson said.

"We never made it in there. Always too crowded. I hear the women are real lookers."

"I wouldn't know," Jackson said. "They don't wear many clothes, so I wasn't exactly concentrating on their faces."

"They have some cute ones," Oliver said. He had removed the rifle stock and was rubbing the barrel with an oilcloth.

"You wouldn't know a cute girl if she came up and slapped you in the face," Jackson said. He looked at the pilots. "We'll go into a bar, and I swear he'll end up with the ugliest girl in the entire place every time."

"I do not," Oliver said. A plane flew low over the treetops and Oliver caught a glimpse of the invasion stripes through the leaves. "One of ours," he reassured the pilots.

"What about that girl in Texas?" Jackson continued. "With the mangy fur coat and that mop of hair."

"She wasn't all that bad," Oliver said as he fiddled with the firing pin.

"Not bad? She had chicken legs! He had his picture taken with his arm around this hag and sent it to his sister. She would have scared my family half to death."

"He's exaggerating," Oliver explained. He added a piece of the rifle to a growing line of parts on a log beside him.

"No, I'm not," Jackson laughed. "He picked up this one girl in Piccadilly Circus and I swear her face could make a steam locomotive take a dirt road."

The pilots were trying not to laugh, but couldn't help it.

"Her name was Ginger," Oliver replied. He looked up from his task. "She had some good points."

"Yeah, two as I recall," Jackson said with a smirk, "and they looked like torpedoes."

"I wasn't planning on taking her back to the states."

"I wouldn't have taken her home to Fido!"

Oliver realized the pilots' faces were a contoured mixture of laughter and pain, so he stopped the banter. "You need some morphine?"

"No," the pilots said, their voices strained. "It's all right. We've seen a few of those girls ourselves. I think they called them the Piccadilly Commandos. They used to take us down into the 'tube' stations and find a little alcove in the wall. They had this crazy idea they wouldn't get pregnant if they did it standing up."

"That's true," Oliver lied as if he were the expert on such matters.

Jackson smiled. "Oliver, you should have gotten yourself a commando. They looked a hell of a lot better than the ones you ended up with."

"That takes all the challenge out of it," Oliver said. He struggled with a spring on the rifle. "Besides, there are plenty of sweet, lonely girls in London."

"With faces to match." Jackson winked. "He just wants the 'first' one to be special."

Oliver rolled his eyes. "They all were."

"Right! The last time we were in London, how many girls did you go out with?"

"Ugh, seventeen."

"We were only there ten days," Jackson explained. "How many did you get past second base with?"

Oliver smiled. "Well," he paused, "a gentleman doesn't say." The spring he had been struggling with suddenly released, scattering parts of the rifle all around them. He got down on his knees and began patting the wet leaves.

"Oh, that's just great!" Jackson said as he got down on all fours and helped gather the errant parts. "Not only is he blind, he has the worst possible luck. Tell them about that night you went out with Miss Torpedoes, Oliver."

"Her name's Ginger," Oliver corrected.

"Whatever," Jackson said. "Wait 'til you get a load of this."

The Windmill
London, March 14, 1944

The Rainbow Corners USO Club in Piccadilly Circus was packed even though it was nearly 11:00 p.m. Fred Astaire's sister, Adele, did volunteer work at the club and a packed house was usually a good sign that she was there. The moment they entered its front doors, Oliver and Jackson had to weave their way through the crowd. Jackson headed toward the bar while Oliver tried to round up a couple of chairs.

A group of English girls were sitting at a table with an empty seat and all turned to look at Oliver when he asked if the chair was taken.

The girl next to the empty seat smiled up at him. "Have a rest, Yank."

She wasn't a raving beauty, but she had pretty eyes and her dress revealed an ample amount of cleavage.

"Don't mind if I do," Oliver said. Jackson could find his own seat.

The girl slid a half-empty glass of warm beer in front of him. "Finish this for me, love. I'm over my limit."

Oliver accepted the beer with a smile. "What's your name?"

"Ginger," she said. The rest of the girls giggled as if this were a running joke.

"Do you live here in London?" Oliver asked.

She giggled. "You want to know if I have an apartment?"

More giggles from her friends.

"You Yanks don't mess around, do you?"

"No, I didn't mean anything by it," Oliver explained. "I'm just new in town and was wondering where I might find a tour guide."

"He wants a guided tour," Ginger said to her friends who erupted in laughter.

Oliver felt a tap on his shoulder and looked up to see Jackson standing behind him.

"Jackson, pull up a seat and join us," Oliver said.

Jackson tipped his aviator's cap. "Good evening, ladies. Please excuse my friend while I have a quick word with him." He smiled and pulled Oliver to his feet.

Oliver winked at Ginger and said he would be right back. Jackson led him through the crowd until they were out of earshot.

"What are you doing?" Jackson asked.

"What does it look like? I'm having a beer with Ginger," Oliver said. "Why don't you join us? She has lots of friends."

"Oliver! Look at her!" He turned toward the table. "She's a commando. They all are!"

"No, she's not," Oliver said. "She's just a girl."

"That's not a girl," Jackson said. He pointed to two beauties sitting at the bar. "Those are girls! The one on the left is with me. The one on the right would like to meet you, and in about five minutes we're going to catch the midnight show at The Windmill, okay? So, go over there and tell Miss Torpedoes and her brood that something's come up."

"I can't do that," Oliver said.

"Why not?"

"It would be rude."

"So is the clap!"

"Look, Jackson, I know you mean well, but that girl at the bar." Oliver shook his head. "I'm not her type."

"Sure, you are. She wants to meet you!"

Oliver glanced toward the bar. "You know good and well that she wouldn't give me the time of day if she wasn't looking for a free ticket to the show."

Jackson started to protest but was cut off.

"And even if she was," Oliver continued, "well, that's the kind of girl you settle down with. I didn't come here for a wife, John. I came here to have a beer and perhaps take a few swings at bat. Ginger, on the other hand, now she's a slugger."

"You know about as much about baseball as you do women, which isn't much." Jackson shrugged. "All right. It's your johnson and your wallet, but if I were you, I'd keep an eye on both of them."

"I'll see you back at base," Oliver said. He returned to the table and sat down.

"So, what did your friend want?" Ginger asked.

"A few of the guys are headed over to The Windmill to catch a show."

"Oh." She glanced at Jackson. "And we're not invited, right?"

"No, that's not what he meant," Oliver lied. "He was just asking if we wanted to go."

"Oh." She didn't sound convinced.

Oliver hesitated a moment. "I told him I was happy right here."

"Well, the theater is always a bit of fun," Ginger said. "You feel up to it?"

"Sure!" Oliver said. "Let's go."

"Give me a sec while I visit the loo." She got up and disappeared toward the Wash Closets.

Everyone else at the table was involved in their own conversations, so Oliver glanced over at the bar where Jackson was now standing between the two girls. They were both beautiful and he couldn't help but wonder if he had made the right decision. *An English wife,* he said to himself. Not exactly the kind of girl who would be content to settle down in rural South Carolina.

Ginger returned after a few minutes and the two of them made their way through the crowd to the door.

"What about your friend?" Ginger said.

Oliver glanced back at Jackson who hadn't moved. "He'll be along."

They walked across the street toward The Windmill Theater where a huge crowd, many in uniform, was standing in line to get in. They stood at the rear of the line for a few minutes and Ginger complained of the cold. Ever the gentleman, Oliver put his arm around her shoulders. He wanted to offer her his coat, but he couldn't because he was in uniform. They kept waiting, and the line wasn't moving.

"It's too cold," Ginger said. "Let's forget the show and take a walk."

"Fine with me," Oliver said. The show probably wasn't worth the ticket anyway.

They walked toward the west end of Piccadilly Circus to an intersection with a circular island in the center of the street. A huge gray object surrounded by thousands of sandbags occupied the entire island and was covered by a great dome of painted plywood.

"That looks important," Oliver said. "What is it?"

"Oh, that's Eros, the sculpture," Ginger said. "I think it was originally intended to be an angel of mercy, but some bloke renamed it after the Greek god of love. They have it covered to protect it from the bombs, so they say. Fat chance of that if one chooses to fall on it. Right, Yank?"

"Right. Is it made of gold?"

"No. Aluminum, believe it or not. Apparently, that was considered a rare metal when the blooming thing was cast. Most of the natives just gather around the base and wonder what all the fuss is about."

She shivered, "It's bloody cold. Want to come up to my flat for some tea? It's only a few blocks."

Right on cue, Oliver spotted a cab and whistled. They entered the cab and it carried them to a street lined with row upon row of old apartment buildings. As soon as they got out of the cab they heard the distant wail of an air-raid siren.

"Bloody hell!" Ginger said. "This is all we need. Come on, the tube station shelters are only a couple of blocks away."

Oliver hesitated. "It's probably nothing but a stray fighter. We've shot down all the German bombers. Goring's Luftwaffe is in full retreat."

"Are you sure?"

"Yeah," Oliver said. "Come on, let's go inside and get warm."

Ginger's apartment was on the first floor, but it was still about ten feet above street level. Because of the blackout, she opened the front door to a hall completely shrouded in darkness. She removed a small flashlight she called a "torch" from her purse to light the way. They climbed the hall steps and entered a small room. She walked to the window, drew the curtain, and lit a gaslight. The light revealed a tiny apartment. There was only the one room. A small bath sink and hotplate served as the kitchen, a tiny table with two chairs, the den, and a bed, no wider than three feet, was her bedroom. "The loo is down the hall," she said, "shared by everyone on the floor."

Ginger lit a small gas heater and Oliver sat on the edge of the bed. It seemed to be sturdy enough, but only large enough if they slept facing each other.

The air-raid sirens were wailing outside from all around the city and he began to hear scattered anti-aircraft fire. The British didn't shoot at illusions; these had to be real bombers.

Ginger handed him a glass of brown liquid.

"Cheers," she said and took a drink from her own glass.

Oliver tried it. Whatever it was, it tasted awful, like a mixture of turpentine, coffee, and gin. It was all he could do to swallow the brew.

She sat on the bed beside him, slipped off her shoes and pulled a pin from her hair, allowing it to fall around her shoulders. "Isn't that anti-aircraft fire we hear?" she asked.

"Yeah, but they'll shoot at anything," Oliver lied. "Nearly blew our squadron commander's plane out of the sky last month."

"Good," she said, pushing him back on the bed and loosening his tie. "I've been waiting for this all evening," she said. She kissed him passionately on the lips.

Oliver felt, rather than heard, the first bomb explosions. They shook the whole block, and they were coming closer.

Ginger sat up, one shoulder out of her dress. "No bloody Luftwaffe, right? Then what do you call that?"

Oliver just looked at her. "Relax," he said. "It couldn't be more than a few planes. The chances of us getting hit are a million to one."

"Right! It will take a lot more than a glass of cheap gin to convince me of that."

He pulled her close. "At least we'll have had this moment together," he said, "and the war will go on around us."

She smiled. "Oh, you're a wicked one, Yank." He felt her relax in his arms.

Second base, here we come, Oliver said to himself.

The crash shook the entire building. The floors above them sounded like they were pan caking down on top of each other. Pieces of plaster broke from the ceiling and fell around them as Ginger let out an ear-piercing scream. She jumped from the bed, the top of her dress hanging around her waist, and ran to the apartment door. Oliver tried to follow, but realized his trousers were around his thighs. He pulled them up with one hand and joined Ginger at the door. She was still topless, but neither seemed to care.

The hall was dark, but it was apparent that the entire staircase leading up to the fourth floor was gone. Above them, he could make out stars shining through the gaping hole in the roof and below them, in the basement, he could see the glowing fires from the magnesium in the bomb.

"One in a million chance, you say?" Ginger screamed. "Bloody hell! Another foot or two and it would have landed in the bed with us. Last time I ever listen to a damn Yank!"

"Look," he said. He tried to put his arm around her, but she pulled away. "It's not that bad. The dust will snuff out the fire. Come on back to bed. It's really the safest place at this point."

She looked at him like he was crazy. "Not that bad? The bloody basement's on fire! No wonder you Yanks won the revolution. You don't have the good sense to quit! Well, to hell with staying here." She grabbed her purse, threw some dresses from her makeshift closet over one arm and headed out the door, apparently oblivious to the fact that she was still topless.

Oliver sat back on the bed and fastened his trousers. "Good grief!" he said. He took a last look around the room, lit by the fires of buildings around them. "That's just great!" he said, as he headed down the remaining steps into the street.

Once he got outside, he saw how bad the fire was growing. In order to help with fire control during the blitz, the Londoners had stockpiles of buckets on every street, usually near a fire hydrant with a spigot attached to one of the ports. Oliver quickly gathered as many residents as he could find and organized a bucket brigade. Within a few minutes they were passing bucketfuls of water hand to hand and throwing them onto the fire in the basement. By the next morning, the fire had been extinguished, and what was left of Ginger's building was saved.

The Attic
November 18, 1991

Downstairs, I could hear that the sounds of the visitors had died down, a clear indication that most had already given their condolences and left. Mom wanted my bother Mike and I to drive her to the funeral home to pick out a casket for my father. For years, he had always said that he didn't want a metal casket or a vault. He thought it was stupid to spend thousands of dollars on a casket that would never be seen again after a burial. "I just want a plain wood box," he would say. "I wish I could just be buried wrapped in an old parachute like all of those fallen soldiers in Normandy were. What difference does it make if a body decays in three months or 10,000 years? No one will ever know or care."

That was so typical of my dad, and of course, Mike and my mom wanted a fancy wooden casket made of oak or walnut. A metal vault wasn't an option. It was required by our cemetery to keep graves from collapsing.

"That's not what he wanted," I insisted. "He wanted one just like that one." I pointed at a rectangular box with a grey felt covering the outside. It was the cheapest one they had.

"But it's so ugly," Mom said. "No wonder it only costs $400," Mike added.

"No one will even see it," I said. "It will be covered with his American flag the entire time."

After the graveside service was over, and the casket had been lowered into the ground, we all agreed that Oliver was right. The casket wasn't even noticed and if that's what Oliver really wanted, we could live with it.

Over those two hours in the attic, my father had spoken to me in a way I had never dreamed possible. In the dim light of that 40-watt bulb, I watched as he joined the army in 1942, trained in an aircraft so unstable it was dubbed a flying coffin, and flew his first combat mission into the nightmare of D-Day. That night he had landed on the front lawn of German headquarters for that area, and narrowly escaped being shot three times. I felt as if I had been thrown into his cockpit, crawled down a wet ditch where even the plants were shooting at you, and taken on a roller coaster ride into the depths of hell.

In one year, my father, Oliver Carmichael Faris, flew five missions into enemy territory, crash landed seven times, and lived to talk about it. To a young man, grieving his dad in a dusty attic, 1944 had become a pretty good year to remember.

A Pretty Good Year won the 2000 Carrie McCray
Literary Award for Best Non-fiction Story/Essay.

Cover design by Mia J. Macy.

Souls of the Abyss – Synopsis

In 1985 a ninety-three year old woman answers a knock on her door and is told that a man she once called the love of her life might still be alive. But that would be impossible, because it had been seventy-three years since she last saw him when they were both aboard the *Titanic*.

SOULS OF THE ABYSS
Fiction

SEPTEMBER 1, 1985

Mattie Conrad lay asleep in her bed, the television set on her bedside table burning bright, a worn and tattered Bible opened across her chest.
Her hands were old and wrinkled and the once-auburn hair was white as
new snow. Her dream of dancing to a long-faded waltz was interrupted
by the voice of Peter Jennings on the nightly news.

"They said that she was unsinkable," Jennings reported, "but seventy-three years after she vanished on her maiden voyage, the most famous
shipwreck in history, the *Titanic*, has been found."

Mattie forced herself back to consciousness. It was not a dream. The
television screen showed ghostly black-and-white images of the wreck
shot from directly above. Search lights illuminated gaping holes where
funnels had once stood tall. Light reflected off broken glass that had
been shrouded in darkness for three-quarters of a century. *Titanic* looked
much like Mattie felt, and neither had aged well.

"God Himself could not sink that ship!" Mattie could still hear her
late husband's voice as she put her fingers to the television screen. She
pictured the moment when she had first heard Connie say those awful
words. She had little doubt that his comment had awakened the wrath of
the Almighty and condemned 1500 souls to eternal darkness.

Between the first and second funnel, the great dome over the grand
staircase had been reduced to a cavernous black hole. Connie and her
had once stood on that very spot and held each other for the last time.
The picture brought back all of those memories she had put from her
mind and she had to force herself to look at it. When she closed her
eyes, she could once again feel the icy current sweeping around her legs
and filling her shoes, the water cold and burning with such intensity that
it might as well have been lava. She remembered the floor dropping
away like an elevator falling down a mine shaft. She envisioned the windows imploding as water filled the room like a rushing wave.

"Hold onto me, Mattie, we'll make a swim for it," Connie had said.

"We're going to die, Connie! There's no time left! Will you not now believe in the Almighty?" she pleaded. "Just pray to Him, Connie, and we'll be joined forever in eternity. All you have to do is believe!"

The icy current cascaded upon them and lifted them off their feet. The ceiling around the glass dome collapsed, and they immediately found themselves swimming underwater. It was so cold that it gave her an instant headache; so much worse than when you eat ice cream too fast. Holding onto Connie's hand, she swam toward the greenish lights in the ceiling. There was just enough trapped air in the paneled recess to raise their heads above the water for a few seconds.

"Take a deep breath, Mattie," Connie said. "We're going to make a swim for it!"

She looked at her husband and pleaded. "If not for me, will you not do it for Daisy?"

A great surge of water pulled her away from him and forced her out through the hole left by the dome. When she surfaced, all she could do was to swim away, knowing that no amount of searching or praying could save him from the arrogance of his own stubborn will.

Mattie opened her eyes, took her hand from the screen, and placed it on her Bible. For the millionth time she said a silent prayer for Connie's lost soul.

A tiny beam of light pierced the blue-green darkness from somewhere far above. Connie Conrad couldn't imagine its source, but it had to be coming from the surface. The lights in the chandeliers had all gone out, their bulbs popping one by one in the frigid seawater. The mounting pressure in his head was a clear indication they were sinking much deeper, but he refused to leave without Mattie. He had to make one more attempt to find her. Again, he put his mouth to the edge of the molding and sucked out a last breath of air trapped behind it. He could feel the icy current flowing past him, filling the inky blackness of the rooms and voids throughout the ship.

The water felt warmer as he swam through the swirling mass of bodies. Maybe it was the coat that had been given to him by his friend, Thomas Hart. Thomas had secured a job as a coal stoker the previous week, but the day before the *Titanic* sailed, he came down with the flu. He had said, "If I'm a no-show I'll never get another job in the White Star line." But if Connie would pretend to be him and take his place, his Certificate of Continuous Discharge book would be Connie's ticket aboard the same ship that Mattie was sailing. It was hard work, but worth it.

Connie's hands were numb as he felt each body in the black water, searching for her dress, her hair, anything to identify Mattie. He held on to this last breath knowing she would desperately need it when he found her.

What was it she had said? "If not for me, will you not do it for Daisy?"

Daisy, had been his first wife, whose cancer had overtaken her in the seventh month of her pregnancy and no amount of praying, could save her or their child. For seven years he had mourned her loss until the day he met Mattie. For a brief moment, Mattie had taken away his pain and again given meaning to his life, but fate had placed them both aboard *Titanic*.

He still recalled Daisy's last words, "Pray for me, Connie. That's all I'll be askin' of ya." It was the one thing he would never do again. To him, God's mercy was only a myth, not worth even these fleeting thoughts.

He tried, instead, to focus on the tiny light and watched it reflect off fine particles of dust suspended in the water around him. The little beam seemed to bend down toward him as though it were searching for someone. How odd, he thought. Were these the imaginations of a dying man or was the light real? It was as if some mighty hand was reaching out and pulling the beam down into the darkness around him as surely as it was pulling this ship toward the bottom of the Atlantic.

If light had mass, then surely one could feel it. What a strange substance; this particle that gives us life, that warms us, that separates night and day and supposedly good from evil. God had claimed to be the light of the world. Perhaps light was synonymous with life, and gravity with death. A schoolteacher had once dropped an egg onto the floor and explained that it had been *pulled* to its demise. What an amazing revelation. To be pulled was somehow different from just falling; pulled meant *no* escape. And now, the fastest thing in the universe was creeping ever so slowly toward a man being pulled to his own demise. He and the bodies around him were headed to a place where light had not reached since the dawn of time. It made him want to touch it all the more, and his final act before the involuntary breath overtook him, was to reach out for those last fading particles.

The man who rang her doorbell that morning looked innocent enough. His hair was white and his skin black and wrinkled. He held his hat in one hand as she cracked the door.

"Excuse me, ma'am," the man said. "Could you tell me where I might find a Mrs. Conrad?"

"What is this about?" she asked.

"It's just a favor for a crazy old man," he said. "Probably nothing. You see, my friend is over at St. Joseph's nursing home. He's never been right in the head. We thought it was senile dementia, but the other night we were watching the news and all of a sudden he starts babbling that he was aboard *Titanic* and was once married to a Mattie Conrad. Well, I saw your address in a phone directory, plain as day, and I just thought I might check it out."

"Connie? You mean he's—"

"Gracious alive!" the man said. "It wasn't just crazy talk. We thought his name was Thomas Hart, but suddenly he claims he's Connie Conrad."

Mattie's coffee cup slipped from her hand and crashed to the floor.

The breath was involuntary. That first gasp of drowning caused icy water to fill his throat, inducing him to gasp more. Had Mattie gone through this terrible ordeal as well? He thought of Daisy's last words, "Pray for me, Connie. That's all I'll be asking of ya!" How could he die without fulfilling that last request?

He couldn't speak, could only mouth the words, "Forgive them, oh Lord, and lift up their souls to Your mercy."

A hand grabbed his shirt, and dragged him upward. Cold air filled his lungs. Connie felt a sharp pain in his head and heard a voice.

"Come on lad, that's a good lad. Now breathe! Maynard, why did ya hit him, you fool? You nearly killed him with that oar."

Another voice answered. "They'll swamp the boat!"

"He's one man! Everyone else is dead you fool!"

"Come on, lad, breathe! Do ya have a name?"

Connie felt a hand reach inside his borrowed coat and remove the leather discharge book. A name was embossed on the cover in gold leaf.

"Says here you're Thomas Hart. Well, Tommy, you'll not die that easy. Ya got a lot of livin' still in ya!"

Connie took a breath and coughed up more water. He looked around and saw that he had been dragged onto an upside-down boat. He had no idea who or where he was, but the sky was unbelievably clear and filled with shooting stars.

"Connie?" the old woman standing over his bed said. "It's Mattie. I've come to take you home."

After all the years, he still remembered her eyes, sky-blue crystals set in a face of porcelain beauty. It was the same eyes he had seen reach out to him and pull him from the cold depths. "Mattie?" he said in a frail voice. "Is it really you?"

"Yes, my love. We're going home now."

"It's been so long and I lost my way."

Tears welled up in Mattie's eyes. "I know, sweetheart. I know."

David "Connie" Conrad died a week later. He was finally home and God Himself had sent Mattie to light his way; a guidepost to guide him back from the souls of the abyss.

Souls of the Abyss won the 2000 Carrie McCray
Literary Award for Best Short Fiction.

Cover design by Stephen Simpson.

Echoes From the Ether – Synopsis

When an old style Morse Code distress signal arrives at the Brunswick Naval Airbase, in April 1996, Commander William B. Heustess has no choice but to step aboard a Lockheed P-3C Orion aircraft to investigate. He is convinced the messages are either a hoax, or an historical reenactment. The problem is, it is still a distress signal, and the vessel refuses to acknowledge the messages to explain their situation. His mission is to find the vessel then have the coast guard identify the culprits, and hold them accountable.

ECHOES FROM THE ETHER
Fiction

Brunswick Naval Airbase, April 1996

Commander William B. Heustess stepped aboard the Lockheed P-3C Orion aircraft and took a seat in the co-pilot's station. Bill Heustess was a man of average build with a slightly balding head that reflected the red cockpit lights. He was soft spoken but quick to snap orders in an emergency. He sifted through the papers in his lap until he found the map coordinates for their destination; a latitude and longitude marking an obscure spot of ocean 1,010 miles to the east. He handed the flight plan to the pilot, Lt. James Pheifer, who entered it into the navigation computer.

"Is it just the two of us, sir?" Lt. Pheifer asked. He was in his late twenties and had been a P-3 pilot his entire career.

"It's a distress call, lieutenant," Bill said. "Let's go!"

"Are you checked out on the P-3, sir?"

"If need be. I was a pilot back in the day."

"Whatever you say, sir."

The four Allison T56-A-14 turboprop engines were brought up to 25% throttle, causing the entire fuselage to rattle from the vibrations. The two men said little as the plane taxied to the end of the 8000-foot runway of the Brunswick Naval Airbase. The rattles increased as the engines were pushed to full throttle. The nearly empty Orion lifted off easily, climbing into the clear starlit sky. The lights from the naval airbase were the only defining marks separating the Maine coastline from the black waters of the North Atlantic.

"What's our ETA?" Bill asked.

"About two hours, sir, but there's a tailwind tonight."

"Good. I want to catch these bastards red-handed and nail their asses to the wall!"

"Sir? I thought this was a distress call?"

"We're treating it like it is, at least for the time being. The Canadian Coast Guard has dispatched a cutter, but we're checking it out first."

"Is there a problem, sir?"

"It's probably a hoax."

"A hoax?"

"It's a long story, lieutenant."

"Well, we go through two time zones to get there, sir, with nothing but stars to look at."

"All right. I'll start at the beginning. At 22:28 hours this evening we received a rather unusual distress call from the Canadian Coast Guard station in Stephenville, Newfoundland. It had been passed along from a ham radio operator in St. Johns who was scanning the lower frequencies when he came across a series of Morse code signals. They caught his attention because the sender was trying to reach someone in Cape Race, with the call letters MCE. His grandfather had once been an operator at Cape Race and MCE was its call sign back in the 1920s."

"Who was the sender?"

"We don't know, but he identified his vessel with the call sign MGY."

"MGY what?"

"That's it. Only three letters."

"That can't be. Some old radio stations may still have three-letter call signs but not any ships."

"Right! There are a few foreign ships that haven't updated to digital transmitters, but they all have four-letter call signs," Bill explained. "The ham operator also said the signal was in Continental Morse and that it sounded like it was coming from a damped wave transmitter, whatever that is. I understand those were replaced in the 1930s and the sound is quite distinctive."

"Yes," James said. "I've studied Morse and once saw a demonstration of an old set at a museum."

"I know. That's why we requested you," Bill said. "At 22:25 hours he heard CQD repeated six times followed by DE which I'm told means 'this is,' and then MGY repeated six times."

"CQD? That's the old distress code."

"You've heard of it?"

"Yes. CQ was 'Attention all stations' and the D meant 'Distress,' but nobody uses that anymore. It should have been SOS."

"We know. He gave his position at 41.44 north, 50.24 west, but later corrected it to our heading."

"Is the CQD why you think it's a hoax?"

"Partly, but whoever the prankster is, he is not alone. There are other ships out there answering him and every one of them is also using a three-letter call sign."

"No way! What's the point?"

"We figured it out when MGY stated that they had struck an iceberg! It's a re-enactment."

"An iceberg? So you saying that MGY is playing the part of the *Titanic*?"

Bill nodded. "We found a copy of *Titanic's* distress signals on the Internet. They match these signals exactly. MGY was *Titanic's* call sign and his culprits are using the call signs of the ships that responded. Someone is doing a major re-enactment!"

"Then why are we bothering to do a fly-over?"

"Because these bastards are not responding to our radio inquiries. Since they won't respond, we have no choice but to treat it as a real distress call!"

"Huh! And they didn't bother to tell us."

"What's worse is they are not answering our warnings."

"Well, if it's a true re-creation, maybe they don't have radios."

"They sure as hell have Morse sets! They have totally ignored our Morse signals to respond and there is no excuse for that."

"I see. So what's the plan?"

"We'll lock onto their signals and identify each vessel. When the Coast Guard arrives, their captains are going to have some real explaining to do!"

"What is their frequency?"

"It's at 500 kilohertz."

James adjusted the radio and turned on the speaker. Suddenly the cockpit was filled with the fuzzy sound of static, interrupted by dots and dashes of code. James heard the familiar three dits, three dahs, and three dits. "He's switched to SOS, sir. Man, this is weird. It's definitely damped wave and almost unreadable. I see why it caught the ham operator's attention."

"Can you tell what they're saying?"

"Yes. MKC is calling with a faint signal. He's asking if they are steering southerly to meet them."

Bill looked up the passage. "MKC was the *Olympic*. That was *Titanic's* sister ship, but she's five hundred miles away."

"That would explain why his signal is much weaker. That also means your culprits are scattered all over the place, sir."

"I'll settle for the one who is sending out the distress calls!"

"Well, MGY's signal is directly ahead."

Over the next hour and a half they continued to monitor the increasingly weak signals of MGY. At 1:48 a.m. they heard DFT (Frankfurt) ask,

"What is the matter U?" MGY responded curtly. "You are a fool, stand by and keep out!" But the signal was so weak they couldn't get a fix on it. Ten minutes later, they dropped down to two hundred feet and circled the empty spot of ocean at 41.46 N, 50.14 W.

"There's nothing here, sir."

"Anything on radar?" Bill asked.

"We have multiple contacts about five miles to the east."

"Do we have enough fuel to check them out?"

"Plenty. The P-3 has a range of 4,785 miles. We can search for about two hours."

"Good! Let's find this sucker and blow his doors off!"

James picked the closest contact and came in at only one hundred feet. Suddenly he jerked the wheel to the left and cried, "Holy cow!" The plane banked steeply, spilling Bill's papers everywhere.

Bill looked up too late to see the problem. "What the hell was that?"

"An iceberg, sir!" James replied, his voice trembling. "A big one! They're all over the place."

He pulled the plane up to five hundred feet and could make out a huge ice field stretching far to the north and south.

"I'm beginning to get a weird feeling about this, sir."

A very weak crackle came over the speaker and the direction needle instantly pointed southeast.

"There he is, sir," James said, pointing to a faint light on the horizon.

"We've got him!"

The P-3 banked south and Bill readied his 35mm camera. The ship was still thirteen miles away when James noticed the odd angle of its lights. They were pointing like a finger into the sky.

"What the hell?" James said. "Look at that!"

Bill saw it, too. A huge ship, its bow already well submerged with four tan funnels still bathed in light. As they approached, the stern of the ship rose almost as high as they were. When they flew past they could see hundreds of human figures in white vests clinging to its railings.

James immediately punched in the emergency frequency of 2182 kilohertz.

"Mayday-mayday-mayday! This is a US naval air/rescue P3-Orion. We are over a large vessel foundering, I repeat *foundering* at 41°43.32 North, 49° 56.49 West. Send everything you've got and for heaven's sake, hurry!"

On their return pass, they watched in horror as the lights suddenly flashed out and the silhouette snapped in two. Within three minutes the ship had vanished beneath the surface, leaving only tiny white specks thrashing about like so many ants.

"Do we have a raft?" Bill asked in desperation.

James shook his head. With all of their modern technology, there was absolutely nothing they could do.

They circled the area for nearly two hours, following the dim outlines of the twenty tiny boats below them. At 04:30 they radioed their last position and headed home.

"Did you get a shot, sir?"

Bill looked down at the camera still in his lap. In all of the excitement, he had forgotten to take a single picture.

The meeting was held in the base commander's office on the following Tuesday.

"You found nothing?" Lt. James Pheifer asked.

"I met with the captain of the Coast Guard cutter who returned from the site this morning. They found only this." Bill held up a piece of elaborately carved wood about four feet in length.

"No bodies?"

"None. No oil slick, no boats, and no other wreckage besides this."

"But what about the transmissions? We recorded them!"

"The tapes are blank. We have nothing to prove it, James, so the Navy's official position is that it didn't happen."

"But I saw it! You were there; you saw it!"

"I know, but how can we prove it? And now I'm not so sure. Last Sunday was April 14th, *Titanic's* 84th anniversary. This year is also a leap year, the same calendar as 1912. Perhaps what we saw was just an echo, or an apparition. Whatever it was, we've been told to just forget it."

"Forget it? What about that piece of wood?"

"One piece of flotsam proves nothing, James. That's a direct order from the Admiral. Don't let this ruin your career. That means you mention it to *no one*. Not your wife or anyone else. Understand?"

James hesitated. "I understand, sir!" He saluted and reluctantly left.

Commander Heustess hated that he had to lie to Lt. Pheifer and showing the newel post to him was probably a big mistake. But, he felt he owed him something if for nothing else to remind the young lieutenant that he wasn't insane.

For twenty-eight years he had planned this flight just to make sure that this was all truly an apparition. What they saw was a total shock, so much so that he had completely forgotten to take any photos. Not that he would have shown them to anyone.

For years, he had imagined that all that would be found would be pieces of wreckage, just like he and his father had found in 1968. That year they had chartered a fishing boat in Newfoundland and were planning to be at the very spot when the time came. What they hadn't planned, was a vast field of sheet ice that blocked their way. It took all night to find their way around the ice flow and the next morning they were rewarded with a huge haul of relics. However, they found no lifeboats and certainly no bodies.

In April 1940, Bill's father was the captain of a World War II destroyer, assigned to escort British convoys across the Atlantic when they encounter those first ghost messages. As captain, he responded immediately to the distress calls but didn't arrive at the site until the next morning. Finding only pieces of wreckage, they assumed that they were just the remains of a torpedoed freighter. Only later, did he examine the pieces closer and realized that he had encountered something remarkable.

Bill opened a book on his desk and compared the newel post to one pictured on *Titanic's* grand staircase. As expected, it was an exact match. He smiled and glanced at the locked closet across the room. It would make a nice addition to his father's collection of artifacts, retrieved over the last fifty-six years. Someday, those relics would make him rich beyond all expectations.

Echoes From the Ether won Best of Issue in the
1999 SC Writers' Workshop Horizons Anthology.
It was this author's very first short story.

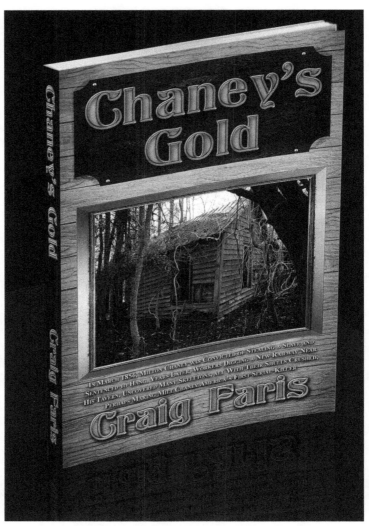

Cover design by James Marshall.

Chaney's Gold – Synopsis

In 1970, this author and his father took a metal detector to a parcel of
land in the panhandle of Lancaster County, South Carolina, in search of
the final location of ill-gotten gold hidden by Milton Chaney in the
1850s. Chaney's Gold is based on a true story of what may have been
America's first serial killer.

CHANEY'S GOLD

Based on a true story

Sometimes I ask myself how I managed to get talked into digging that hole. There I was, a fifteen-year-old boy who should have been out shooting hoops with my friends on that clear, cool Sunday afternoon, but no, I was knee deep in a hole in what must have been the rockiest, root-filled dirt I had ever laid a shovel to. Daddy, on the other hand, was sitting on a boulder tinkering with his newest toy, a metal detector he'd picked up at the pawnshop.

"The man said this thing would detect a twenty-dollar gold piece through six inches of solid quartz rock," Daddy said proudly as he turned a knob and swung the metal detector in my direction. It didn't come with an owner's manual so he had no idea what most of those dials and knobs were for.

"How could a twenty-dollar gold piece get inside a quartz rock?" I asked.

My father gave me a weird look. "That's not the point, son. It means it can detect a coin up to thirty feet underground. Understand?"

I rolled my eyes. "No way am I digging down thirty feet!"

He shrugged and went back to his knobs. There was something about that time of the year; between seasons. My daddy's name was Oliver but most folks called him Rev because he was named after a preacher. He was a part-time farmer, and at that time of the year, when it was too early to plant the fields but too warm to feed the cows, he would get these notions in his head. The latest had come that morning.

"Let's go see if we can scare up Ole Chaney's gold," he said.

I couldn't believe I had fallen for that line three times. The first two times we'd poked and prodded around this boulder-filled landscape for over two hours. I never knew why. He proudly showed me the ancient Charlotte to Camden roadbed where supposedly George Washington himself once traveled. He told Momma he was giving me a history les-son, which I suppose was true if you call traipsing around a leaf-covered ditch instructive.

Daddy said there used to be a village near here called Os-ce-ola, which has since been completely swallowed by kudzu. Kudzu vines grow about a foot a day, and if you believe the propaganda, it was imported from Japan about the time Osceola vanished from sight. They said it was to control erosion, but everyone knew it was obviously a Yankee plot to once again bury our Southern heritage.

Daddy pointed to a mass of green vines and said, "Your Grand-mamma Secrest attended grade school right over there."

I frowned and said, "Right!"

We were about a hundred yards to the southeast of the corner of Highway 521 and Highway 75 and we had no idea whose property this was. Daddy said, "Don't make no difference unless we find something."

He had gotten this notion from Murph Crosby, who seemed to be a prime source for notions that forced me to dig up the surrounding countryside. The previous year we had been ankle deep in poison ivy, scaring up some old Indian mound that Murph's second cousin had discovered as a kid. There was no sign of the mound, but we found lots of snakes and chiggers.

The Crosbys lived two doors down the road and had at least eight kids. Every Saturday you could spot the cloud of dust as they swept the front yard, which had this huge oak tree in the center, but not the first blade of grass. Mrs. Crosby liked a tidy yard even if it was only dirt. I imagined the Crosbys all sitting around at night, slapping each other on the back and telling stories about the latest wild goose chase that Murph had planted in Rev's head. What a hoot!

"This one's true," Daddy swore. "I looked it up." As I shoveled, he began reading from the *Lancaster Book of Folklore* he'd borrowed from the county library. "Milt Chaney operated a tavern on this very spot of land back in the 1850s," Daddy said. "He was a giant, bearded man who would greet weary travelers with a broad smile, a hot meal, and a warm place to sleep for the night. If the traveler was obviously alone and headed south to Charleston with bales of cotton or slaves, Chaney never charged for the lodgings. He only asked that they promise to stop by and pay him on the return trip north. Trouble was, many of those who returned to Chaney's Tavern were never heard from again."

I stopped shoveling. For once, Daddy had my full attention.

"You see, son," he explained, "on the way south they had no money, but on the return trip their purses were full. Relatives would start tracing back the last places their missing loved ones were seen, but the trail always seemed to end right here." His finger was pointing at the hole I was standing in and for once this was turning out to be a pretty interesting notion.

"You mean he killed them?" I asked.

Daddy nodded and continued. "In 1855," he said, "a slave named Ole Toney claimed that Milt Chaney stole him from the neighboring plantation of Dr. R.L. Crawford, took him to northern Virginia, and sold him to a Mr. Powell. It took years, but eventually Ole Toney told his story to the local sheriff, hoping that he would be sent back to Dr. Crawford's plantation. Eventually, he did."

Daddy closed the book. "That much of the story was documented, but according to the legend that Murph Crosby heard, Ole Toney saw firsthand what Chaney was up to. The only reason why Toney was allowed to live was because he was a slave, and therefore, more valuable alive than dead."

I began to wonder what exactly we were supposed to find in this hole.

"According to Murph," Daddy said, "One day Ole Toney was hoeing a garden on a piece of land that boarded Chaney's place. Toney said that he saw Chaney walk out the back door of his tavern toting a heavy burlap sack over his shoulder. For years, there had been rumors about people disappearing. Toney later said that he thought it was odd because the sack looked very heavy and Chaney was headed up a hill towards a field that would never be plowed. You see, that field was full of huge boulders and rocks, ones far too big to be moved with teams of horses."

I looked around at all of the huge rocks and boulders where we were digging. "Like here?"

"Exactly," Daddy said. "So, Toney followed Chaney at a distance, because he didn't want to get caught spying on him. He saw Chaney put the bag down near a rock, about the size of a wheelbarrow. Chaney then took an iron rod and used it to leaver the rock to one side where he dropped the heavy sack into what must have been a hole under it, and then returned the rock to its rightful position. Toney was so frightened by this, he hid until Chaney had passed by. But the next day, while Toney was again hoeing, he said that Chaney suddenly appeared behind him, so perhaps he had been spotted."

"That's when he stole him?" I asked.

"Well, it was probably too risky in daylight, especially if there were other slaves in the field. Murph said that Chaney started asking Toney questions about his treatment by Dr. Crawford. Toney replied that the doctor was a good master, but then Chaney claimed that his tavern was part of the Underground Railroad and if Toney ever wanted to escape to the North, he could get him and his family up to the Mason Dixon line.

He told Toney to come by the tavern that night and he would tell him more."

Even though Toney was treated well, he was still a slave, so that night he apparently decided to go see what Mr. Chaney had to say."

I was so engrossed in the story that had completely forgotten about digging which suited me fine.

Daddy described the night Ole Toney went to Chaney's tavern. Getting no answer when he knocked, he cracked the door to call inside, then something hit him in the back of the head. He woke up, hog-tied to one of Chaney's chairs. Toney watched as Chaney stood on a chair and figured that Chaney was going to hang him. Instead he got an old, broken anvil down from a trap door in the attic, which was directly above the bed pillow of a nice rope bed with sheets and blanket. Toney later testified that the anvil was covered with dark brown stains, and Chaney had said, "This has killed better men than you, boy. You say a word about this and I'll squash your head like a rotten tomato." That would have been enough for me to rip out my own tongue, but Ole Toney, he must have been some mighty brave because he told the sheriff all about the anvil, the trap door above the bed, and those folks who went missing.

The sheriff wrote to Dr. Crawford, who confirmed that Ole Toney had been stolen. When he was returned to Dr. Crawford's, Milt Chaney was arrested, but not charged with murder. There were no bodies to be found, and even though a trap door was found exactly where Ole Toney had described, there was no anvil; no murder weapon. However, Chaney was convicted of stealing a slave and sentenced to hang.

According to a *Lancaster Ledger* article Daddy found, on July 11, 1856 a large crowd gathered before the courthouse gallows expecting Chaney to confess all. He never did. Instead he addressed that crowd for an hour and a half, read a poem to his toothless wife, and ignored shouted pleas to confess. The hangman finally got tired of his ramblings and dropped him. For years, folks tried to decipher the message they assumed was hidden in Chaney's poem, but to no avail. Chaney was dead, buried, and forgotten until 1888 when the railroad cut through the hill behind the site of his old former tavern and began unearthing dozens of human skeletons; all had their skulls crushed in.

"No one ever found the gold Chaney supposedly took from those people," Daddy said, "and since Ole Toney was just a slave, no one believed his story."

Murph's legend said Ole Toney never described where the rock with the hole under it was located. He only said that the field was so covered with rocks and huge boulders it would never be plowed, and that the rock was as big as a wheelbarrow. Toney never went looking for this prize. Such was his fear of ill-gotten gold and the ghosts of the murdered.

The hole I was standing in had been directly beneath such a rock, and on hearing this I began to dig with renewed vigor. Like Chaney, we had used iron rods to move the rock and each time my daddy passed that new metal detector over the hole it screamed out its high-pitched whine of buried wealth below. The signal was getting stronger. The earth was an unnatural brown color compared to the surrounding red clay and smelled odd.

"Just a couple more feet, son," Daddy kept saying. At that point I would have dug thirty feet. I think we both nearly jumped out of our skins when I cut through the last root and my shovel hit something hard with a heavy, metallic clank.

"Hot damn!" Daddy said with the detector's needle maxed into the red. "We done found Chaney's gold!"

It's been nearly fifty years since I stepped out of that hole. I sometimes walk past Murph Crosby's old place and wonder if he is still planting notions in my Daddy's head up in heaven. Chaney's gold was like that rusty spigot they used to have driven up in their front yard as a joke to make folks think it had running water. You opened the tap expecting one thing, only to hear hoots of laughter coming from inside the house. Lord, I miss those boys. They were good folks. Always had a kind word, a glass of sweet tea, and a friendly joke. I used to think Daddy looked down on the Crosbys, but then I saw his tears at Murph's funeral and heard him whisper, "He was my best friend."

I really think Murph Crosby believed the story passed down over the years from Ole Toney. And even if he didn't, he still gave my daddy and me an afternoon filled with wonder, sweat, and a little bit of history.

Somewhere around the old home place Daddy kept Chaney's greatest secret locked away. I remember times he would proudly display it for all those who were willing to listen to the tale. It wasn't golden, but to Daddy, far more valuable.

I will always wonder where he hid that piece of an old broken anvil we found three feet under a rock. I guess some treasures are just better off buried.

Gold won Best of Issue in the 2002 South Carolina
Writers Workshop, Horizon's Anthology Collection.

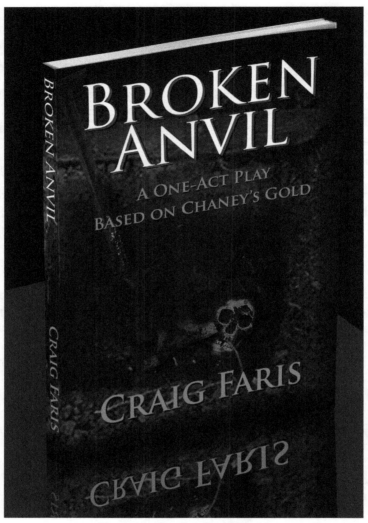

Cover design by Craig Faris.
Photo by Craig Faris.

Broken Anvil – Synopsis

Broken Anvil is a one-act play based on the events described in the previous short story, *Chaney's Gold*. However, this play focuses on the trial of Milt Chaney. Since I have been unable to locate a transcript of the original trial of Milt Chaney in March 1852, this is a fictional account based on real events.

BROKEN ANVIL

A One-Act Play

SETTING

SCENE 1: The court chambers of the county courthouse in Lancaster, South Carolina.

SCENE 2: Outside the Lancaster County Jail.

TIME

SCENE 1: Morning, March 1856.

SCENE 2: Mid-afternoon, three months later. July 1856

CHARACTERS

MILT CHANEY   Big man with a beard, worn work clothes,
                              late forties

JUDGE FROSCHER   Wears a white wig and black robe, fifties

OLE TONEY (Tŏ-knee)   Slave, in work clothes, thirties

DR. R. L. CRAWFORD   Graying hair, nice suit, early fifties

MR. MCGEE   Chaney's lawyer, suit, twenty-three

MR. COOK   Solicitor, suit, twenty-nine

JOHN STEELE   White trash, old dirty work clothes,
                              thirty-five

COURT CRIER   Dressed in colonial style with a wig,
                              twenty

ACT ONE

SCENE 1

The courtroom bench is center stage, a witness chair beside it. Dr. Crawford sits in the witness chair. Milt Chaney and his lawyer, Mr. McGee, sit at a table, stage right. The Camden District Solicitor, Mr. Cook, stands in front of his desk, stage left. The slave, Ole Toney, sits at the desk behind the Solicitor. The Court Crier is out front, center stage.

COURT CRIER:

Here Ye, Hear Ye, Hear Ye! The Camden district court of Lancaster County is now in session. Draw near all who have business with the court to these chambers, this thirteenth day of March, in the year of our Lord, 1856. The Honorable Judge Buford N. Froscher presiding. All Rise.

> (The Judge enters and sits at his bench, stage center. He wears spectacles and a white wig. He raps his gavel on the desk.)

JUDGE FROSCHER:

Mr. District Attorney, in the case of the people versus Milton M. Chaney, charged with stealing a slave, are you ready to proceed?

MR. COOK:

We are, your Honor.

JUDGE FROSCHER:

Dr. Crawford, may I remind you that you are still under oath.

> (Crawford nods.)

MR. COOK:

Dr. Crawford, you own a slave by the name of Toney. Is this correct?

DR. CRAWFORD:

That's correct, sir. We call him Ole Toney.

MR. COOK:

And would you mind pointing him out for the benefit of the jury?

DR. CRAWFORD:

He's sitting right over there.
                    (Crawford points toward the plaintiff's table.)

MR. COOK:

(To Toney)

Stand up so we can get a good look at you. Let the record state that the doctor pointed to the slave identified as Toney.

MR. COOK:

How long have you owned this slave?

DR. CRAWFORD:

He was born and raised on our farm, sir. I've known him his whole life.

MR. COOK:

Would you know of any reason why Toney would want to run off?

DR. CRAWFORD:

No, sir. Toney is like one of the family. My children adore him.

MR. COOK:

Yet, three years ago, he disappeared. Isn't that correct?

DR. CRAWFORD:

Yes, sir. It was Christmas Eve. We sent Ole Toney out to fetch us a holly bush so that my wife and children could decorate the house for the holidays. He never came back.

MR. COOK:

Did you go looking for him?

DR. CRAWFORD:

Yes, sir. We searched the entire place. We found the axe he was toting down at the creek that borders our property with Chaney's.

MR. COOK:

You are referring to Milton Chaney, the defendant?

DR. CRAWFORD:

Yes, sir.

MR. COOK:

And did you ask Mr. Chaney if he had seen Toney?

DR. CRAWFORD:

Sure did, and he denied it. And him with poor Ole Toney tied up inside his tavern all—

MR. MCGEE:

Objection!

JUDGE FROSCHER:

Sustained. Mr. Cook, you know better.

MR. COOK:

Sorry, your Honor.
(to Crawford)
When did you first learn of Toney's whereabouts?

DR. CRAWFORD:

It was last fall, sir. The Lancaster County sheriff came by and showed me a letter he had received from a sheriff up in King William County, Virginia. The letter stated that a Mr. Powell had bought a slave about three years back from a man fitting Chaney's description. The slave called himself Toney, and claimed to have been stolen from Dr. R. L. Crawford of Lancaster district. He tried Lancaster Counties in other states and finally stumbled upon us.

MR. COOK:

And that's when Toney was returned to you?

DR. CRAWFORD:

Yes, sir, but first I had to promise to compensate Mr. Powell for the money he had paid Chaney.

MR. MC GEE:

Objection! There is no proof that my client was the man who sold the slave to Powell.

JUDGE FROSCHER:

Sustained.

MR. COOK:

No further questions, your Honor.

JUDGE FROSCHER:

Mr. McGee, do you wish to cross-examine?

MR. MCGEE:

Yes, sir.
(He stands but stays at his table.)
Dr. Crawford, this slave, does he ever give you any trouble?

DR. CRAWFORD:

No, sir. Ole Toney is a hard worker.

MR. MCGEE:

Old Toney? He doesn't look that old. Young bucks like him like to run off, don't they?

DR. CRAWFORD:

I wouldn't know, sir. My children gave him that name, and he loves them like his own.

MR. MCGEE:

Isn't it true that you have to whip your slaves on a regular basis?

DR. CRAWFORD:

(Mad)
No, sir! None of my slaves has ever done anything to deserve a beating. I would no more beat Ole Toney than a prize horse.

MR. MCGEE:
Is that so? Shall I have the slave remove his shirt in the courtroom to verify that fact?

MR. COOK:
Objection! May I remind the court that Toney is <u>not</u> the one on trial here!

JUDGE FROSCHER:
Sustained.

DR. CRAWFORD:
Sir, any scars on Toney's back were inflicted during his time with Mr. Powell, not by me.

MR. MCGEE:
So you say, but isn't it true that Toney came to my client, Milt Chaney, seeking help in reaching freedom in the North?

DR. CRAWFORD:
That's not what he told me. He said Chaney stole him, tied him to a mule, and sold him up north like he owned him.

MR. MCGEE:
And you believe the word of a Negro slave over a White?

DR. CRAWFORD:
Yes, sir. In this case, I sure do.

MR. MCGEE:
<u>(in disgust)</u>
I have no further use for this witness.

JUDGE FROSCHER:
Dr. Crawford, you may step down. Solicitor, you may call the next witness.

MR. COOK:
If it pleases the court, we would like to call John Steele to the stand.

(Steele enters from stage left. He is an uneducated
White man with a patch over one eye.)

COURT CRIER:
(Approaches the witness stand)
Put your right hand on the Good Book.

(Steele places his left.)

Do you swear to tell the truth and nothing but, so help you God?

MR. STEELE:
Shownuf do.

MR. COOK:
State your name and occupation for the court, sir.

MR. STEELE:
John M. Steele. I's a planter.

MR. COOK:
Mr. Steele, do you know the defendant, Milt Chaney?

MR. STEELE:
Show do. He be's a neighbor.

MR. COOK:
Where is your cabin in relationship to Chaney's Tavern?

MR. STEELE:
I wek-con his place be about a half mile down the road a piece.

MR. COOK:
Did you have an occasion to observe Milt Chaney on or about
Christmas Day three years ago?

MR. STEELE:
I reckon I did. I's out fetching some firewood about the break of dawn,
and here I seen Chaney on horseback leadin' a mule up the road in front
of my place.

MR. COOK:
Did he have anything on the mule?

MR. STEELE:
Shownuf did. I see's he has a slave mounted on that mule.

MR. COOK:
Did you recognize this slave?

MR. STEELE:
No, saw. It still be's dark and the slave, he had like a rope or somethin'
tied around his mouth, and his hands, they's tied to the saddle. I's
figured he might be a runaway that Chaney caught, so I axs him. Chaney
says one of his lodgers done paid him with the slave and he gonna gives
him to some folk up in Nawth Carolina as a Christmas present.

MR. COOK:
He told you one of his tavern guests paid him with a slave? That's a
pretty expensive night's sleep, don't you think?

MR. STEELE:
Don't seem that odd. Chaney done that lots. He'd put up a whole
family, when they's headed south. Not charge a penny till they comes
back through from sellin' they goods. Folks talked 'bout how nice the
place wuz. He only allowed three to a bed and makes um take off their
muddy boots 'fore gettin' in. I hear's he'd ratchet up those bed-ropes
every night, so they's always sleep tight.

MR. COOK:
Lots of those folks disappeared after stopping at Chaney's, didn't they?

MR. MCGEE:
Objection, Your Honor!

JUDGE FROSCHER:
Sustained. Mr. Cook, please confine your questions to the case at hand.

MR. COOK:
No further questions, Your Honor.

JUDGE FROSCHER:

Mr. McGee, your turn.

MR. MCGEE:

(McGee approaches the witness.)

So, you have no idea who that slave was, correct?

MR. STEELE:

Naw, sa. Didn't see his face.

MR. MCGEE:

And folks spoke well about Chaney's Tavern, didn't they?

MR. STEELE:

Shownuf did. I seen him myself out back washn' the sheets once a month, whether they needs it or not and he always put tha mattresses on anthills to get rid of tha lice.

MR. MCGEE:

No further questions.

JUDGE FROSCHER:

Mr. Steele, you're through. Please step down.

(Steele returns to his seat.)

Call your next witness, Mr. Cook.

MR. COOK:

We'd like to call the slave, Toney, to the stand, sir.

MR. MCGEE:

Objection, Your Honor! We object to the testimony of a slave being offered against that of a White man.

JUDGE FROSCHER:

Overruled. Toney, you come on up here.

(Toney approaches the witness chair and raises his right hand.)

COURT CRIER:
(Stands in front of Toney)
Put your right hand on the Bible.

(Toney does.)

Do you swear to tell the truth and nothing but, so help you God?

TONEY:
Yas, sir.

MR. COOK:
State your name for the court, please.

TONEY:
Dr. Crawford, he calls me Ole Toney.

MR. COOK:
Toney, would you please tell the court what happened on Christmas
Eve, three years back?

TONEY:
Well, sah, Dr. Crawford sent me out to fetch some holly bushes, so's his
kids can fix up the mantle for Christmas. I remember's seenin' a bush,
down by the crick that borders Misa Chaney's place, so's I fetch an axe
and heads down there.

MR. COOK:
What happened when you got there?

TONEY:
Well, I see's Misa Chaney come out the back of one of the corncribs he
uses as a tavern and he's toting a heavy sack over one shoulder. He
comes right at me, so I hide's behind a big tree and watches him. After
he's passed, I follows along. Directly, he comes to a field that ain't never
gonna be plowed.

MR. COOK:
Why is that?

TONEY:

It's a full of big rocks and boulders. I sees him stop at one rock and he looks around, like makin' sure no one's lookin'. Then he uses a pole to leaver the rock to one side. Rock wuz just big enough for a man his size to move. Then I sees him drop that whole sack into what must'a been a hole under the rock.

MR. COOK:

What happened next?

TONEY:

He puts the rock back and starts down toward the crick. After I's sure he's gone, I goes back to cuttin' on the holly bush. Directly, I hear Misa Chaney's voice right behind me. Scares me purt near to death.

MR. COOK:

What did he say?

TONEY:

He axs me what I'm doin'. I tell's him that I'm cuttin' Christmas holly for Dr. Crawford's kids. He smiles and axs me how would I like a Christmas gift. I says that'd be mighty neighborly. He says he knows folks who hides slaves and helps 'em escape up north to free country. Says I can earn enough up there in a month to buy my whole family free.

MR. COOK:

What did you say?

TONEY:

I told him that I's happy at Dr. Crawford's. But directly, ole curiosity, it gots the better of me, so I axs him how they goes about hiding these slaves. He say's for me to walk on up to the big house with him and he'd show me. So, I left the axe and followed him.

MR. COOK:

What happened next?

TONEY:

Soon as I walks in the door, Chaney knocks me out. When I comes to, I's tied with rope to a chair. Chaney climbs up on a stool directly above one of his beds. He opens a trap door to the attic and gets a piece of an

A DEN OF RHYME - SHORT STORY COLLECTION   141

old rusty broken anvil down.

MR. COOK:

This trap door was over the bed?

TONEY:

Yas, sir. Directly over the pillow.

MR. COOK:

And then what?

TONEY:

He holds that anvil right in front of me, likes he gonna smash it into my face. He grabs my hair and makes me look at it. It's all covered with dark brown stains and Masa Chaney say's, "This has killed better men than you. You say a word about this, and I'll squash your head like a rotten tomato."

MR. COOK:

Did he say anything else?

TONEY:

He says the only reason I's still alive wuz because I's a slave and worth more alive than dead. I sat in that chair all night, scared to death. Didn't dare move a finger. Everyone knows the stories 'bout folks that went missin' after stoppin' at Chaney's.

MR. MCGEE:

Objection!

JUDGE FROSCHER:

Sustained.
Toney, Mr. Chaney's not charged with murder. He's charged with stealing you. Understand?

TONEY:

Yas, sir. But that don't comfort all those poor widow women who stopped at our house, lookin' for their missin' loved ones.

MR. MCGEE:

Objection!

JUDGE FROSCHER:
Sustained. Just answer the questions, Toney.

MR. COOK:
You can continue, Toney.

TONEY:
Next day, he ties me to a mule and that's when I sees Masa Steele. I's so scared. I knows that Chaney got a loaded shotgun under his cape pointed right at Masa Steele's heart. So, I stays quiet for four days until he sells me up north to that Masa Powell.

MR. COOK:
He claimed that he owned you and sold you to Mr. Powell. Is that correct?

TONEY:
Yas, sir.

MR. COOK:
No further questions.

JUDGE FROSCHER:
Mr. McGee.

MR. MCGEE:
Just one question. If you supposedly were so scared of this man, why did you go along voluntarily to his house?

TONEY:
Freedom, sir.! Masa Chaney done says that's he wuz part of this underground railway. No matter how nice a place is or how good the masa treats ya, I is still a slave. And every man dreams of being free.

SCENE 2

<u>Afternoon. Four months later. Mr. Cook is standing
outside the Lancaster County Jail, center stage,
looking toward the audience. Dr. R. L. Crawford
enters from stage left and stops beside Mr. Cook.</u>

MR. COOK:
Good afternoon, Doctor. There's not much anyone can do for him now.

DR. CRAWFORD:
Quite a crowd. Did he ever confess?

MR. COOK:
No. He rambled on for an hour and a half with the noose around his
neck before they dropped him. He read a poem to that toothless wife of
his. Everybody figures he hid some secret message in the poem that
gives the location of where he buried the gold.

    We tried to make a deal with Chaney. Judge told him if he
confessed all, he'd spare his life, but he wouldn't budge. I guess we'll
never find where he buried their money now.

DR. CRAWFORD:
I guess not. All those missing people. How many is it up to?

MR. COOK:
About thirty families have come forward, mostly brothers and wives.
Every one of them tracked their loved ones all the way down to
Charleston and back up, but no further. Looks like Chaney tricked them
into coming back by being real generous with free room and board on
the way south. Their purses were fat after selling their goods, so it's
only logical that they stopped by and paid Chaney a visit on the way
north. That's where the trail always ends.

DR. CRAWFORD:
Looks like Ole Toney got the right man. I'm thinking about freeing him,

since it was he who sent Chaney to the gallows.

MR. COOK:

That would be mighty generous considering the risks he took to get back here. If you offer him wages, I'd bet he'd stick around.

DR. CRAWFORD:

Hopefully. I'd hate to see him go, and my kids just love him.

MR. COOK:

The whole town turned out for the hanging. Where were you?

DR. CRAWFORD:

Ole Toney took me up to that field where he saw Chaney bury that stuff under a rock.

MR. COOK:

Did you find anything?

DR. CRAWFORD:

We dug down three feet, finally came upon an old burlap sack.

MR. COOK:

What was in it?

DR. CRAWFORD:

A broken piece of a rusty anvil, and part of a skull with a big hole in it.

MR. COOK:
(surprised)

You found the murder weapon! Where is it?

DR. CRAWFORD:

What difference does it make? The murderer is dead.

MR. COOK:

It's proof that he did it!

DR. CRAWFORD:

How does that prove anything?

MR. COOK:

Well, if nothing else, it might provide some comfort to those people to know the truth.

DR. CRAWFORD:

Those people know what happened. That's why they're all here. If that anvil were solid gold, it wouldn't matter.

MR. COOK:

I guess you're right.

DR. CRAWFORD:

Some treasures, Mr. Cook, are just better off buried.

(Fade)

Broken Anvil won Best of Issue for Play in the 2003 Catfish Stew Anthology Collection (a juried regional competition).

AUTHOR'S NOTE:

For more information on this crime and its results, you can read an article by Mrs. Louise Pettus, entitled *Dark Doings at Chaney's Tavern online* at: www.scgenweb.org/lancaster/history/index.htm .

For a fictionalized novel based on real places and real bodies, surrounding this story, I recommend:

Milt Chaney's Taven
By Don L. McCorkle © 2015
ISBN: 978-0692705964

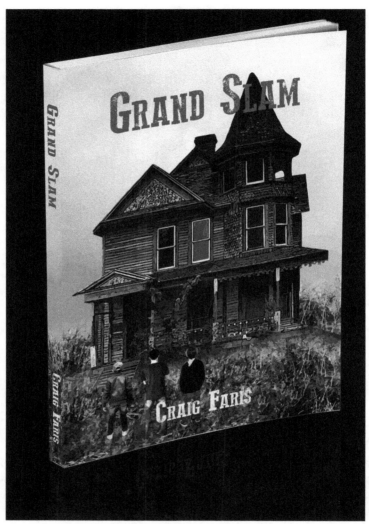

Cover design by Michaela Krug.

Grand Slam – Synopsis

Grand Slam is a darker story about three thirteen-year old boys who mistakenly hit a softball into the overgrown yard of an elderly man's home at the end of their cul-de-sac. This prompts the kids into an impromptu treasure hunt, resulting in them finding the last thing they ever expected.

GRAND SLAM

Inspired by a short story,
WHAT WAS IN THE BOX
(1959) by Richard Matheson

The three boys had grown up together on this street, in this neighborhood, and had played together since birth. They were all thirteen and usually played video games, but after a long hot summer that had kept them inside, they were enjoying a cool November day, playing softball. With the country suddenly focused on the World Series and the Chicago Cubs, baseball had caught their attention.

Among the three of them, they only had one softball, a metal bat, and one glove. Their ball field was their street with the end of their cul-de-sac serving as the outfield. It was Kirk's turn to have the glove in the outfield, with Joey at the pitcher's chalk mark in the street. Kerry took his place at home plate, also drawn in chalk, and rested the bat on his shoulder. Joey's first pitch sailed past him, but there was no need for a catcher since the street ran downhill toward the pitcher's mound. Strikes were only called with a swing and a miss. Kerry tossed the ball back and once again Joey took aim. This pitch was underhanded, but surprisingly fast. Kerry's bat connected with a resounding "ping" and the ball sailed high over Kirk's head, veered to the right, and disappeared into a lot filled with briers and weeds, and surrounded by an old, rusty iron fence.

The old Victorian house had been there long before the cul-de-sac was built. Any paint applied decades earlier had long since vanished, and the lapboards were almost black with age. Shutters hung askew from some of the windows and every tree in the yard was dead with bare limbs. An old garage stood out back with a '50s-era car visible inside, but worn tire tracks on the grass leading out to the street indicated that the car still ran.

The three boys stood outside the rusty iron gate and surveyed the yard.

"Well, Kerry, you hit the ball; go get it," Joey said.

"I'm not going in there," he said. "My parents said the only reason this place is still standing is because a light comes on in a second-floor window every evening."

"My dad told my sister to stay away from here," Kirk said. "He says this whole area once belonged to the old man who lives there. They say he's crazy."

"Mom saw him driving that old car one morning, but the windows were so dirty and yellowed that she couldn't even see what he looked like," Kerry added. "Just his shadow."

"Well, it's my ball, and it's the only one we've got," Kirk said. "Let's all look."

They lifted the gate latch and pushed. The rusted hinges squealed in protest but they got it open enough to squeeze through. The weeds and briers were as tall as they were and caught their bare legs and socks as they spread out to look for the ball. Most of the scrollwork on the porch columns had rotted away and the gray floor boards were warped and covered with leaves. They searched the thicket for at least fifteen minutes before Kerry spotted it near the edge of the porch.

Reaching down to pick it up, he got a whiff of odor that smelled like wet carpet and cat pee. Looking onto the porch, he saw a moldy, cracked-leather shoe. In the shoe was a gray pants leg and above that, a leathery, wrinkled hand with yellowed fingernails protruding from the sleeve of a threadbare dress coat. A wild gray beard covered the top of the coat and pale blue eyes stared down at him.

Kerry straightened and held up the ball. "Ugh . . . sorry, mister," he muttered, "we were just looking for our ball."

Kirk and Joey were frozen in place, their mouths agape. Slowly, each of them began backing toward the gate, never taking their eyes off the old man.

The old man's voice was like gravel. "So, you boys like baseball, eh?"

"Ugh . . . yeah. We watched the World Series," Kerry said.

"Ever heard of a grand slam?"

Kerry began to relax. "Yeah. The Cubs hit one in the sixth game in 2019."

The old man raised his left arm and extended an arthritic finger. "You see that huge hickory tree on top of that hill? There's an old brick chimney up there. Five o'clock this afternoon, walk six paces due west from its northwest corner, dig down four feet; that's where you'll find it."

"Find what?" Kerry said.

"Things that dreams are made of," he hissed, "but tell no one. It's our secret!"

They left him standing on the porch, still pointing toward the hill, and ran toward their respective houses where they gathered a pick, shovels, and a compass. The hill had once been a cow pasture and most of it was still covered in tall grass. Reaching the top shortly after 2 p.m., they found part of a brick chimney and foundation stones where a house had once been. The huge hickory tree stood nearby with limbs shading the entire area. Joey used his compass to measure six paces from the chimney's northwest corner and Kerry marked the spot with Kirk's softball that he had stuck in his pants pocket.

The first six inches of topsoil was removed quickly only to reveal hard-packed red clay beneath, laced with hickory roots. As they chopped and dug, the wind picked up, swirling leaves around them. A cold front was moving in from the south, covering the blue sky with gray clouds.

An hour after starting, they were only down about twenty inches. Kirk stepped out of the hole and wiped the sweat from his face. He glanced down the hill toward the old man's house and thought he saw a glint of light in one of the windows. "You know," he said, "I think this is a total waste of time. That old man is probably watching us with binoculars and laughing his head off. He got three kids to come up here and dig a hole, just to punish us for coming into his yard!"

"Then why was he so specific on the time, the exact place, and how deep to dig?" Kerry asked.

"I don't know. I'm getting hungry and it's about to rain. Let's come back tomorrow and finish."

"Tomorrow it might be gone," Joey said. "We've done the bulk of the work and he might come up here tonight and retrieve his treasure."

"Who said anything about a treasure?" Kirk said. "He called it *things that dreams are made of.*"

"He also said it was a *secret,*" Kerry added. "Why would a hole in the ground be a secret if it didn't contain anything valuable?"

"Whatever it is, it can't be worth much. Look how he lives."

"But at one time, he owned this whole valley," Kerry said. "He didn't just give it away."

"Look, I'm tired and I have chores to finish before Dad gets home." Kirk picked up his ball and headed down the hill with his shovel.

"It your loss," Joey called.

"Let him go," Kerry said. "A two-way split is better than three."

Now that they were below most of the roots, they made better progress. They continued to dig for another hour and a half, and a large mound of loose clay and rocks surrounded the hole and was growing with every shovelful. The clouds were getting darker and the wind whipped leaves from the hickory like flocks of birds.

"It's starting to rain," Joey said, leaning on his shovel. "Surely we're down four feet."

Kerry took his tape measure and checked. "Another six inches and that's it."

"You know, Kirk might be right about one thing," Joey said. "That old man has got to be at least ninety years old. He knows he could drop dead at any minute."

"So?"

"So, he got three kids to come up here and dig him a grave in the exact spot where he wanted to be buried!"

"You're saying that he knows he's going to die at exactly five o'clock?" Kerry said.

"Maybe he's going to take poison."

"Or maybe he needs the jar of money he buried here to pay for his funeral," Kerry said, the rain now pelting their shirts. "Come on, we're almost there."

Joey ignored him and scrambled to the top of the mound "Kerry, there's nothing here but dirt. Are you coming or not?"

"I'm not leaving until I find it," Kerry said, "and you'll lose your share."

"You can have my share of all the mud and rocks you find," Joey said. "If this keeps up, you could drown in that hole." He took his shovel and compass and left.

Kerry threw his shovel down. "I'll show you!" He picked up the pick, swung it high over his head, and slammed it into the hard clay floor of the hole, but it stopped short with a hard clank. No matter how hard he pulled, he couldn't free it. "JOEY!" he yelled. "This is it! We've found it!" But Joey was gone.

Using the shovel, he cleared away the clay and found the point of the pick embedded in what appeared to be a crack in concrete. He shoveled frantically until he uncovered a seam in the concrete running straight from the pick until it made a right turn. It was obviously some sort of lid about two feet square. He dug until he found another corner, and then another. He couldn't believe the lid was centered directly where the old man had said. By the time he got all the clay cleared off the lid, his hair and clothes were soaked. It would soon be too dark to see, but he was determined not to quit. He stuck the point of the shovel into the seam and worked it all the way around the edge to try to loosen it, but the head of the pick had it wedged shut. Then he pulled on the pick handle with all his might. It suddenly gave way and he fell back against the slick mud on the sides of the hole. To his astonishment, the lid slowly began to rise on its own. He stood up against the clay wall as a strong, stale odor escaped from the inky black opening before him. He could see hinges under the lid and then his eyes grew wide when something seemed to move within the cavern.

Trying to scramble back up the embankment, his shoes slipped on the wet clay. Suddenly, he was sliding feet-first directly into the opening. Frantically, he clawed at the lip, and his head struck the concrete lid as he disappeared into darkness.

The fall felt much longer that it lasted, but he landed on something soft and spongy. The only light was from the dark grey square of sky above the opening. He rubbed his head where it had struck the lid, but he couldn't see if it was bleeding or not. Looking up, he saw rainwater dripping from two springs attached to hinges. No wonder the lid had risen on its own. As his eyes adjusted to the darkness, he began to see round shapes all around him. He picked up one of them and realized it was a nearly deflated soccer ball. "Thanks a lot, mister!"

He tried standing, but it was hard to keep his balance on the uneven surface. The opening with the springs underneath was out of his reach. He yelled, "Help!" then realized that his cell phone was still in his pocket. He took it out and held it up toward the opening, revealing that it had plenty of battery left, but no signal. He texted HELP to his mom, anyway. No answer. With the pile of clay around the top of the hole, he had to be nearly ten feet underground.

He turned on the flashlight app and shined it at his feet. The entire floor was covered with hundreds of softballs, baseballs, basketballs, tennis balls, soccer balls, old bats, gloves, and mitts. All of them had turned green with mildew and mold. "Some treasure!" The old man must have thrown every ball that had ever landed in his yard down here. But how? Was there another entrance?

He shined the camera light around him. The whole room was about eight feet square with concrete walls. The only entrance was above him. A faded sign on one wall had a black circle containing three upside-down triangles, with "FALLOUT SHELTER" stenciled above it. He had read about backyard shelters in history class. The only way out of here was up, unless another door was buried under the pile. Jumping didn't work because the ball floor was so soft and spongy he couldn't push off. Then he spotted his shovel leaning against the embankment wall, right outside of the hole. With it, he might could hook the shovel's blade between the lip and the lid and pull his way up the handle. He grabbed a couple of baseballs and threw them at the shovel's upper handle, hoping to make it fall into the opening. But every time he threw a ball, clods of clay and loose dirt fell in. He had to dodge large clods, and rocks that he knocked loose. On the fifth throw, a larger clod or rock fell into the hole and hit him in the back of his head. It stunned him, and when he opened his eyes, a human shadow was peering over the edge of the hole.

"Joey? Thank God. Is that you?" But his cell phone light revealed the wet bushy beard of the old man with the blue eyes.

"Ugh, hey, mister," Kerry said. "I guess we found your secret."

The man cackled with laughter. "Were you surprised?"

"Well, yeah. But not exactly what we hoped for. Hey, could you hand me that shovel there? I seem to be stuck down here."

"You wanted a grand slam," he said, reaching down to grab the shovel, "and I always keep my word." He then took the shovel and pulled up on the lid. "The greatest slam of your lives!" he cackled. The springs clicked and the lid crashed down.

Kerry could still hear the man laughing as shovelfuls of mud and dirt began landing on the lid.

"Laugh on, old man," Kerry said, sitting down. "You'll hear the slamming jail bars to your own concrete box soon enough. There's plenty of air in here, and both Joey and Kirk know exactly where I am. As soon as I'm missed, my parents will call his and a search party will be up here within the hour."

The spot on the back of his head ached, and when touched, it felt sticky. The phone light revealed blood on his hand, but it also reveled that some of those moldy white balls had what appeared to be eye sockets, and many of those shapes he thought were baseball bats, actually looked more like bones. Spinning around, he was shocked by what he saw and instantly remembered what the old man had said, "The greatest slam of *your* lives!" It wasn't mud clods that had hit him. It was the severed heads of Joey and Kirk.

Kerry collapsed to his knees. The old man had sealed his fate along with his friends.

Then, his phone vibrated. It was a text message:
Where are you? Mom.

Billboard design by Jillian Pauline.
Cover design by Craig Faris.

Guatemala – Synopsis

Guatemala is a comedy, but it is also based on a true story. Mark Nunn is a friend, and an engineer who works for Hartness International, a company that manufactures case packing machines and conveyors for businesses all over the world. In 1992 Mark was sent to Guatemala to repair some of Hartness's equipment. This is his story.

GUATEMALA

Based on a true story told by Mark Nunn

1992

I was sick; so sick the airline brought a wheelchair down the boarding ramp to roll me off the plane and through the concourse. I barely remember identifying my luggage as I lay in the chair, head to one side, and beads of sweat rolling off my brow. The airport attendants bumped me through half-opened doors, and nearly shook my teeth out as the hard rubber tires bounced across the rough, asphalt parking lot. Somehow, I was deposited at my car with a vague memory of a bus ride along the way. The wheelchair was leaned forward and I literally fell into the driver's seat. The airport attendant reached in, pulled me into an upright position, and extended a hand for his tip. I gave him my wallet, and he removed a few bills.

"You need to see a doctor," he said, smiling a little too broadly and handing me back a much lighter wallet.

How I managed to drive home is anyone's guess, but I remember thinking that a quick head-on collision might provide some relief from the bug that was frying my brain. I could envision my tombstone: Mark Nunn, born 1961. Eaten alive by unknown Guatemalan virus, 1992.

Once home, my wife, Kathie, helped me from the car and into bed. When she returned from calling the doctor, she informed me that they could see me Thursday.

"Three days?" I said. "You'll be attending my funeral in three days!"

Faced with the prospect of being a thirty-something widow, she managed to get me worked in that evening. Once there, I was so weak I stretched out on the floor of the emergency room. Kathie kept her head buried in a magazine, too embarrassed to claim me.

I awoke sometime later as the doctor stuck probes into my mouth, nose, and ears, all the while interrogating Kathie on how I might have come down with this unknown disease. "Has he traveled anywhere?" I heard the doctor ask.

"He just returned from the jungles of Guatemala," Kathie announced.

The look on the doctor's face spoke volumes. *She might as well have said I was swimming in the E-bola River*, I thought. He quickly adjusted his mask and fled from the room.

When the doctor returned, he looked like he was prepared to enter the reactor of a nuclear power plant. Dressed from head to toe in disposable paper robes, he had donned a filtered mask, plastic face shield, and gloves. "I'm sorry," I heard his muffled voice say, "but we're going to have to quarantine you and your husband."

Oh, that's just great! I thought. *Twin tombstones.*

He pointed a light into my eyes and said, "Now, tell us what happened in Guatemala."

My company manufactures case packers, machinery that puts a variety of products, from beer cans to cigarettes, into cases. Our client, Coca-Cola, needed one of our engineers, me, to go to Guatemala and adjust a machine at a remote plant in the village of Retalhuleu. My first glimpse of Guatemala from the air showed a beautiful country of vast, green, banana forests, hills dotted with coffee plantations, and active volcanoes that reached nearly 13,000 feet. We landed in Guatemala City and I waited at the airport for my driver from Coca-Cola to pick me up.

My courier arrived in an old beat up Toyota pickup that looked like it had just had a rear-end collision with a telephone pole. The driver introduced himself as Pedro, said something in broken English that sounded vaguely like an apology, and explained that he had just been rear-ended by a bus. Having established great confidence in his driving skills, he threw my luggage in the back, and we set off on a ninety-mile journey toward the western coast.

The highways leading out of the capital are only paved in the academic sense. They once had been covered with tar and gravel that now only clung to a mound of dirt between deep ruts. The ruts were so gaping that Pedro drove with one wheel in the middle and one on the shoulder, causing the truck to lean to one side at about a fifteen-degree angle. This afforded me a great view of the countryside and the peasants who make a living alongside the road. The road itself provided employment for entire families who would spend hours hammering away at huge boulders. The gravel they created was sold by the bucketfuls to stranded tourists whose vehicles became grounded or stuck in the ruts.

The poverty was incredible. All the makeshift houses we passed were old school busses from the United States that had broken down, and then were shoved off the highway to become instant roadside homes to families of twelve or more.

Pedro seemed to know everyone, and along the way, he kept stopping to pick up passengers, who would climb in the back with bikes, kids, and various farm animals.

After about thirty miles, Pedro suddenly veered off the main road, down a logging trail through a forest of banana trees. Despite the huge bumps, he didn't slow down and I was fairly certain that Pedro was using this opportunity to lighten the load by bouncing a few passengers out the back.

"Are you sure this is the right way?" I asked.

"Sí, señor," Pedro said. "The rebels, they blow up bridge over river. We go this way."

"Rebels? Funny that my boss failed to mention this."

"Oh, sí, señor. The rebels, they rob and kill you!"

The forest opened onto a huge field of sugarcane that was perhaps ten feet tall. The road cut straight through the middle, the gap barely wide enough to accommodate the truck's side mirrors, which hit the sugar-cane on either side. I felt like one of Pharaoh's soldiers following Moses into the depths of the Red Sea. Pedro had the truck floored and peasant workers ahead of us were literally leaping for their lives.

"Why are we going so fast?" I asked.

"The rebels, they lay down in road to stop us. Then rob you, señor," Pedro explained. "We go fast, they know we not stop." He pushed down on my shoulder. "Best lay down, so they not see you."

A few miles downstream from the wrecked bridge, we came to a ford in the river. There, rocks the size of riprap had been laid across the riverbed, with huge boulders on the downstream side. I soon learned why as water poured into the cab of the truck and we began to float, the boulder being the only obstacle keeping us from being swept away. Pedro opened his door, allowing the cab to fill enough for the tires to again find enough traction to carry us to the far side.

After draining the cab of water, we made our way back to the main road, and stopped at the Guatemalan equivalent of a convenience store. It was a cinder block building with a thatched roof. The gas pump was an elevated fifty-five-gallon drum with a hose attached. Pedro gassed up by repeatedly filling one-gallon plastic milk jugs and pouring them into the tank. He paid, and returned to the cab, smelling like gasoline and holding two tortilla La Cheeseburgers.

"You eat now, señor," he said, giving me one as we sped off in a cloud of dust.

We reached Reu, the town's English nickname, at dusk and the hotel was surprisingly nice, the executive suite costing only six dollars a night.

I was thrilled at such a bargain, until I discovered the windows had no glass or screens, only shutters. Pedro carried my bags up to the room, turned down sheets, and swept several spiders and centipedes off the bed before tucking in the mosquito netting.

I gave Pedro a generous tip of twenty dollars and he said he would return each morning to shuttle me to the plant.

I settled into the room only to discover that a diesel generator in the hotel courtyard, belching an oily black smoke, provided the only electricity since the rebels had also blown up the power plant. The electric current flowed in waves causing the black-and-white TV and 20-watt overhead light bulb to continually fade in and out. The one channel aired endless episodes of La Isla de Gilligan in an incomprehensible Aztec language. I finally gave up and read a book by candlelight.

Fighting off dreams of giant centipedes, I awoke the next morning and stepped in the shower. Guatemala's idea of hot water was a bare heatng coil wrapped around the showerhead, with a power cord and 240-volt plug inside the shower stall. Needless to say, I took cold showers.

The Coca-Cola plant was quite modern and I was able to fix the problem in a few days. However, everyday I awoke feeling worse, despite the fact that I drank only bottled water from the plant, and ate most of my meals from the vending machines.

The day I was scheduled to leave I became deathly ill with Montezuma's revenge. On the way back to Guatemala City, I asked Pedro to stop at what appeared to be a restaurant so I might find a restroom. I was astonished to find that I was directed to a wooden stall, in the middle of the room, surrounded by tables and guests. From inside the stall I could see the feet of the patrons eating their meals. The sounds and odors that surely escaped would have sent Americans fleeing, but when I emerged, all I saw were concerned and smiling faces.

"You okay, señor?" one of them asked.

"Oh, yes," Embarrassed, I lied with a smile.

Returning to the truck, Pedro informed me the bombed-out bridge was now fixed, which was good, since the river was now too high to ford. The steel structure crossed the Rio Guacalate, a raging river filled with boulders that emptied out of twin 12,000-foot volcanoes. The eighty-foot middle span of the bridge that had been destroyed was now a sagging hulk, rebuilt from whatever material they had found or salvaged from the river. The whole mass seemed held together with c-clamps, vise-grips, and an abundance of rope. Since we were the first to cross, the workers stood around taking bets to see if our truck would make it across.

"You wish to walk across first, señor?" Pedro asked.

I shook my head since my stomach was killing me and I have a terrible fear of heights.

I got in, and said a prayer. Pedro started across the bridge at a snail's pace and I could feel it sagging beneath us.

"Go!" I yelled.

"Bridge may fall, señor. We go slow."

I slammed my foot on top of his, flooring the gas pedal and lurching the truck ahead. "No, we go fast. Bridge may fall!"

I opened my eyes to the intense gaze of the doctor. "Other than that," I said, "it was pretty uneventful."

"You said you had a cheeseburger?" he said.

"Yeah, but I only took a couple of bites before tossing it. All the bouncing had my stomach unsettled."

"Was the meat pink?"

"Maybe."

"Ah!" He pulled off his face shield. "You have bacterial gastro enteritis, not a jungle virus. That, we can treat."

"But Pedro ate his entire burger and was fine," I insisted.

"Natives have immunities you don't," he explained. "We've lost ours."

Three days later, I was well enough to go home. As the orderly rolled me down the hall, I heard a lady complaining about her non-private room. Another person grumbled about her pillow being too hard, and someone had left a completely untouched dinner on his tray. Exiting the sterile environment of the hospital, I was struck by how weak we Americans have become. We have so much and they have so little, yet never once did I hear the good people of Guatemala complain. Smiling children would run up to the rich American and beg for a penny. When given a dollar, they acted like it was a fortune. For them it probably was.

I suppose I haven't changed. I still waste food, dream of fancy cars, and think I'm underpaid. But sometimes when I see an old school bus I think about Pedro, the peasants making gravel, and the smiling faces of those children. That's when I find myself longing for the simple treasures of Guatemala.

Guatemala won the Third Place award for best short story in the
2004 Catfish Stew Anthology Collection.

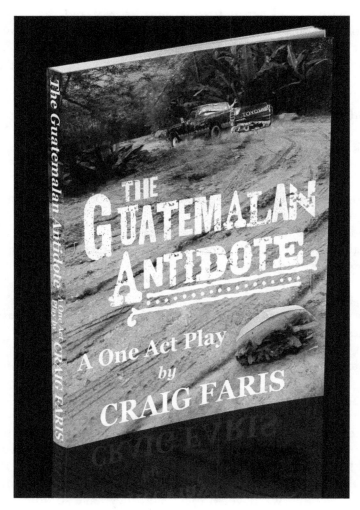

Cover design by Meghan Bushbacker.

The Guatemalan Antidote – Synopsis

This is a one-act play based on the short story Guatemala as told by Mark Nunn.

THE GUATEMALAN ANTIDOTE

A One-Act Play
By Craig Faris

SETTING

SCENE 1: A doctor's office in a large southern city
SCENE 2: In Mark's home

TIME

SCENE 1: July 1993
SCENE 2: Present

CHARACTERS

MARK NUNN	Big man with a beard, forties
KATHY NUNN	Mark's wife, thirties
DR. ORR	Medical doctor, thirties
DR. SIMPSON	Medical doctor in full lab suit, fifties
PEDRO	Hispanic man, twenties
PEASANTS	Various ages

ACT ONE

SCENE 1

Inside a doctor's examining room with a door. There are two chairs stage center with a five-foot bench behind the chairs. Mark Nunn is lying on the floor in front of one of two chairs. He is on his back, his head turned away from the audience. His wife, Kathy, sits in another chair, her face buried in a magazine.

KATHY:

Mark, get up off that floor; the doctor will be in here at any minute.

(She clenches her teeth.)

This is so embarrassing!

MARK:

(He looks toward her and groans.)

If I sit up, I might throw up again. Is that what you want?

KATHY:

You don't have anything left to throw up, Mark. It's on the road between here and home.

MARK:

No, actually, it's on the plane I took from Guatemala.

(Kathy helps him into a chair.)

MARK:

What could be taking them so long? I'm dying here.

KATHY:

You're not dying. It's just a stomach virus. You'll feel fine in twenty-four hours.

MARK:

(He leans his head to one side of his shoulder.)

In twenty-four hours, you'll be attending my funeral.

KATHY:

Good. I can't wait to sell your Harley-Davidson and paint the den pink.

(There is a knock on the door and Dr. Orr
enters, wearing a white lab coat, a stethoscope
around his neck. Kathy stands to greet him. Mark
stays seated.)

DR. ORR:
(He extends his hand which Kathy shakes.)

Hi, I'm Dr. Orr.

KATHY:

I'm Kathie Nunn and this is my husband, Mark. He claims he's dying.

DR ORR:

Well, let's see what he has.
(He takes out a small flashlight.)

KATHY:

I think he has a stomach virus. He's been throwing up and going to the bathroom ever since he got home.

(The doctor opens Mark's eyelids and shines the
flashlight into one.)

DR. ORR:

Any headaches or fever?
(Dr. Orr puts his hand on Mark's forehead.)

KATHY:
(To Dr. Orr)

Yes. Headaches, fever, diarrhea, nausea, you name it.

DR. ORR:

He feels pretty hot. How long has he had these symptoms?

KATHY:

He says they started about a week ago, but it got much worse today on the plane.

DR. ORR:
(He takes out a tongue depressor and leans close
to Mark's open mouth.)
Say 'ah.'
(To Kathy)
So, where has he been?

KATHY:
He just returned from the jungles of Guatemala.

(Dr. Orr straightens and turns to look at Kathy
with raised eyebrows.)

DR. ORR:
Guatemala?

KATHY:
It was a business trip. His company has a packaging plant in Rau.

(With the tips of his gloved fingers, Dr. Orr
drops the tongue depressor in a garbage can.)

DR. ORR:
Ugh, please excuse me for just a moment.

(Dr. Orr bolts for the door. Mark looks at
Kathy.)

MARK:
Oh, that's just great. You might as well have said I was swimming in the
E-bola River!

(A speaker somewhere offstage begins repeating
CODE PURPLE, CODE PURPLE, CODE
PURPLE.)

KATHY:
Well, that's where you were. Maybe you picked up something in
Guatemala.

MARK:

Obviously! But you didn't have to make it sound like I was traipsing through jungles.

KATHY:

Any of those jungles contain scantily clad women?

MARK:

Believe me, that's the last thing I've had on my mind.

(There is another knock on the door. Dr. Orr returns with a second older doctor. They are both dressed from head to toe in Hazmat suits of disposable paper, their faces donned with filtered masks, plastic face shields, and gloves.)

DR. ORR:

This is Doctor Simpson. I'm afraid that we are going to have to quarantine both you and your wife until we can determine the source of this bacteriological agent.

KATHY:

Me? But I haven't been near Guatemala!

DR. SIMPSON:

But you've been exposed to him for several hours. It's just a precaution.

KATHY:

I need to use the bathroom. Is there one with a window that opens to the outside? I really could use some air.
(She gets up and leaves stage left.)

Dr. ORR (to Mark):

Why don't we start with Guatemala. What happened there?

MARK:
(Gets up and sits in the chair to his right and addresses the audience.)

My company manufactures machinery that puts products like soda and beer cans into cases. One of our clients needed an engineer to adjust a machine at a remote plant in Guatemala. It's a beautiful country with

vast banana forests, coffee plantations, and active volcanoes that
reached nearly 13,000 feet.

(The lights begin to fade, with a spotlight on
Mark.)

I landed in Guatemala City a week ago and waited at the airport for the
limousine service to pick me up.

(Pedro, the driver enters and stands beside
Mark's chair.)

My courier finally arrived in an old beat-up Toyota pickup that looked
like it had just backed into a telephone pole at 30 miles per hour.

PEDRO:

Sorry, señor. A bus, it slammed into me when I stopped too quickly.

MARK:

Having established great confidence in his driving skills, Pedro threw my
luggage in the back, and we set off on an eighty-mile journey toward the
western coast.

(A cardboard cutout of the front of a truck in
rolled out in front. Pedro sits in a chair behind
the cutout to Mark's left and pretends to be
steering.)

MARK:

The roads in Guatemala are only paved in the academic sense. They
once had been covered with tar and gravel that now only clings to a
mound of dirt between deep ruts. The ruts were so gaping that Pedro
drove with one wheel in the middle, causing the truck to lean to one side
at about 20-degree angle.

(Both Mark and Pedro lean to Mark's right.)

MARK:

The poverty was incredible and most peasants lived in old broken-down
school buses that had become instant roadside homes. They scratch out
a living by hammering huge rocks into gravel. I asked Pedro why.

PEDRO:

They sell bucketfuls of rock to stranded American tourists who get stuck
in ruts.

MARK:

Pedro seemed to know everyone, and he kept picking up passengers, who climbed in the back with bikes, kids, and various farm animals.

> (Passengers appear holding various animals behind Mark and Pedro's chairs and pretend to climb aboard and sit on the bench behind them.)

MARK:

After a few miles, Pedro suddenly veered off the main road, down a logging trail through a forest of banana trees. Despite the huge bumps, he didn't slow down.

> (Mark, Pedro, and passengers begin to bounce wildly and then the passengers fall out with the animals.)

MARK:

(Shrugs)

I figured he was trying to lighten the load. I asked him if he was sure this was the right way.

PEDRO:

Sí, señor. The rebels, they blow up bridge over river. We go this way.

MARK:

My boss failed to mention that there were rebels. The forest opened onto a huge field of sugarcane that was perhaps ten feet tall. The road cut straight through the middle, the gap barely wide enough to accommodate the truck's side mirrors which hit the sugarcane on either side. I felt like one of Pharaoh's soldiers following Moses into the depths of the Red Sea. Pedro had the truck floored and peasant workers ahead of us were literally leaping for their lives.

> (A peasant tumble-rolls in front of the truck cutout. Mark and Pedro react with wide-eyed expressions.)

MARK:

I asked why we were going so fast.

PEDRO:

The rebels, they lay down in road to stop us. Then rob and kill you, señor. We go fast, so they know we not stop.

(Pedro pushes Mark's head down.)

Best lay down, so they not shoot you.

MARK:

We forded the river a few miles downstream and made our way back to the main road, where we stopped at the Guatemalan equivalent of a convenience store. It had a thatched roof and the gas pump was an elevated 55-gallon drum with a hose attached.

(A cardboard cutout of a barrel with a short garden hose, sitting on top of cinder blocks rolls out beside the truck. Pedro stands to pretend to gas up the truck.)

Pedro got gas, paid, and returned with two tortilla La Cheeseburgers.

PEDRO:

(He exits left and returns with a paper bag with fake burgers.)

We eat now. You look pale, señor.

MARK:

I wasn't very hungry. Soon we arrived at the town of Rau and stopped at the Hotel Modelo.

(Pedro stands and gathers imaginary luggage.)

MARK:

The hotel was surprisingly nice and the executive suite costs fifteen Diarios, about six US dollars, per night. Pedro carried my bags to the room, turned down the sheets, and swept the spiders and centipedes off the bed before tucking in the mosquito netting.

PEDRO:

Goodnight, señor. I take you to the factory tomorrow.

(He exits.)

MARK:

(Smoke starts to enter from stage right.)

The rebels also blew up the power plant and the only electricity came from a smoking diesel generator in the courtyard. The power came in

waves that caused the black-and-white TV and 20-watt overhead light bulb to fade in and out.
(Lights begin to flicker.)
The one TV channel aired endless episodes of La Isla de Gilligan in an incomprehensible Aztec language. I finally gave up and went to sleep.
(Beat)
As promised, Pedro was out front the next morning.

PEDRO:
You sleep well, señor?

MARK:
I dreamed of giant centipedes and when I stepped in the shower I discovered a bare heating coil wrapped around the showerhead.

PEDRO:
(Smiles)
Ah, hot water, señor. Good, no?

MARK:
Not so good. In order to have hot water, I had to plug a power cord into an outlet, inside the stall!
(Beat)
Cold showers aren't really that bad.
(Beat)
Our plant was quite modern, and I was able to fix the problem in a few days. However, every morning I awoke feeling worse, despite the fact that I drank only bottled water from the plant, and ate most of my meals from the vending machines.

PEDRO:
You not look so good, señor.

MARK:
This morning, when I was scheduled to leave, Pedro told me the bombed-out bridge was now fixed. It was a steel structure that crossed a boulder filled, raging river that emptied out of twin volcanoes. The eighty-foot middle span of the destroyed bridge that had been destroyed was now a sagging hulk, rebuilt from whatever material they had salvaged from the river. The whole mass appeared to be held together with c-clamps, vise-grips, and rope.

PEDRO:

I think they just finish. You wish me to go first, señor, then you walk across?

MARK:

I have a terrible fear of heights. Even though the bridge workers appeared to be taking bets to see if our truck would make it, I told Pedro no, and he started across the bridge at a snail's pace. I could feel it moving.
(Beat)
I asked why we were going so slow.

PEDRO:

We go slow, señor. Bridge may fall.

MARK:

I stomped my foot on top of his, flooring the gas, and said,
(To Pedro)
We go fast. Bridge may fall!
(Beat)
We made it, but Montezuma's revenge was catching up with me. When we got to Guatemala City I asked Pedro to stop at a restaurant so I could use the restroom. They had a big lunch crowd and I was directed to a wooden bathroom stall in the middle of the room, surrounded by tables and guests.
(A cardboard cutout of a bathroom stall with the door closed is pulled in front of Mark, Only his bare legs are visible.)
From inside the stall I could see the feet of the patrons. No telling what they thought, but when I emerged, all I saw were concerned and smiling faces. Pedro was standing a couple of feet away.
(The stall is pulled away.)

PEDRO:
(He smiles.)

You okay, señor?

MARK:

They were all genuinely worried about me, and no one seemed to care that I had ruined their meal. I told them that I was okay, and thanks for caring.

(Pedro exits.)

(Mark sits. Lights come up and the doctors still in hazmat suits return.)

MARK:
(Speaking to Dr. Orr)
Other than that, it was pretty uneventful.

DR. SIMPSON:
You said Pedro gave you a cheeseburger?

MARK:
Yes, but I only took a couple of bites before tossing it. All the bouncing had my stomach unsettled.

Dr. ORR:
Was the meat pink?

MARK:
(Beat)
Maybe.

(Both doctors pull off their face shields.)

Dr. ORR:
You have bacterial gastroenteritis, not a jungle virus. That we can treat.

MARK:
But Pedro ate his entire burger and was fine.

DR. SIMPSON:
Natives have immunities you don't. We've lost ours.

(Fade)

SCENE 2

Mark Nunn is standing, facing the audience. His

wife, Kathy, sits in a chair, her face buried in a magazine.

After all these years, I've never forgotten the lessons I learned in Guatemala. When I was well enough to go home from the hospital, I heard a lady complaining about her non-private room. Another grumbled about her pillows being too hard, and someone left a completely untouched dinner on their tray. As I left that sterile environment, I was struck by how weak we Americans have become. We have so much, and they have so little, yet never once did I hear the good people of Guatemala complain. Smiling children would run up to me and beg for a penny. When I gave them a dollar, they acted like it was a fortune. For them, I suppose it was.

KATHY:
(Looks up from the magazine)
You ate a cheeseburger and almost died down there, Mark. Now you want to go back?

MARK:
(To audience)
I suppose I haven't changed. I still waste food, dream of fancy cars, and think I'm underpaid. But sometimes when I see an old school bus parked alongside the road, I think about Pedro, the peasants making gravel, and the smiling faces of those children.

KATHY:
(Gets up)
Forget it, Mark. We're not going there on vacation!
(She exits.)

MARK:
It's times like these that I find myself longing for those simple treasures of Guatemala.

(Fade to black)

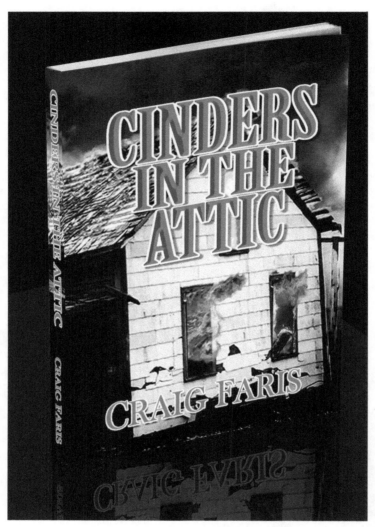

Cover design by Stanley Todd Robertson.

Cinders in the Attic – Synopsis

Under a shade tree in the back yard of Albert Williford's home, a Forth of July tradition of cooking a Catfish Stew is being prepared. While the guests wait, Albert tells the story of how the wood frame house that used to sit where his concrete block house now exists, burned to the ground in 1950.

CINDERS IN THE ATTIC

1970

Albert Williford was what some folks would call a pillar of the community. Not the marbled pillars of a big city, mind you. He was more like the rough creosote timbers that held up the Southern trestle over the Catawba River.

Everyone depended on Mr. Williford because he could fix most anything. From well pumps to electric stoves, nothing stumped him. One look at the trunk of his car, which was filled to the lid with every conceivable tool, proved it. I was only fifteen, but even then I knew what an honor it was to live next-door to a man of his talents.

It was Independence Day, and the whole community was in our side yard eagerly awaiting The Stew. Every year, Daddy and Mr. Williford would turn over the old cast iron wash pot we kept in the backyard and build a fire under it. This, according to Daddy, would kill all the black widow spiders and bugs that didn't have the good sense to leave. Into this pot, Mr. Williford would add several gallons of water, a hunk of fatback, various vegetables from his garden, whether they were ripe or not, gobs of onions, and the main ingredient—catfish. I've often wondered how they managed to get the entire community excited about coming over on a hot summer day to eat boiled fish. Not only did they come, they actually brought Mason jars to take the brew home with them.

Daddy filled my bowl to the rim. Eating catfish stew was a lot like a riverboat adventure. You never quite knew what lay beneath the surface. Between the bones, kernels of corn and stewed tomatoes, I often found objects that looked curiously like fish eyes. If I complained, Daddy would crush a handful of saltines over the surface and tell me it was impolite to stare at the stew. Other than that, it was pretty good.

After the feast, we would gather around the picnic tables in the shade of a live oak tree while our stomachs decided how best to process this concoction. This was the most exciting part of the festivities, because Mr. Williford was about to tell the kids one of his stories.

"Son," Mr. Williford said. It didn't matter if you were eight or eighty, he called everyone "son." "Run in the house and fetch me a cold Co-Cola from the Kelvinator."

I hated to fetch anything in Mr. Williford's house, because he had apparently experimented in a new form of wiring where you served as the ground wire and completed the circuit whenever you touched anything metallic. His hands were so thick with calluses that he must have been totally oblivious to both electricity and pain. I once saw him plug a wire into a live socket before cutting it in two with his pocketknife, preferring to let the blade burn its way through the copper. My tender hands had no such immunity and his refrigerator was like an electric chair. All I could do was grit my teeth, open it fast, and kick it shut with the sole of my sneaker.

As I walked through the house, I noticed that other than the furniture and a few pieces of molding, there was no wood. The floor was a bare concrete slab with rugs, and the walls concrete brick. *All the better to conduct electricity through unsuspecting strangers*, I thought.

Mr. Williford downed the Co-Cola with one swig and took out his pipe. He filled it with tobacco, packed it, and lit it with a glowing ember he lifted from the fire with his bare hands. I'm sure he did this just to amaze us kids.

I decided this was a good time to ask why a man with all of Mr. Williford's endowments would choose to live in a concrete torture chamber. But I didn't exactly put it that way.

"Mr. Williford, was there a shortage of wood when you built your house?"

He chuckled. "Well, son, just sit yourself down there and I'll tell you all about it." He puffed on his pipe as we gathered closer.

"It was twenty years ago come September 20th," he said. A bead of sweat rolled down Mr. Williford's nose and dangled on the end. I waited for it to fall, but it hung there.

"Since what?" I asked.

His daughter, Bernice, and her husband, William, were sitting at the next table. "I ran barefoot up to your house and told your momma," Bernice said. "Good thing, too, because your house almost went."

I was totally confused.

William laughed. "I remember Elmer Shugart grabbed that trunk of his and dragged it all the way down to the creek. Came back with only one shoe. Never did find the other one."

"What was in the trunk?" Mrs. Crosby asked.

"Dynamite." William said with a grin. "He worked on the county road crew and that's where he kept the sticks to keep them dry."

"No wonder he took it to the creek," Daddy said. "That would've taken out the whole block."

"Now y'all wait a minute," Mr. Williford said. "You're getting ahead of the story."

Laura Williford came out of the house with cups of homemade ice cream on a platter. Miz Laura was Mr. Williford's wife and he affectionately called her "Snook." She always insisted I give her a kiss on her cheek whenever she saw me. She smelled like talcum power and had the softest cheeks I ever felt. "What are y'all talking about?" she asked.

"Albert's telling the boys about the fire," Daddy said.

"Lord have mercy. Why would you want to talk about that?"

"What fire?" I asked.

"Our house," Mr. Williford explained. "It used to sit right over there." He nodded toward the torture chamber.

Daddy piped in. "It used to be the old Caldwell place before they put Joe's momma in the nursing home."

Mr. Williford continued. "The whole house was built out of old-growth heart pine. Kindling. So volatile you could light a two-by-four with a match. Just put a new roof on it. The porch wrapped around the front, down one side, and around the back. No upstairs, but it had a huge attic."

"What started it, Albert?" Mrs. Crosby asked. Some of the adults had overheard the conversation and gathered around.

"Can't say for sure," Mr. Williford said. "Probably a short in the wiring."

"I always thought it was a cigarette," Mrs. Sparks said.

Mr. Williford exhaled a cloud of smoke and shook his head. "Couldn't have. It started in our closet about midnight."

The drip of sweat still dangled from the tip of his nose.

"A case of shotgun shells in the closet started exploding and woke me. I saw the yellow glow coming around the cracks of the door and told Snook to fill two buckets of water at the kitchen sink."

"Albert was sitting on the edge of the bed calmly tying his boots when I returned," Miz Laura added.

Mr. Williford nodded. "Can't put a fire out with bare feet."

"He branded his hand on the doorknob when he opened it," Miz Laura said.

"The first bucket put most of it out. The second bucket got the rest," Mr. Williford said. "I stuck my head in and looked up. The ceiling of the closet had burned away and that's when I heard popping in the attic."

He turned and looked at Miz Laura as if in a trance.

"Get everyone out, Snook," he said. "Take what you can carry. She's gone."

The images in Mr. Williford's words played through my mind as clear as the screen of our new RCA Victor: Bernice, barefoot, pounding on our front door. Daddy dialing the fire department. His shocked face when the fire department wanted a hundred dollars since we lived in the country. Daddy agreeing to pay it. Miz Laura in her housedress, holding little Ricky while Mr. Williford, William and Daddy carried furniture and set it in the yard. Mr. Shugart on the side porch, wearing only one shoe, heaving a trunk out his window, then dragging it down in the woods. A hand-made cedar chest filled with William's war mementos, unnoticed be-side the door. They walked past it ten times while they saved the Kelvinator, some furniture, and a stove.

The fire department arriving too late and pouring water on our house and the Crosbys'; steam rising off boards so hot that the sap was weeping. They never laid a drop on the fire.

Bernice and Miz Laura, huddled on our screen porch, watching sparks, millions of them, swirl into the night sky. Tears streaking down Miz Laura's soft cheeks.

"All we could do was watch it burn," I heard Miz Laura say, and opened my eyes. "Ruth lost all her clothes in that closet."

"That's right" Bernice said. "My sister came up that weekend. I'd forgotten that. We picked up her dry-cleaning and she left them in there."

A frown formed on William's face. "Wasn't there a light bulb in that closet, Albert?" he asked.

Mr. Williford nodded.

Daddy's eyes widened. "Dry-cleaning fumes were flammable back then."

Mr. Williford put his hand on his face. The drip of sweat fell from his nose, and formed a dark stain on the knee of his pants. "She must've forgotten to switch off the light."

That was our last Fourth of July Stew. A few months later, Mr. Williford and Miz Laura packed everything they owned, including the car, in the back of a U-Haul truck and moved to Florida. They moved back a few years later, but I was older then and didn't see them much.

After Daddy died of cancer, Momma sold the house. One of the last things I got from the old home place was the cast iron wash pot. It sat in my yard for thirty years, unnoticed, before I decided it was time to try out the old recipe. We caught fifteen pounds of catfish and Momma filleted some of them. My wife gathered the vegetables and I invited the neighbors. To my surprise, most everyone came and seemed to enjoy it. Everyone, that is, except my daughter and my little boy.

Katie found an entire vertebra in her bowl and refused to eat another bite.

Charlie handed me his bowl and said, "Dad, what's that?"

I took one look, grabbed a handful of saltines, and remembered Daddy's words. "It's impolite to stare at the stew, son."

"But Dad, it's staring back."

Cinders in the Attic won an Honorable Mention in the 2003 Catfish Stew Anthology collection, published by the South Carolina Writers Workshop, now the South Carolina Writers Association.

Cover design by Craig Faris.

A Catfish Stew – Synopsis

A Catfish Stew is a one-act play based on the short story Cinders in the Attic.

A CATFISH STEW

A One-Act Play

SETTING

SCENE 1: Under a shade tree in Albert Williford's yard, Catawba, South Carolina

SCENE 2: Thirty-three years later under the same shade tree

TIME

SCENE 1: Noon, July 1970

SCENE 2: Late afternoon, July 2003

CHARACTERS

ALBERT WILLIFORD   Big man with a pipe, dressed in
brown coveralls, mid sixties

OLIVER   Next door neighbor. farmer's
overalls, mid fifties

CRAIG   Oliver's son, thin, tall, fifteen

LAURA (Snook)   Albert's wife, old dress with an
apron, sixty

BERNICE COSTNER   Albert's grown daughter, forty-five

WILLIAM   Bernice's husband, fifty

ANN CROSBY   Albert's other neighbor, dress with
big apron, sixties

MRS. SPARKS   Another neighbor, big apron, fifties

NEIGHBORS' KIDS   Kids of various ages

KATIE   Craig's daughter, years later, eleven

CHARLIE   Craig's son, years later, eight

ACT ONE

SCENE 1

(There is an old iron wash pot center stage with a
boat paddle in it and a water hose that leads off
to stage left. Oliver is adding water to the pot
and rubbing the paddle around the inside. His
son, Craig, is on his knees, adding firewood
under it. A picnic table sits at stage right with a
big oak tree behind it. The corner of a cinder
block house is at stage left with a screen door.
Mrs. Sparks and Ann Crosby sit on the
doorsteps, shucking corn.)

CRAIG:
Daddy, don't you think that's about enough water to rinse out the pot?
You're gonna get the firewood wet.

OLIVER:
No need, son. Any black widow spiders and bugs that didn't have the
good sense to leave won't even be noticed once we get the corn, taters,
onions, and fatback added.

CRAIG:
Are you just going to leave them in there?

OLIVER:
(Shrugs)
Don't make any difference. Were boiling it.

CRAIG:
Yuck! That is just gross. How can you eat this stuff?

OLIVER:
Aw, son, you just wait until we get a good fire roaring. The smell of

those veggies cooking in amongst all those taters and fish, why it will just make you plum forget about that little bit of protein that was crawling around.

(Craig cringes.)

(Mrs. Laura Williford comes out the screen door, dumps a platter of potatoes in the pot.)

LAURA:
(Yells offstage right)
Albert! You about finished skinning those fish? The neighbors will be here directly.

ALBERT:
(Answers from offstage right)
Hush ya griping, Snook. I'm coming.

LAURA:
Well, be sure to whack 'em upside the head before you throw them in. I hate seeing 'em sloshing around while they's cooking.

ALBERT:
I took their guts out, Snook. They ain't lively.

(Mrs. Laura goes back in the house.)

CRAIG:
Double yuck! No way anyone's eating this!

OLIVER:
Sure they will. Ain't no better eating than catfish stew at a July 4th picnic. There's something about the smell of boiled fish that just brings out all the neighbors. You watch, they'll bring Mason jars, and there won't be a drop left by six this evening. I guarantee.

CRAIG:
That's 'cause they don't know what's in it!

OLIVER:
Oh, they won't care. Son, eating catfish stew is a lot like a riverboat

adventure. You're never quite sure what lies beneath the surface. Between the bones, kernels of corn, and stewed tomatoes, you can find some pretty interesting things in there.

CRAIG:

Yeah, I heard about the fish eyes.

OLIVER:

Nothing a handful of crushed Saltines won't fix. Besides, it's impolite to stare at the stew. Now go in yonder and fetch Albert's lighter. We gotta get this fire going.

CRAIG:

Aw, Daddy, I hate going in that house. It's like a concrete torture chamber.

OLIVER:

Why is that?

CRAIG:

'Cause his refrigerator shocks the hound out of ya. Mr. Williford's hands are so thick with calluses that he seems totally oblivious. I think we serve as the ground wire to complete the circuit.

OLIVER:

A tickle won't hurt ya. Oh, never mind, here he comes now. Albert, loan us ya lighter.

(Albert Williford enters from stage left and dumps a bucketful of catfish into the pot. He sits on the picnic bench, takes out his lighter, and hands it to Craig who starts the fire.)

ALBERT:

Son, how about running in the house and fetchin' me a cold Coca-Cola from the Kelvinator?

(Craig rolls his eyes and slowly heads toward the house.)

ALBERT:

(Speaking in a low voice to Oliver)

Did he believe that story about the bugs?

OLIVER:
(smiles)
Yeah, and the one about the fish eyes, too.

(They both chuckle.)

ALBERT:
You wait, he's like you. He'll be cooking the stew before long and telling the same stories to his younguns.

> (Mrs. Sparks and Ann Crosby, their aprons full of corn, walk to the pot and add it to the brew. They sit at the picnic table. Craig returns from the house with a six-ounce bottle of Coca-Cola which he gives to Mr. Williford.)

CRAIG:
(Sarcastically to Oliver)
I had to open the Kelvinator with the sole of my sneaker!

> (Mr. Williford downs the Coca-Cola with one swig. Albert's daughter, Bernice, and her husband, William, come out of the house and sit at the table.)

CRAIG:
Mr. Williford, was there a shortage of wood when you built your house? Other than the furniture and a few rugs, I don't see a stick of wood in the place.

ALBERT:
Well, son, just sit yourself down there and I'll tell you all about it.

> (The neighbors' kids gather around as Albert takes out his pipe, fills it with tobacco, and lights it with a glowing ember he lifts from the fire with his bare hands.)

MRS. SPARKS:

You going to tell us about the fire, Albert?

ALBERT:

Yep, it was twenty years ago come September 20th. That was 1950.

CRAIG:

What fire?

BERNICE:

You weren't born yet, but I ran barefoot up to your house that night and told your momma.

WILLIAM:

Good thing, too, because your house almost went.
            (To Albert)
I remember Uncle Elmer Shugart grabbed that trunk of his and dragged it all the way down to the creek. Came back with only one shoe. Never did find the other one.

BERNICE:

What did you say was in Uncle Shugart's trunk?

WILLIAM:

            (grins)
Dynamite! He worked on the county road crew and that's where he kept the sticks to keep them dry.

OLIVER:

Well, no wonder he took it to the creek. That would've taken out the whole block!

ALBERT:

Now ya'll wait a minute. You're getting way ahead of my story.

(Laura Williford comes out of the house with a platter of chopped onions and tomatoes which she adds to the pot.)

LAURA:

What are y'all talking about?

OLIVER:

Albert's telling the boys about the fire.

LAURA:

Lord have mercy. Why would you want to talk about that?
(She sits with the others.)

CRAIG:

What fire?

ALBERT:

Our old house. It used to sit right over there.
                    (He nods toward the cinder block home.)

OLIVER:

Used to be the old Caldwell place before they put Joe's mamma in the
nursing home.

ALBERT:

The whole house was built out of old-growth heart pine. Nothing but
kindling. So volatile you could light a two-by-four with a match. Just put
a new roof on it, too.

ANN CROSBY:

I remember it had a porch that wrapped around the front, down one
side, and around the back. Wasn't it two stories, Albert?

ALBERT:

Nope, but it had a huge attic.

MRS. SPARKS:

What started it, Albert?

ALBERT:

Can't say for sure. Probably a short in the wiring.

CRAIG:
                    (Whispers to Oliver)
You can say that again.

ANN CROSBY:

I always thought it was a cigarette.

ALBERT:

Nope, wasn't a cigarette. It started in our closet about midnight. A case of shotgun shells went off in that closet and shook the whole house. I woke up, saw the yellow glow coming around the cracks of the door, and told Snook to fill two buckets of water at the kitchen sink.

LAURA:

(She shakes her head.)

I remember Albert was still sitting on the edge of the bed calmly tying his boots when I came back with the water.

ALBERT:

Can't put a fire out with bare feet, Snook. Everybody knows that.

LAURA:

He branded his hand on the doorknob when he opened the closet. I can still feel it on his palm.

ALBERT:

I didn't even notice. The first bucket put out the burning clothes. The second bucket got the rest. But when I stuck my head in and looked up, the ceiling of the closet had burned away. That's when I heard the popping in the attic.

LAURA:

Lord, I still remember Albert's words like it was yesterday. "Get everyone out, Snook," he said. "Take what you can carry. She's gone."

OLIVER:

I called the fire department when Bernice pounded on our door. They wanted a hundred dollars 'cause we lived in the country. I told them to come on.

BERNICE:

All we had were our housedresses. Mama was holding little Ricky while Daddy, William, and Oliver carried furniture outside and set it in the yard. William, you remember that cedar chest with all of your war photos?

WILLIAM:

Shoot, I made that cedar chest by hand and it sat right there while we walked past it ten times to save a stupid Kelvinator, some furniture, and a stove. I could've kicked it out the door. I lost half my life in that trunk.

ALBERT:
The fire department arrived too late to do anything but pour water on Oliver's house and the Crosbys'. I can still see the steam rising off boards so hot that the sap was weeping. They never laid a drop on the fire.

BERNICE:
We huddled on Oliver's screen porch, and watching sparks, millions of them, swirl into the night sky. Momma's tears had streaked her soft cheeks and there was no water to clean them.
(She dabs her eyes.)

LAURA:
Well, all we could do was watch it burn. Ruth lost all her clothes in that closet.

BERNICE:
Wait a minute. That's right. I'd forgotten that my sister came up that weekend. We picked up her dry-cleaning that day and she put them in daddy's closet because ours was full.

WILLIAM:
(Frowns)
Wasn't there a light bulb in that closet, Albert?

ALBERT:
Now that you mention it, there sure was.

OLIVER:
And as I recall, dry-cleaning fumes were highly flammable back then.

ALBERT:
(Shakes his head)
For twenty years I've wondered what started it, and it comes down to something as simple as switching off the light. Don't that beat all.

LAURA:

(She stands and moves to the pot)
Well, something smells mighty good. Albert, I'll fetch the Saltines if
you'll start serving the stew.

ANN CROSBY:
That sounds like a grand idea. Laura, I'll help you with the bowls.
           (She follows Laura into the house. Oliver pats
           Albert on the shoulder as he gets up. The others
           shake their heads.)

SCENE 2

           (The old iron wash pot sits rusted and upside
           down in center stage. The oak tree looks older
           now with weeds grown up around it and the
           house. Craig, at 48, sits in a rusty chair center
           stage with a bowl in his lap and a Mason jar filled
           with a brown liquid. His son, Charlie, and his
           daughter, Katie, sit on the ground beside the
           overturned pot.)

CRAIG:
That was our last Fourth of July stew. This is where we used to gather.

KATIE:
So, what became of Mr. Albert and Mrs. Laura, Daddy?

CRAIG:
A few months later, Mr. Williford and Mrs. Laura packed everything
they owned in the back of a U-Haul truck and moved to Florida. They
moved back a few years later, but I was older then and didn't see them
much. They eventually passed on, like we all will.

CHARLIE:
You lived next door in that house right up there?
           (He points off stage right.)

CRAIG:
That's right. After Daddy died of cancer, Momma sold the house. One
of the last things I got from the old home place was our cast iron wash

pot, just like this one. It sat in my yard for thirty years, before I decided it was time for you two to try out the old recipe.
>(Craig unscrews the lid from the Mason jar and pours some into a bowl.)

KATIE:
No way I'm trying that. I heard what went into that stuff. Yuck!

CRAIG:
Oh, come on, Katie. (beat) Charlie, have one bowl with me. It's good. Just try it!

CHARLIE:
>(He takes the bowl, looks down at it, and glances back at Craig.)

Dad, what's that?

CRAIG:
>(Craig looks and quickly crushes a handful of Saltines into the bowl)

It's impolite to stare at the stew, son.

CHARLIE:
But Dad, it's staring back.
>(Fade)

A Catfish Stew won the Third Place award in the 2003 Catfish Stew Anthology Collection published by the South Carolina Writers Workshop, now the South Carolina Writers Association. It has never been preformed.

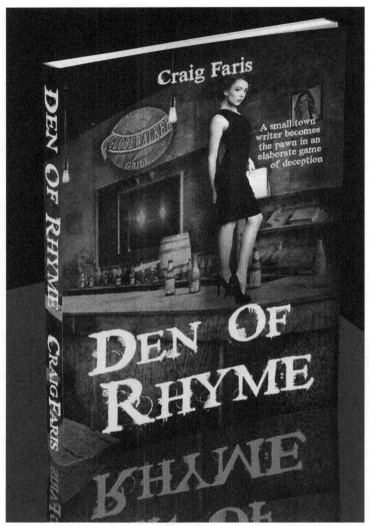

Cover design by Megan Bushbacker.

Den of Rhyme – Synopsis
The tranquil world of a southern writers group is forever changed when a provocative young writer joins, bringing her extraordinary talent along with some personal baggage. Now, a decade later, an injured author revisits the site of the tragic event that tore the writers group apart, only to discover that things may not have been what they seemed in this literary forsaken den of rhyme.

DEN OF RHYME
Fiction

2010

The old building was just as I remembered, despite the wisteria vines covering part of the rusted tin roof. Paint peeled from the clapboards above the front porch and the sandblasted sign that hung over it. The sign was round, carved to look like the Earth. Wood letters surrounding it proclaimed the building as the former home of the *Globewalker Arcade and Grill*. It served as a general store until the '70s when the traffic moved to the interstate. In the '80s, the owner's son, Ed Glasscock, renovated it as the *Globewalker*, but that too had failed.

A cool November breeze swirled leaves around my car like a flood of memories as I got out. I grew up here, rode to school every day, and stopped at this store for snacks on the way home. Down the road was the church we attended and where I got married. The best times of my life were spent in this community, but those fond memories intermingled with more recent images.

The *Globewalker* had been empty for years before Ed suggested we use it for our local writers' meetings. An aspiring writer himself, Ed cleaned it up and served sandwiches and spirits when the crowd was large enough. It usually was, and for five wonderful years, the Thursday evening critiques at the *Globewalker* stretched late into night. That is, until one Thursday, a decade ago, when a new member arrived.

JULY 1999

She told us her name was PJ, and like the rest of us, she had difficulty finding her way into the building that first time. Ed posted a wooden sign over the front door which read: *There are no doors into the Globewalker. Knock on the window.* Having missed the sign, she almost left, but I caught up with her in the parking lot and invited her inside.

She was young for our group, probably in her late twenties with shoulder-length, brown hair and hazel eyes. Gwen, our chapter president, told her she was allowed to attend and read at three meetings before joining. Membership was forty dollars, and I got the feeling PJ would have trouble scraping together that sum.

That night, PJ brought several poems and, being late, she read last. Halfway into her work, I knew she was an extraordinary writer. Her word choices and descriptions filled us with vivid images. Our critiques covered her pages with checkmarks and words like "fabulous" and "wow." I longed for more and felt slightly jealous.

By the time we adjourned, most of us nursed a glass of wine or beer, but PJ sipped only a soft drink. She thanked several members, and then lingered to ask if I would walk her to her car. "There's no streetlight," she said. "Would you mind?"

"Of course not," I said. We headed outside toward the far end of the lot. "Do you live around here?"

"Not too far. We have a place at Cedar Valley."

Cedar Valley was a mobile home park. "So, where did you learn to write like that?"

"I'm usually home alone, so I read a lot."

"That's essential for writing. You have a real talent."

"I wrote in high school." She walked slowly, as if prolonging the conversation. "I had pretty good grades in English, especially in creative writing."

"Your poems are excellent," I said. "I'm not into poetry, but I know great similes when I see them."

She smiled. "You really think so?"

"It's not just me. Just wait until you read those critiques. Everyone loved them."

"That's a sweet thing to say." She unlocked the car door and faced me.

"Are you coming back?"

"This is the first time in years I've heard compliments on my writing. I'm hooked."

"Good. I'm looking forward to more."

"Thanks for showing me the entrance."

I extended my hand and she squeezed it. Maybe it was only my imagination, but it felt like she didn't want to let go.

2010

Although Ed had moved to Columbia with his family, he still owned the building. The day I phoned, our conversation was brief. "You mind if I look inside the *Globewalker*?"

"Go ahead," he said. "Take a flashlight. The fuse box is in the back closet. Switch it off when you leave."

"Do I need a key?"

Ed chuckled. "That front door is like Fort Knox. You know how to get in."

Three iron pipes supporting the front porch grew out of cracked concrete where ancient gas pumps once stood. Wooden steps ran the full width of the building where Ed and I used to eat ice cream as kids. They were worn deep below the twin front doors attesting to the thousands of patrons who had passed through. The rusted screen doors had chrome push bars and still advertised Royal Crown Cola and Moon Pies as the "working man's lunch."

The skeleton key to the brass door locks had long since vanished and rather than replace the locks, Ed opted for an alternate entrance. On either side of the doors were solid, wooden shutters with a steel bar diagonally across them. The bar was secured with a foot-long pin that ran through one end into the wall. I twisted and pulled the pin, and it came free. Behind the shutters was a tall window, its bottom sill only three inches above the floor. A slight pull at the sill sent the counterweighted lower sash up six feet, and I stepped inside.

Using my cell phone flashlight, I located the fuse box and switched on the power. A row of dusty light bulbs dangling from long, twisted wires flickered to life, revealing a beadboard ceiling high above. During the *Globewalker's* renovation, Ed added dark green felt wallpaper, and the long grocery counter was refinished as a soda fountain and bar. A thin layer of dust covered everything including the green barstools and tables with ladder-back chairs still hanging inverted from them.

The bar became symbolic of our rite of passage into the publishing world. Tradition required that you stand on top of the counter and spew forth your greatest published achievement. On the faded walls, darker rectangles marked where pictures once hung of those who achieved that goal. A few remaining photos stared down from dust-shrouded frames. There was Millard, holding his award-winning poem, and Melissa with her long blonde ringlets. She was the first to perform the rite: climbing onto the bar, only to discover that it was best not to wear an above-the-knee skirt.

Here, in this literary forsaken den, we had gathered, spilling out our hearts and emotions onto twenty-pound bond in double-spaced black ink, always in an attempt to move closer to the edge of the publishing abyss. Those of us who made it worked our poems and prose onto a hook as one might an earthworm and flung them as far as we could into the swirling maelstrom of unpublished manuscripts. Some only got a nibble; some a bite, but in landing our catch, each of us was careful that the literary trophy bass we longed for wasn't a bottom-feeding carp.

1999

By late August, PJ was a regular in the group and never failed to astound us with her writing talent. She said she was working on a novel, but the only selections she read were from short stories and poetry. She usually sat by me, and we exchanged notes about the boring or grammatically challenged critiques we suffered through. However, she showered my work with an array of accolades like "outstanding" and "brilliant."

She called me her mentor. It was flattering, especially to an overweight, middle aged man, but in truth, I thought she was the better writer. In one particular story, she placed her character inside an hourglass, using her fingers to push the sands of time back up through the neck, instead of a cliché about reversing the hands on a clock.

"Where do you get those images?" I asked, walking her to her car.

"I don't know. There's plenty of inspiration in my neighborhood."

"You mean Cedar Valley?"

She nodded. "It's a trailer park."

I smiled. "What a venue for literary intrigue. No wonder you write so well."

"Are you married?"

The question took me aback. We had grown close but never shared these basics. "My wife is a teacher. We have two kids."

"I thought so, but you never wear a wedding band."

"It doesn't fit my fat finger. I see a crease on your ring finger, but never a ring."

"I never wear it until he gets home. So, you liked my story?"

It was obvious that "he" wasn't her favorite topic. "Yes. I think it could win a literary award."

"Really?"

"There's a competition at the Myrtle Beach writers' conference in October. You could win hands down, but you have to register in order to enter."

"How much does it cost?"

"The room and fees are $150, but there's absolutely no better place to find an agent or editor."

She frowned. "Money is a little tight right now."

"If you win first place, you'll get a check for a hundred bucks."

She mumbled almost to herself. "Maybe I could tell him I'm visiting my cousin Sheri in Murrells Inlet." She threw both hands into the air and screamed, "Billy works the night shift in October!" Then she turned and planted a kiss directly on my lips.

2010

I remember thinking it was nothing, but her impulsive reaction startled me. I should have known better and said something to my wife right then, but that's not the kind of discussion that ever ends with "That's nice, dear." It creeps into conversations, is always present in an argument, and awakens you repeatedly at three o'clock in the morning. The truth was, that I was attracted to PJ, yet torn between the woman I truly loved and the prospect of this exciting temptation.

My eyes turned to the beadboard ceiling of the *Globewalker*, to the very spot I had focused on a decade earlier. PJ's final words came flooding into my thoughts. *I'm so sorry. This wasn't supposed to happen.*

"Hello!" A deep baritone voice snapped me from my trance. "Is anyone in there?"

"Detective Lee?" I called toward the store front. "Come through the window."

SEPTEMBER 1999

We had plenty of discussions in the weeks that followed. PJ apologized for the kiss and said that she couldn't imagine how Billy would react if he found out.

"Is he abusive?" I asked.

"Not physically, but he yells and ignores my needs. He hasn't read any of my stories since high school, and he treats me like some life support system for his sex toy."

"Have you considered divorce?"

"Of course, but I have no job, no money, and my parents haven't spoken to me in years." She nodded at the pages in her lap. "The only positive thing in my life right now is this."

"Are you reading that tonight?"

"No, it's part of my novel. I've been working on it for years, but it's not ready to present."

"I'd love to read it sometime."

"Well, maybe after the conference. What are you working on?"

I fingered my pages. "It's the beginning of a new book. Actually, it's about all of us, our group and this place where we meet and share critiques, but I'm struggling with the ending."

She took the pages and studied the cover. "*A Den of Rhyme*. I love the title."

"Yeah, so far that's as good as it gets."

"Maybe your ending hasn't happened yet. Just let it flow." She laughed. "Like I'm the expert. You've won how many literary awards?"

I looked down, embarrassed. "You'll be next. We meet two weeks after the conference, and it will be your turn to stand on the bar. Be sure to wear jeans."

She smiled and poked me in the side. "If I win, I'm wearing the shortest black skirt you've ever seen, and everyone can admire my red panties because *I won*, and I won't *give a damn!*"

2010

I met Detective Robert Lee only once, back when he was the sheriff's department investigator assigned to the case. I helped him navigate the window entrance and we sat at the same table again. "Thanks for bringing the file."

"For what it's worth," Lee said, "this case was closed years ago. So, you found her?"

"I'm not sure. Even though we were friends, I never knew PJ's real name. Her husband's name was Billy. I can't remember his last name."

Detective Lee opened the file and flipped pages. "Billy Joe Ratford. His nickname was Rat. PJ's name was Pamela Jane Ratford."

Pam seemed too quaint for her, but it confirmed my findings. "Was her maiden name Woodbridge?"

"It doesn't say. How did you find her?"

"Years ago, I outlined a novel about a writers' group, but it didn't have a climax. Before our 1999 writers conference, I told PJ the basic storyline, but after the incident I quit writing. Three years ago, I found the perfect ending and finally finished it. I always do an internet search on titles before sending out a manuscript. That's when I discovered that a New York novelist, Pamela Jane Woodbridge, had received a six-figure advance for her book, *The Den of Rhyme.* The synopsis is almost exactly the same plot as my novel, and that was *my* title."

"She stole your story?" Lee said.

"The plot idea. It was only an outline."

Lee began flipping through the case file. "There are a lot of unanswered questions here. What exactly happened at that conference?"

OCTOBER *23, 1999*

On Saturday evening, all of the conference attendees gathered in the main ballroom for dinner, drinks, and the keynote speaker's address. Six members of our chapter sat together awaiting the announcement of the writing competition winners. Everyone cheered when Melissa's poem, *Hellfire Hath No Fury Like the Backseat of a '48 Ford,* won first place. My entry, *Silent Assault,* was the nonfiction winner, and we all held our breath to see if PJ's story would place in the short fiction category. When they announced her name as the first-place winner, she shrieked, and we cheered her onto the stage. I've never seen anyone get so excited about a certificate and a hundred-dollar check.

Afterward, Gwen hosted a party for us in her room with several agents and editors in attendance. PJ was on top of the world and shared the news of her award with anyone who would listen. She came up behind me as I refilled my drink in the kitchen and whispered, "I brought my novel. Help me find my room, and I'll let you have a peek."

She seemed tipsy and, despite my misgivings about going to her room, I was curious about the novel, so I agreed. However, in the elevator and walking down the hall, I began to feel uneasy. PJ appeared sober and easily found her room and key. She opened the door, but I remained in the hallway.

"I should head back down."

"Quit being silly," she said, nodding over her shoulder. "My computer is right there on the table. Go take a look while I visit the restroom."

I followed her to the table where she opened an expensive laptop and scrolled down to chapter six. "I think you'll find this interesting."

I sat and began reading, but this story was unlike anything PJ shared at our meetings. The scene was erotic, and the further I read the more the main character's description began to look like me.

"So, what do you think?" she said, her voice inches behind me.

"Uh, I think if my wife ever—" My words froze as I saw her reflection in the dresser mirror. I stood and turned to find her completely nude.

"You wanted a peek," she said, moving closer.

Her stunning beauty was every man's fantasy. She pressed her mouth to mine, wrapped one leg around my thigh, and ran fingers through my hair. I tried to say "no," but her lips covered my words and her hand slid down past my belt. It took all of my moral strength to push her away.

"I'm sorry," I said. "I can't do this."

"Come on, let's celebrate," she whispered. "We'll do it here on the floor. I need someone who makes me feel cherished. No one will ever know."

"I'll know! "PJ, you know I like you . . . but if we do this, I'll lose everything—my wife, my kids, and I'll never forgive myself."

She watched as I straightened my clothes, saying nothing, nor bothering to get dressed. When I reached the door, she said, "Don't tell anyone, okay?"

I nodded and left.

2010

Detective Lee stared at me, transfixed by the story. "So, you're saying you two never had sex?"

"That's all that happened," I said.

"Did you see her again?"

"I planned to let PJ have her celebration and afterwards to stop attending. She was too great a temptation. I thought about it for two weeks before deciding to attend the next meeting."

"This is all starting to make sense," Lee said.

November 4, 1999

True to her word, PJ showed up at the *Globewalker* in a mid-thigh-length, black dress. She sat beside me and whispered, "Don't worry. That won't ever happen again."

I told her we needed to talk, and then she announced to the group that she had to leave early and asked if she could read her piece by 8:00 p.m. We critiqued others for a half-hour and while Melissa was climbing onto the bar, PJ excused herself to use the restroom out back. When she returned, Melissa was finishing up.

PJ climbed onto the bar, revealing that the red panties were actually her high school cheerleader shorts. A few minutes into her story, we heard the deep rumbling of a truck engine outside, followed seconds later by pounding on the front door. Gwen went to investigate, and PJ yelled, "Lock the window!"

A man looking to be in his late twenties threw up the window sash with such force that it cracked the pane. He stepped inside and surveyed the room. "What the hell is this?" He glared at PJ on the bar. "What, are you stripping now?"

"Go home, Billy," PJ growled. "It's not like that."

"We're a writers' group," Gwen interrupted. "She's reading her—"

"Shut up, bitch!"

"You need to leave," Gwen said, brandishing her cell phone.

Billy pulled a snub-nosed revolver from his waistband and pointed it at Gwen's face. "You got anything else to say?"

Gwen shook her head, and we all shrank into our chairs.

"That slut up there is my wife, and we're both leaving."

"I'm not going anywhere, Billy," PJ said. "I filed for divorce today."

Billy pointed the revolver at her. "I know what *you've* done. I read your story, you whore!"

"That's nothing compared to what I'm going to do once I'm rid of your sorry ass."

"Here's your divorce, bitch!" The gun exploded with a deafening sound. PJ crumpled and fell off the far side of the bar. Screams filled the room, and everyone ran for cover.

Then Billy spotted me. "There you are, you bastard!"

I raised a hand. "Look, I didn't do anything. I—"

"I saw what you did to my wife," he hissed, the revolver pointed at my chest.

"Freeze!" a voice yelled, "and drop your weapon!" A sheriff's deputy stood by the front window, his pistol aimed at Billy's back. "Now!"

Billy just grinned at me and squeezed the trigger.

2010

"Being shot feels nothing like I imagined," I said. "The impact knocked me off my feet and a sharp, burning sensation pierced my left shoulder. I remember lying on the floor looking up at red lights reflecting off the ceiling. Someone said, 'He's dead,' and I wondered if Billy had killed me. I was so angry at Billy for shooting his wife, angry at PJ for dragging me into their relationship, but mostly angry at myself for getting involved. Someone pressed down on my left shoulder, and then PJ leaned over me, saying, 'I'm so sorry. This wasn't supposed to happen.'"

"That's not what Gwen heard," Detective Lee said.

"What?"

"Gwen was holding a bandage to your wound. She heard PJ say, *It wasn't supposed to happen this way.*"

"What's the difference?"

"*This way* implies premeditation," Lee said.

"You mean she planned it?"

"Absolutely. The first round in Billy's revolver was a blank, and PJ claimed she *fell* off the bar. When questioned, she said Billy always kept a blank in the gun to scare off burglars, but that sure was a convenient excuse."

"A damn clever one if she replaced the bullet," I said. "But how could she know that the sheriff's deputy would show up right before Billy squeezed off a live round?"

"Our 911 operator got a domestic disturbance call at 7:50 p.m. It came from the pay phone outside."

"Her restroom break?"

"Yes. She claimed she suddenly remembered leaving the laptop on and was afraid that Billy might see it when he got home. Her testimony that she was trying to *prevent a crime* was key to her case with the insurance adjustors."

"What insurance?"

"She collected a million-dollar life insurance policy on Billy that was purchased in July. Plus, when we investigated their trailer, Billy had smashed her laptop screen with his fist. It had a camera attached, and we found a video on the hard drive showing *you* reading her story and then her, naked, kissing you. The scene of you leaving was missing, but there was a scene with just her legs sticking up from the floor in a V-shape, with her moaning your name and giving you some rather interesting directions . . . Convincing stuff. We thought it was you, but obviously it was edited for someone to assume that. We also found evidence that she was supplementing her erotic writing income with an amateur porn site."

My mind spun in disbelief. "She wasn't broke? She left that video where Billy would find it?"

"Right beside the divorce notice. We also found a printed copy of that erotic chapter you mentioned, along with *your* business card. It had the *Globewalker's* address scribbled across it."

"I gave her that card the night we met," I said, her scheme becoming clear. "She used that story and the video to infuriate Billy, then called the cops knowing he wouldn't back down. She set all this up to *get rid* of him."

"Why not you as well?"

"Me?"

"Someone needed to die to make sure Billy either got life or the needle," Lee said. "Plus there was that fabulous story idea with only *you* in the way."

It wasn't supposed to happen this way, she had said. "I wasn't supposed to live?"

"Probably not, but either way it still worked in her favor. Billy got the grave, and you quit writing."

"Can she still be indicted?"

"With what? She didn't kill anyone. Billy shot you. The insurance company couldn't even prove causation. But you might have a civil case with your book."

"No." I sighed. "You can't copyright an idea or a title."

I thanked Detective Lee for his research, then turned out the lights and closed the shutters on the *Globewalker Arcade and Grill* one last time. As we shook hands, he said, "PJ's plan was flawless except for one thing."

"What's that?"

"You lived. She may have gotten away with it, but she isn't the only one who can write."

2012

The New York bookstore on Broadway was huge with several areas designated for author book-signings on the first floor. I waited in a line behind an overweight, dark-haired woman, a burgundy sweater covering her rounded shoulders. She had PJ's novel clutched in the crook of her arm and I caught a glimpse of a quotation printed on the back of the dust jacket. The words were familiar, spoken as my angry response to PJ's *I'm-so-sorry* line while I bled on the floor, *I just want to get the hell out of this literary forsaken den of rhyme and go home to my family.* Those words, *my words,* now graced banners and the covers of stacks of books around us.

Over the years my anger had faded into regret, unaware that PJ had built her deception as one might a rock wall, stacking layer upon layer, turning each stone until it fit perfectly. Detective Lee's statement had reignited that fire, and in my arms was all the ammunition I would ever need.

Burgundy Sweater collected her signed copy and moved away, revealing that Pamela Jane was still attractive, a little pale, but had barely aged. Her hair was now shorter, gold-rimmed glasses were perched low on her nose, but she looked like she had a head cold or the flu, a box of tissues within reach. Looking up, she gave me an unrecognizing smile and took the novel from my hands.

PJ frowned at the title and said, "This isn't my—" her mouth froze as she read my name on the cover. She struggled for words. "Oh . . . so you . . . finally wrote a book."

"My second," I said, glancing around. "Since you quoted me in yours, and *stole* mine."

"It wasn't . . ." she coughed. "It was only an idea."

"Yeah. *My* idea and *my* title!"

"You can't—"

"Copyright an idea? I know. This is my new book: a gift for you, since we were such *close friends*."

"Oh." PJ opened it. "Self-published?"

"Hardly. They expect five thousand copies could be sold by next month. Tomorrow I'm doing the morning news circuit."

She swallowed hard. "What's it about?"

"It's right there on the dust jacket." I recited the line aloud. "An aspiring young writer sets up her husband's death-by-cop, collects his insurance, and then steals her lover's story."

Her face paled. "You can't prove that."

"Relax, PJ. It's only a novel."

"I was . . . cleared of any—"

"Wrongdoing? Detective Lee says they have a new tech lab with some *amazing* equipment. They were able to salvage an erased video from your old hard drive, along with my deleted outline."

She stared at me, her mouth agape.

"They also found some kind of checklist that you wrote a week before the shooting. It was quite detailed. He's contacted your insurance company and publisher. They seem *real* interested."

"But . . . you never wrote it."

"I didn't?" I pointed to my quote on her dust jacket. "It seems that legally only a few lines are grounds for plagiarism."

Her cheeks were now white, her lips blue. "I . . . I have an attorney."

"Good. You'll *need* one."

PJ put a hand over her mouth and tried to stand. Then heaving, she threw up on a stack of her new novels.

"Well, it's time for me to sign *my books*. Good luck in prison."

I walked away feeling much lighter on my feet. A line was already forming in front of my table, now joined by those escaping from the odor and mess at PJ's.

Someone asked, "What was that about?"

I gave him my novel. "It's called *A Murder in Prose*."

Den of Rhyme was a 2012 Semifinalist in the William Faulkner/ William Wisdom Short Story Competition, was a 2014 Finalist in the William Faulkner/William Wisdom Short Story Competition, and placed forth in the 2021 York County Literary Competition.

Cover design by Craig Faris.

The Spectrum Conspiracy – Synopsis

Special Agent Devrin Crosby is consumed by his past addictions, and one lethal mistake. Suspended and reduced to pushing papers, he is on the verge of leaving the FBI when the President's assassination on live television pulls him back. Everyone saw who did it, but Crosby uncovers a far more sinister plot, a conspiracy involving a secret Government agency, a nuclear Trojan Horse, and amateur thieves.

In order to save thousands of lives, he will have to unravel their secrets or risk losing everyone he loves. The clock is ticking, no one is listening.

THE SPECTRUM CONSPIRACY
THREE CHAPTER SAMPLE

PART 1
CHAPTER 1

12:25 a.m, Alexandria, VA

Beyond the iron gates that guarded the entrance to the property, beyond the manicured lawn and hedges that lined the driveway, the senator's home loomed in the darkness. Upstairs in the master bedroom, a phone warbled two sets of triplets, the pattern indicating the encrypted line.

"The President knows," the caller said.

"What?" Senator Luther mumbled, still asleep.

The message was clearer this time. "He knows about Spectrum!"

Eyes wide open, the senator lifted himself onto one elbow. "Who is this?"

"Viper," Norman Trexler replied. "He knows."

"How much?"

"All of it. He has a full report."

The senator swung his legs off the bed, fully awake. "How did it get out?"

"How the hell should I know? Someone leaked it to his Press Secretary."

"When?"

"An hour ago. I just got out of the meeting at the White House," Trexler said.

"Did you explain the implications?"

"Of course. Why do you think I'm calling? He went ballistic. He's scheduled a press conference for tomorrow at noon."

"Good Lord!"

"We'll all be indicted," Trexler choked on the last syllable.

"That idiot. Who else knows?"

"Just the Chairman of the Joint Chiefs and the Press Secretary. He wants to go public with it himself."

"The Chairman's not a problem," the senator said. "Has he contacted the FBI?"

"Hell no. Director Gregory's office leaks like a screen door. He's afraid if it gets out before tomorrow the media will accuse him of being part of it. He's beating them to the punch."

"There must be some way to reason with him."

"Believe me, I've tried. You know how righteous he is." Trexler sighed. "It's over. Spectrum is finished and so are we."

"Not necessarily." The senator glanced at his alarm clock. "Where's the press conference being held?"

"In the White House Briefing Room. Why?"

The Senator didn't answer.

"You're not serious? It can't be done!"

"I'll discuss it with Raptor."

"You've got to be crazy. It's *in* the White House!"

"Are you certain he's told no one else?"

Trexler's voice was shaky. "I can't say for sure, but I know his wife is out of town, and he wants to make damn sure the media hears it from his lips. That's all I know."

"Go home and get some rest. Call for further instructions in the morning. With any luck we'll be one step ahead of him." The senator disconnected and punched in Raptor's speed dial number.

•   •   •

Across the Potomac River, the Secretary of Defense, Norman Trexler, hung up his phone and steadied his trembling hand. He had never met the man they called Counselor, and had no idea to what extent he would go to protect the project. They considered themselves patriots, but selling weapons to a terrorist state was a treasonable act, and hiding their true identities was crucial. By midday the President would expose them all and his political career would end behind iron bars.

Perhaps Counselor did have the power to stop the speech. His political future might yet be saved, and if anyone could pull it off, it was the man they called Raptor.

•   •   •

DuPont Circle, Washington, DC

The beer cradled between his palms was warm, the foam long gone. Special Agent Devrin Crosby never liked beer, but the smell of alcohol was still tempting. FBI agents were expected to remain sober even when off duty, but Crosby was a recovering alcoholic, a disease that had nearly cost him his job. If his boss so much as smelled it on him at work, he would be cleaning out his desk the same day. The beer was a self-imposed test, a ritual he went through every Sunday evening. If he could resist the urge to taste despite its aroma and proximity, he knew he could remain sober for another week.

The glare of the bar television reflected the mirrored image of 12:34 a.m. onto his beer mug and Crosby glanced across the room at the corner of Goodtime Charlie's lounge. There, a shiny black Baldwin grand piano stood with ivory keys and a touch much finer than the electronic piano he kept in the tiny bedroom of his apartment. The lounge had a regular pianist on weekdays, but on Sundays the bench was empty. Crosby played well but his addiction had robbed his confidence, so he preferred to wait for the other patrons to leave. This evening, he had hovered over his warm mug for an hour as a young couple stubbornly remained.

The couple seemed an odd match to Crosby. The woman was blonde, well endowed and strikingly beautiful, but the man was short, bald and in a rumpled black suit. *Must be an expensive date,* he thought.

"Go ahead, Devrin," the bartender said. "They won't care."

"I'll wait. What's my latest time on the cube?"

The bartended placed a Rubik's Cube in front of Crosby and turned a few pages in his small notebook. "One minute, forty seconds. You were off pace last week."

"Depends on the starting point." Crosby studied the layout. "You ready?"

The bartender clicked a stop watch and Crosby's fingers began spinning the faces. He only glanced at what he was doing, as if each set of fingers had memorized the pattern and acted independently of each other, turning sections without even rotating the cube.

"How do you do that?" the bartender said.

Crosby shrugged, fingers flying. "It's algorithms designed to change parts of the cube without scrambling the others. Once you learn the patterns, it's simple."

"Looks impressive."

"These cubes are easy. You wouldn't believe the really complex ones. What was my best time to date?"

The bartender flipped back a few pages. "Forty-four seconds."

"Was I sober?"

"You came in looking like you had slammed a half-bottle of scotch."

"That figures. Almost there," Crosby said with a final spin. "Time?"

The completed cube sat on the bar, each color arranged perfectly.

"Fifty-eight seconds," the bartender said. "Not bad."

"It's a far cry from the world record."

"You're way ahead of everyone here." The bartender closed the notebook.

Crosby glanced up at a muted news segment on the television. A reporter was standing in a park with blooming flowers behind her, and in the distant background, the White House.

She's in Lafayette Park, he thought. Images of the park flashed through his memory. The shouted warnings, the recoil of his Glock, and tiny red spots on yellow daffodils.

Even as he refocused on his beer, a smell of cordite remained. A year had passed since the incident, and there was no one to blame but himself. Well, almost no one.

•   •   •

Senator Christian Luther had no choice but to use his regular phone to make the call. He had tried Raptor's secure line, but apparently his unit was switched off. The phone rang twice before he heard a rough voice.

"What is it?" Harold Sanders said curtly.

"It's Counselor," Luther replied. "There's a storm."

Sanders waited a beat to respond. "Serious?"

"A squall line is approaching."

"Where?"

Luther hesitated, remembering his unsecure line. "Sixteenth and Pennsylvania."

Sanders remained silent for a moment. "Give me a minute. I'll call you back."

Only seconds later the senator's encrypted line rang.

"Tell me about it." Sanders voice lacked any hint of emotion.

"The President knows about Project Spectrum," Luther said. "He has a detailed report that he's going to reveal tomorrow in the Press Briefing Room. All attempts to reason with him have failed."

"You're sure?"

"Yes. Stalker is working on the confirmation."

"What time is the briefing?"

"Noon."

Sanders paused, apparently checking his watch. "Short notice."

"What choice do we have? The report is lethal to the project. He must be stopped!"

"Which plan?"

"Proceed with Operation Sweep."

"I'll need executive authorization."

"You'll have it," Luther said. "Can it be done?"

"What's the collateral damage?"

"One witness and some documentation. Stalker will handle the documents. The witness will have to look like a coincidence."

"Won't work," Sanders said. "Better to make it a consequence. Who is the witness?"

"The Press Secretary. You have someone in mind?"

"I'll see if Mig is available."

"Approved," Luther said. "The identity package is being prepared."

"What about his wife?"

"Out of town. Stalker is accessing her cell. What else do you need?"

"Stalker will have to place the propaganda material in the sponsor's home. I'll handle the camera equipment and seeding the sponsor's clothing and locker. I need access to the storage facility and the station's news van."

"Both keys will be in the package. What time?"

"By 0200," Sanders said. "See that the primary cameraman calls in sick. Give him something that's untraceable."

"I'll try not to make it too contagious."

"Whatever. Just make damn sure he doesn't show up. And one other thing."

"What's that?" Luther asked.

"Find out what time the cleaning crew vacuums the Briefing Room."

"Why?"

"Just do it."

CHAPTER 2

CROSBY

In Goodtime Charlie's lounge the couple at the bar finally got up to leave. The bartender nodded toward the piano. "Better hurry, Devrin. I'm closing at one a.m."

Crosby sat at the piano and examined his haggard face in its mirrored finish. He imagined his mother's reflection looking over his shoulder as she had during his years of piano lessons. *What would she think?* He was forty-four, but he felt ten years older. He had gained fifteen pounds since the incident in Lafayette Park, but at least his sandy blond hair hadn't grayed.

His fingers moved over the keys and the melancholy strains of a piece called "As for Us" filled the room. He had no sheet music, just a knack for picking out tunes from memory. Above the soft melody he heard the door chime and, glancing up, saw a man rush in. The man stopped at the bar, his hair soaking wet and his suit dripping on the floor. He glanced at Crosby, ashen faced, hands trembling, and clutching a manila envelope close to his side. He said something to the bartender who poured him a shot and pointed down the street. The man downed the drink, slid money across the bar and dashed back into the storm, the envelope still at his side.

Twenty minutes later, Crosby stepped out under the awning, and the bartender switched off the neon lights behind him.

"Who was that?" Crosby asked.

"I think it was Tim Cook, the White House Press Secretary," the bartender said. "He wanted directions to the nearest mailbox."

"I thought he looked familiar."

"He left you a tip." The bartender handed him a twenty dollar bill.

Crosby smiled. "Whoa. I must have sounded okay."

"That's what I've been saying, Devrin," he said, locking the door. "See you next week."

"Thanks, Charlie," Crosby replied. It was raining hard, so he hustled down the dark familiar path toward his tiny apartment two blocks away.

• • •

Charlotte, NC

Kathryn Froscher leaned closer to the wheel trying to see through the streaks left by her windshield wipers. She was on I-77 just north of the Panthers Stadium, still in the dress she had worn to her father's wake earlier that evening. He had been terminally ill for over a year, but the news of his death had brought out far more mourners than even she anticipated. From seven until ten p.m. she had stood in the receiving line shaking hands with people she had never met and never expected to see again. Afterward, a couple of girlfriends had taken her out for a late dinner and a drink.

The dress was new, expensive and looked great with her pale skin, brown hair and green eyes. At twenty-nine she still had a great body and could have taken home any of the guys who kept eyeing her long legs under the table. *Wasn't getting laid while your father was in an open casket a sin? Surely he would know.*

A flash of lightning followed by the crack of thunder refocused her attention on the road and seemed to confirm her thoughts. *Right decision.* Her older brother, Chuck, was flying in from Oak Ridge early in the morning. There simply wasn't any time to deal with a strange guy in her bed, no matter how cute he might be.

The steering wheel began to vibrate, and she felt the rear of the car pull to one side, the unmistakable signs of tire trouble.

Oh great. The interstate was busy, the rain blinding with no emergency shoulder in sight. She spotted a bridge overpass and guided her Acura TSX to an exit ramp under the bridge hoping it might afford her some shelter from the rain.

It didn't. It was a railway bridge that let as much rain through it as around it. To make matters worse, the ramp led to another interstate and trucks were flying past her at sixty miles per hour.

She eased off the roadway as far as the guardrail would permit and turned on her emergency flashers. She found her triple-A card in her purse, but when she opened her cell phone, it beeped for a second and went dead.

"Damn it." She rifled through the glove box, failing to find the battery charger and realized that her only option was to get out and survey the damage. She glanced down at the new dress. "Just my luck."

When she cracked the door, a huge truck flew past, rocking the entire car and coating the windows in a dirty mist.

Katie slammed it shut and threw the cell phone into her purse. *Wrong decision,* she thought realizing how close she had come to having a man who could change the tire in the seat beside her. She thought about the "driving test" she would sometimes give a male passenger if he was especially cute. The Acura had a five-speed manual transmission and she would place his left hand on the stick shift and say, "Let's see if you can follow directions." She would then put her right hand down his pants, grab his joystick, and change gears by remote control.

Truck lights appeared in her rearview mirror and came to a stop behind her. Fear gripped her as she watched a man open his door. Ignoring the rain and oncoming traffic, he walked toward her car. He might be an off-duty policeman, or a psychopath.

He knelt down beside her flat tire for a second before approaching. She looked around the car searching for something she could use as a weapon and grabbed the heaviest thing in her purse; the useless cell phone.

The man tapped the glass, his mocha-colored face at her window. Rain had already soaked his dark curly hair, and water was dripping from his nose. She cracked her window and said, "Thanks for stopping, but I'm—" She brandished the cell phone. "My husband should be here any second."

"You have a blowout, ma'am," the stranger said. "Do you have a spare?"

"Uh, I suppose."

"Pop the trunk and I'll check."

She hesitated, wondering if he could get into her car through the trunk. The rear seat could be folded down, but it locked from the inside.

He smiled. "It's okay, ma'am. You can trust me."

Wasn't that the psychopath's motto? He seemed nice enough and good looking, but so was Ted Bundy. If there wasn't a spare, she wouldn't have to ruin her new dress to find out. She pulled the trunk release.

Within a minute, she felt the car being jacked up and heard the squeal of loosening lug bolts. She lowered the window enough to yell, "Sir, you don't have to do that." Another truck rocked the car, showering her face with specks of mud and the smell of diesel fuel. She raised the window. *If he's crazy enough to change the damn tire, let him.*

The rain slowed and she adjusted the side mirror so she could see what he was doing. To her astonishment, the man was on all fours, his legs in the lane of traffic. Trucks were passing within inches of them, yet he seemed unconcerned. *A total stranger risking his life?*

The car was lowered and the flat placed in the trunk. Katie looked through her purse, but found only a ten-dollar bill, hardly sufficient to pay the man for his kindness. The trunk slammed shut and the stranger wiped his hands on his now filthy jeans.

"That should do it," he shouted and gave her a goodbye salute.

Lowering her window again and waving the money, she yelled, "Wait a minute."

The stranger came back to her door. He was handsome, a thirty-something version of Denzel Washington. She felt ashamed she had not lowered the window further the first time.

"Yes, ma'am?"

"How much do I owe you?"

"Nothing."

"But your jeans are soaked. At least let me pay to have them laundered."

He laughed. "I have a washer and dryer."

"You risked your life. Those trucks could have taken your legs off."

She noted that he wasn't wearing a wedding band when he turned to watch a car speed past where his legs had been.

"It's a matter of faith, ma'am," he said with a smile.

"How can I thank you?"

"You just did. Have a nice day."

Within seconds he was back in his truck and had pulled into traffic. He had been a shining example of human decency and had said more with that single act of kindness than a thousand sermons.

I didn't even get his name, she thought as she started the car.

•   •   •

Huge letters on each side of the van proclaimed NBC-6 to its viewers. Harold Sanders unlocked the back door and closed himself inside. With a small key he opened a storage locker containing two video cameras, one older and the other almost new. He removed the older one, opened his black bag and took out a duplicate camera, pausing to check that they were identical. He zipped the station's older camera into his bag, and placed the duplicate in the locker. To ensure that the newer camera wouldn't be chosen, he removed it from the locker, held it about three feet off the floor, and let the $55,000 camera drop. The impact did little visible damage, cracking a UV filter and denting the lens cowling. He returned the broken camera to the shelf, making certain it was turned so the damaged lens would be visible the next time the locker was opened. He checked his watch as he locked the van door. It was 2:14 a.m.

•   •   •

Gerald McMullen had stripped out of his wet clothes and taken a shower before climbing in bed. He was tired and his flight back to Washington left at six a.m. He thought about the girl's left hand. No wedding ring. *My husband should be here any second,* he recalled her saying. That was smart, given her situation. People were naturally suspicious of strangers. But when she offered him money, her smile had given him an overwhelming feeling that she wasn't married. It was only a chance encounter, but Gerald had learned to trust his feelings.

Perhaps it was hopeful thinking, or the way the light reflected off the letters as he slammed her trunk, but when he closed his eyes, a clear image of her personalized license plate remained.

•   •   •

Wesley Heights, Washington, DC

The canvas-draped Corvette was parked in front of apartment 301 in building 4174. The man, dressed in black, emerged from his truck holding a briefcase. He lifted a corner of the canvas and focused a penlight on the candy red fiberglass quarter panel. *Drives a red Corvette,* he recalled from the file. *D.C. License plate, REBA, the subject's favorite singer.* He checked the personalized license plate and spotted the NBC-6 parking sticker. He returned the penlight to his pocket and gazed at the faint light coming from a second floor window. *Nightlight in the bathroom,* the man thought.

After moving quickly to the top of the exterior staircase, he checked to make sure no one was around then unscrewed the light bulb by the door. He opened the lid of the wall-mounted mailbox and pointed the penlight at the name, Chad Stillwell. *Subject is single. One cat, no dogs,* he recalled, picturing the apartment layout he had studied. *Single bedroom, second floor apartment. Door opens into a small den. Kitchen on the left. Bedroom and bath facing the parking lot.* No direct access was available to windows from the exterior staircase. The door's threshold would have to do.

The man squatted, opened the briefcase, removed a gasmask and placed it over his head. He inserted a length of clear plastic hose connected to a metal wand into the crack under the door and attached the other end to a small yellow cylinder. He opened the valve releasing the viral agent through the tube and waited. A clear, odorless gas containing a cocktail of a genetically altered zoonotic influenza virus, THC, and carbon monoxide flowed through the tube. It would give the subject a severe headache followed by flu-like symptoms. Since the bedroom was fifteen feet from the front door he had to use the entire canister to ensure the desired results. The whole process took less than a minute.

• • •

By 3:45 a.m., Raptor's van was outside the gates of a storage facility located less than three miles from the sponsor's apartment. With a gloved finger, he punched the entry code on a keypad and the gate opened. The rows of cinderblock storage buildings, lit by the orange glow of sulfur-vapor street lamps, revealed the pale outlines of numbers painted on the roll-up doors. Storage locker K-11 was identical in size to the rest. Harold Sanders got out of the van, carrying a cardboard box that contained the now disassembled parts of the station's video camera. The sponsor's palm print, lifted from a microphone in the van, had been placed conspicuously on one of the camera parts.

He inserted his key into the Master lock, removed it, and lifted the door. Inside the space were stacks of cardboard boxes, flags, tent poles and what appeared to be folded white sheets. He ripped open one of the boxes, removed a handful of brochures, and pointed his penlight at the cover.

A Message of Hope and Deliverance for White Christian America, he read. *Compliments of The Imperial Knights of The Ku Klux Klan.*

Sanders put a few of the brochures into his coat pocket. He placed the camera parts on a workbench at the center of the room and relocked the door.

• • •

The White House, 5:50 a.m.

As head of the White House Secret Service detail, Harold Sanders walked the halls with total confidence. He was tall and lean with salt and pepper hair, and a ruddy face, the result of severe teenage acne. He entered the press corps offices located near the rear of the Briefing Room and nodded to the fellow agent on duty. In his hands were two cups of coffee, and under one arm, a folded newspaper. He offered the paper and a cup to the duty agent.

"Thanks," the agent said. "You're here early."

"Got a call," Sanders said. He stood opposite the duty agent and looked down the hall into the darkened and near empty Briefing Room. "Something's up."

"Haven't heard anything," the duty agent said, taking a sip. "Good coffee."

"Yeah." Sanders watched the cleaning crew running a carpet shampooer near the podium at the far end of the Briefing Room. The rest of the room was dark. "They have Danish down in the Navy Mess. Want some?"

"I'm too fat already," the agent said. He put down the coffee and opened the newspaper.

"Nothing's on the morning schedule," Sanders added, noting that the duty agent was already involved in the headlines. "Must be the President."

"Maybe he's going to address this Argentine mess," the agent said. "Ever since the coup, their self-appointed president has been making noise about leading them into the nuclear age."

"He's a mile wide and an inch thick," Sanders said. "All surface."

"I don't know. They say his father was killed in the Falklands war and he keeps talking about taking back what's theirs. I guess we'll find out soon enough," the agent replied, never looking up.

"I'm going to ask around, maybe get some Danish," Sanders said, as he stepped back into the hall that led into the Briefing Room. "Be back in a minute."

"Okay."

Sanders watched the agent from the hallway for a moment. He was still reading, oblivious to anything else. Sanders found the cord of the carpet shampooer plugged into a wall socket beside the door. It ran down the right aisle toward the front of the Briefing Room between banks of video equipment mounted on various stands. He spotted the NBC-6 video camera attached to a tripod near the aisle. It took only a second to make a loop in the cord and hook it high on one leg of the tripod.

•　　•　　•

7:00 a.m.

"NBC-6," the receptionist said into her headset. "How may I direct your call?"

"Gina." The voice sounded weak. "It's Chad."

"Chad? You don't sound good."

"I've come down with something," he replied coughing. "Anything on the schedule?"

"The White House called. The cleaning crew knocked over our camera. The President is scheduled to speak at noon and we need a replacement."

"Oh, great!" Chad said. "There's no way I can make it, Gina. I'm sorry. I've thrown up twice already and have a splitting headache. To top it off, my cat died."

"Miss Reba's dead?"

"Yeah. She was fifteen. Died in her sleep."

"Oh, Chad, I'm sorry."

"Call Billy for me, will you?"

"Sure," Gina said. "Can he handle setting up a replacement camera?"

"He knows the drill. There's a spare camera in the van. He'll have to fill in for me."

"I'll take care of it," she said. "You should go back to bed."

"I am. Thanks, Gina."

"You take care, Chad."

CHAPTER 3

THE FOURTH ANGEL

It was a clear Monday morning, with a slight breeze to carry the scent of the freshly mowed grass into the portico of the White House. As the April sun climbed into the sky, the moist heat rose, hinting that soon the muggy days of summer would follow. President William Joseph Barnett had begun his day like every day, by reading a passage from his Bible. He had chosen an unusual verse; Revelation 16:8. The words seemed so appropriate that he added them to the first paragraph of the speech he would deliver at his noon press conference.

President Barnett was an honest pious man and vowed that he would once again make the office of President beyond reproach. He was a born-again Christian, a former minister, and an African-American—the first direct descendent of slaves to achieve the office of President. Barnett was fifty-six, married with three children. His youngest daughter, Alma, lived with him and his wife, Phyllis in the White House. Alma would soon begin her freshman year at the College of William and Mary. The First Lady, had taken Alma to Williamsburg for orientation, and they were scheduled to return the following evening. He had called Phyllis earlier but her cell phone signal kept fading out. At least he knew they probably had slept well and that Alma loved the campus.

Barnett had been up early, polishing his speech. Unlike most modern presidents, he preferred to write his own and he packed them with as many Southern clichés and jokes as he pleased. His admirers said it made him sound "down home," and his return to ordinary language caused a soar in his approval ratings after every speech. His critics rolled their eyes and sneered behind his back, but even they admitted that Barnett knew how to reach people.

He looked over the pages, committing them to memory. He moved the announcement terminating Norman Trexler to the third paragraph. He always considered his Secretary of Defense a friend, but the web of deceit Trexler had woven was inexcusable. Trexler had gone to great lengths to cover up the covert military operation called The Spectrum

Project. Even when confronted with the physical proof of its existence, Trexler continued to lie. That was the one thing that Barnett never tolerated. Trexler acted as though the operation was above the law and his actions were exceeded only by his arrogance. Trexler would have to go.

The President paused at a mirror outside the Oval Office to straighten his favorite blue tie, a birthday gift from his daughter. His shirt, white with blue pinstripes, contrasted well with his navy suit and dark skin and would look great at his next portrait sitting.

• • •

Special Agent Devrin Crosby entered Woodbutcher's Deli a little before his lunch appointment. He wore the trademark Hoover Blues business suit of the FBI, but his tie was loosened, the top button of his shirt undone. Crosby hated ties and couldn't understand how starting the day with a noose around one's neck had ever come into fashion.

The hostess was young and in deep conversation with a waitress. She ignored Crosby.

He cleared his throat to get her attention.

She reluctantly excused herself. "How many?" she said with all the enthusiasm of a mortician.

"Two," Crosby said, nodding towards a darkened section. "We'll take that booth in the back corner."

"Sorry. That section is closed."

"Then please tell Louie that Special Agent Devrin Crosby of the FBI would prefer to have his usual table in the corner," he said in a firm tone. In any other city the title alone would be enough to warrant a degree of respect, but not in Washington. This city was crawling with "agents" of this or that, and if the title meant anything to the hostess, she wasn't showing it.

"Just a minute!" she said through clenched teeth and disappeared.

Crosby glanced around and saw a table of young women look at him and whispering something among themselves with raised eyebrows. To his left he caught a glimpse of his profile in a mirror and the slight pouch above his belt. Instinctively, he sucked it in and heard muted chuckles coming from the table.

Within moments, the owner emerged from the kitchen, took the menus from the hostess with a dismissive nod. "Agent Crosby!" he said with a Greek accent. "Your usual booth?"

Crosby nodded.

"You have a guest joining you?"

"Just one." Crosby gave the hostess a smirk as they walked into the closed section.

She marched back to her station mouthing, "Whatever!"

"College kids," Louie said, putting down the menus. "They think they own the place. I'll send a waitress when your guest arrives."

"Thanks, Louie. He has wavy black hair and looks like a model."

"My pleasure."

While Crosby waited, he looked over the laminated menu. It was clean and bore none of the tiny brown spots roaches leave when they walk across them at night. Louie ran a tidy ship. With that assurance, Crosby considered the selections against their respective calories. His stocky build had added a few pounds since he was reassigned to the Violent Criminal Apprehension Program and started spending his days in front of a computer. Surely his friend, Gerald McMullen, had put on weight as well.

They had hardly spoken at all since the incident that had landed Crosby his desk job. During the first Gulf War, Crosby's Humvee loaded with wounded prisoners had gotten lost in the darkness and wandered into a mine field. The explosion killed everyone aboard except Crosby, whose lacerations had saved his life since the Iraqi's assumed he was dead. Gerald's helicopter was one of three sent out to locate them. When met with hostile fire, the other helicopters held back, but not Gerald. His courage was the only reason Crosby was still alive.

"Devrin?" a voice said.

Crosby saw Gerald standing a few feet away. "Hi Gerry," he said getting out of the booth. The two men gave each other an awkward hug.

"You've put on a few pounds," Gerald said patting Crosby's belly.

Crosby noted that Gerald's abdomen was flat as a board. If anything, he had lost weight. Crosby had spent most of the previous afternoon at the gym at Quantico in a vain attempt to sweat off thirty pounds in three hours. He sucked in his stomach as he slid back into the booth. "It's no bigger than *normal* people in their mid forties."

"You have a girlfriend cooking for you?" Gerald said as he sat.

"I work for the Bureau, remember? The only women in my life pack a Glock and can kill you with their bare hands."

"Some women think guns are sexy."

"Yeah, but their idea of a hot date is a five-mile run to a firing range," Crosby said. "So, how's your love life?"

"Who wants a beach bum like me?"

Crosby surveyed the room, expecting a sea of waving arms from every woman in the place. "I figured you moved to the Caribbean and were feasting on turtle soup."

"Someday, buddy, I'm going to find me an island with an all-female staff and an endless supply of soup and margaritas." He took a sip of water. "Speaking of which, how long has it been?"

"I've managed to stay on the wagon for almost two months," Crosby said.

"That's good to hear."

"Are you still at the *Post*?"

"That's one of the reasons I called. I flew down to Charlotte yesterday for a job interview. The *Observer* offered me an editorial position."

"The *Observer*?" Crosby said. "I thought you loved Washington."

"I don't have a choice. Mom's cancer returned."

"Oh . . . sorry, Gerald."

"Who knows, it could be six months or six years. Ned's moved in with Mom, but with his aerial business he can't be with her all the time."

Gerald's mother was Portuguese, his late father Jamaican, and his dark wavy hair and chestnut skin was the same as theirs. Crosby had met Gerald's mother and his brother, Ned, when Gerald won the Scripps Howard Journalism Award for his story on Gulf War helicopter pilots.

"I need to spend as much time with her as I can before the end." Gerald said, a hint of sadness in his voice.

Crosby changed the subject. "Does Ned still do aerial photography?"

"No, just traffic reports. It's steady work, and he also flies air-rescue choppers when needed." Gerald leaned closer. "The thing is, as soon as all of this is over, I'm planning on coming back to the *Post*. That's where you come in, buddy."

"Me? How?"

"Are you still in that tiny apartment near DuPont Circle?"

"Of course," Crosby said. "What else could I afford?"

"How would you like to move into my condo while I'm gone?"

"Right. On my salary?"

"Here's the deal. If Mom goes into remission, I could be in Charlotte for years. If I rent my place, who knows what will happen to it, plus I would prefer to have it available when I come back to town on assignments. It's three bedrooms and most of my furniture can go into storage. There's plenty of room for your stuff and you can use the spare bedroom for your piano."

"Sounds interesting," Crosby said, "but I can't afford it."

"If you cover the utilities, I'll lease it to you for a dollar a month."

"A dollar! What about your mortgage payment?"

"I'll be living with Mom."

"Yeah, but she's sick. You'll still have this mortgage on top of her medical bills?"

"Insurance and Medicare. She planned well. You would be doing me a big favor, Devrin. What do you say?"

"Can I pay a year in advance?" Crosby said.

Gerald laughed. "Sure. Deal?"

"Deal!" Crosby said with a handshake.

"By the way, my boss thinks I'm having lunch with my inside source at the FBI," Gerald added, "so lunch is on me."

Devrin laughed. "I've never leaked any secrets."

"They don't know that."

The waitress arrived. "What'ya havin'?"

"I'll take a Cobb Salad and bottled water," Gerald said never bothering to look at the menu.

A salad and water? Devrin thought. "What tha hell! Give me a Philly with extra cheese."

Gerald smiled. "No wonder."

•   •   •

U.S. Secret Service agent Harold Sanders examined the professional video camera carefully before placing it in front of the electronic scanner, which would X-ray it and check the lens for anything unusual. This was an old camera, not unlike thousands he had seen come through the White House security check before. A large label with the letters "NBC-6" was pasted on its side with the television station's call letters, WBC-TV. The station was a frequent visitor to the Briefing Room, but the cameraman was not their usual operator.

"Name?" Sanders asked.

"Billy Ray Anderson." He held out his press pass. Sanders examined it for authenticity.

"You have a driver's license or other ID?"

Billy Ray handed the agent his wallet. Another Secret Service agent ran a portable metal detector over Anderson's body as Sanders typed the name into a computer. Billy Ray's name popped up on his screen. His clearance was just over three years old, but his job function listed him as a soundman.

"Remove your shoes and belt and place them on the scanner."

Billy Ray complied.

"How long have you been assigned to the press corps?"

"Three years, two months."

"You're listed here as the soundman. Where is your regular cameraman?"

"He called in sick. I'm his backup."

"I'll need his phone number," Sanders said. "Have you ever operated a camera in the Press Briefing Room before?"

"A while back, but I usually handle the sound."

"You're familiar with the protocol?"

"Yes, sir. I'm the backup."

The station's NBC correspondent, herself being scanned with the metal detector spoke up. "Sir, Billy's been with the station for twelve years."

Agent Sanders knew the correspondent's face, and her comment added the credibility he needed. "Sign here," he instructed and turned his attention to the equipment. "Why the replacement camera?"

"Don't know," Billy Ray said. "I was told to pick up another camera before coming in."

The correspondent explained. "Your cleaning crew got a power cord entangled in our tripod last night. The camera was knocked over and damaged. Your office called the station manager this morning."

Sanders already knew this, but he needed the correspondent to explain it in front of the other agents for the record.

"Write that out on this form and sign it," Sanders said, handing her a clipboard. He looked at Billy Ray. "Turn on your camera, please."

Billy Ray picked up the camera, attached a portable battery from the camera bag and switched it on. The blue-gray light glowed from the viewfinder, and he handed it to Sanders.

Sanders put his eye to the viewfinder and ran his hand in front of the lens. He noted the auto focus and the remote zoom control. Both were common options on professional cameras of this type. He tested various switches, and they all functioned as expected.

"You may proceed," Sanders said, handing the camera, belt and shoes back to Billy Ray. He slipped a camera remote into Billy's jacket pocket while he put on the belt. The camera seemed flawless and short of taking it apart, he had given it an extensive examination. Spectrum's technicians had done an excellent job.

• • •

Norman Trexler returned from his morning jog and waited to catch his breath before calling Counselor. He had put off calling but time was running short. He punched a four-digit speed dial number into his secure phone and waited through two rings.

Senator Christian Luther's voice came on the line. "Yes."

"Counselor, this is Viper. Are we scrambled?"

"Yes."

"Have you heard from Raptor?"

"We are go. You are to proceed with operation SWEEP."

"*Holy Mother.*" Trexler mumbled. Even though he knew it was coming, the confirmation sent shock waves through him. His father had been a Tennessee congressman who had lost his seat in a bribery scandal and was now serving a seven-year sentence in federal prison. He remembered his father's advice: "Your reputation's all you got," but his reputation had landed him a view of a razor-wire fence from a six-by-nine cell.

Today could bring Trexler a similar fate. He struggled to regain his composure. "What are my instructions?"

"The documentation has been deleted from the subject's computer and replaced with an appropriate but harmless report," Luther said. "A backup copy of the speech has been removed from the private residence safe. The subject has the final copy on his person. Your objective is to secure that copy. A replacement is already inside the podium and will be discovered afterwards. Your window of opportunity will be brief. Use it and be careful in positioning yourself. This video will be studied frame by frame."

Trexler felt sick as he hung up the phone. One screw-up and he could spend the rest of his life in a federal penitentiary. He thought about his father, his wife and their daughter. How would they ever understand? There was still time to act. He could save the President and perhaps even himself. With a little luck he might even avoid prosecution, but he knew it wasn't an option. Counselor had given him his assignment and there was no turning back now. Raptor would make damn sure of that.

• • •

Crosby took another bite of his sandwich and listened to Gerald expound about his upcoming move to Charlotte. They had both attended the University of North Carolina, but never met while there. Gerald played varsity basketball, and his one claim to fame was that he had once blocked Michael Jordan's shot in a scrimmage game.

"My boss wants to know what's up at the Bureau?" Gerald said smiling.

"Not my favorite subject," Crosby said. "Let's talk about something else."

"What's wrong, Devrin?"

Crosby shrugged. "I'm thinking about leaving."

"Leaving? The last time we talked, you said it was the greatest job in the world."

"I was reassigned. Now I sit at a computer all day profiling suspects."

"When did this happen?"

"A year ago," Crosby said, "and I fell off the wagon soon after." He again thought of the red spots on yellow daffodils.

"So that's why you stopped calling," Gerald said. "What happened?"

"I'm not supposed to talk about it."

"Come on, Devrin. I'm your best friend."

"The usual reasons. I screwed up." He pictured the slamming doors of the surveillance van; the suspect with the briefcase ignoring the shouts to stop; the White House looming two blocks away.

"That's nothing new. Anyone who falls asleep at the wheel of his Humvee during the middle of a battle should be accustomed to screwing up."

"I wish it was that simple." Crosby waited a long moment. "I blew an innocent man's face off."

Gerald's smile vanished. "*Good Lord.* Were you sober?"

"Yeah, but I had to prove it."

"That must have been rough."

"It still is," Crosby explained. "We mistook his identity and I shot the wrong guy."

"That's an accident."

Crosby shook his head. "It doesn't matter. I gave the order. After the FBI screw-up at Ruby Ridge, someone *always* takes the blame. I happened to be the most convenient."

"Can you appeal?"

Crosby resumed eating, a clear sign that his part of the conversation was finished.

•   •   •

Inside the super-secure domain of the Briefing Room, Agent Harold Sanders checked his mic and earphone. As chief of the White House Secret Service detail, it was his responsibility to make sure everything was ready.

"Okay, people," Sanders said, his voice almost as rough as his face. "Five minutes. Let's call them in."

"Penn Avenue entrance, clear," the agent reported. A series of responses followed as each agent reported the status of their area and ended with, "Tunnel, clear."

Sanders notified the team leader of the President's security detail. "Scout One, Briefing Room is secure. Send in the clowns."

Through his left earphone, he could monitor the President's movements.

"This is Scout Three; POTUS is in the elevator. I repeat, POTUS is in the elevator and moving. Stand by, Scout Two."

"This is Scout Two. Back hallway is clear. POTUS is now leaving the elevator. Briefing Room, he's yours in sixty seconds."

"Roger Scout Two," Sanders said. "ETA in one minute."

Everything was ready. Sanders moved his hand to his waist and unplugged one of his microphones. He then switched on a second wireless set, encrypted and programmed to an ultra-high frequency. He checked his new equipment. "Scout One, do you read? Over."

There was no response.

"Scout team? Scout team, do you read, over?" He waited ten seconds for a response. There was none. If anyone was scanning the frequencies, the only thing they might hear would be static.

"Raptor." Counselor's voice was calm through Sanders' right earphone. "Signal is scrambled. You are authorized to proceed."

• • •

Their napkins lay in their plates, drinking glasses empty. The waitress had either forgotten them or was siding with the hostess.

"So what was that other thing you wanted to ask me earlier?" Crosby asked.

"It's a personal favor." Gerald slid a scrap a paper across the table.

"What's KT-GIRL mean?"

"It's a North Carolina license plate number. I was in a driving rainstorm in Charlotte last night and helped change this girl's flat tire. She was outstandingly beautiful! Only problem is I don't know her name or where she lives. All I've got is her license plate number."

"I see." Crosby smiled. "Still chasing skirts."

"I tried the DMV's website and hit a wall. I thought you might be able to suggest an agency I could contact."

"This is probably illegal." Crosby leaned forward. "But I might be able to get a name."

"I don't want to get you fired, Devrin. It's not that big a deal. For all I know she could be married."

"What the hell. I'm leaving the Bureau anyway. I'll see what I can do."

• • •

Harold Sanders spoke softly to minimize the movement of his lips.

"Roger, Counselor. Switching to visual."

Sanders reached into his breast pocket and put on a pair of aviator-type sunglasses. The sunglasses were standard Secret Service gear, and since a potential assailant could not see their eyes, the agents wore them inside as well as out. To the other agents, the putting on of the sunglasses had always been their final signal to Scout One that the team was in place.

But Sanders' glasses were different, and as soon as he put them on, his visual point of view was transferred to the center of the room. A virtual image filled his lenses, shot from a news video camera twenty feet away and tapped into the signal from the video control bank located in the back. The image showed the empty podium with the White House logo in blue and white mounted on the wall behind it. Sanders took an ink pen from his pocket and casually twisted the head of it to focus the camera's lens on the logo. With the pen, he could also make the lens zoom in tighter, but it had no control over panning from side to side. A remote pan control might arouse the suspicions of his fellow agents as well as the cameraman. The job had to look like the work of one man. Additional controls were an unnecessary risk. With only a click of the pen's head, the shutter would release at exactly the right moment.

• • •

Billy Ray's hands were sweating. This was his first time as cameraman on a live presidential shoot, and he was sure that he had forgotten something vital that might ruin the broadcast. If so, it would forever kill his chances for a repeat assignment. He knew how to do this, having watched the regular cameraman, Chad, for three years. He had been a soundman for twelve years, and this was his big chance to move up.

There was something odd about this camera, though. He was sure that he had switched off the autofocus, but somehow it kept refocusing as though it had a mind of its own. This was an older model, and it was probably a faulty switch. Chad must have dropped the newer camera he found in the van, so he was forced to use this one. It was heavy as hell, and he was glad it was mounted on a tripod for the duration.

"Billy, you ready?" his NBC correspondent said.

"Yes," he replied.

"Five seconds," the director called from the control room.

Billy put his eye to the viewfinder and pressed the record switch.

• • •

At the same moment a symbol in Sanders' sunglasses notified him that the camera was recording.

"Standby Counselor," Raptor said. "We are armed and ready."

•   •   •

Billy Ray watched as Tim Cook, the President's Press Secretary, entered the room followed by several members of the Cabinet. The chairman of the Joint Chiefs and the Secretary of Defense took their place to the right of the podium.

"Thank you for coming," the Press Secretary said into the microphones. "I'm sure you are curious about the nature of this meeting, so without delay— The President of the United States."

The attendees erupted with applause as President William Barnett entered the room. Beside him was a surprise visitor, the Reverend Jebadiah Johnson. The President shook hands with several of the reporters, took his place at the lectern, and waited for the applause to fade.

Billy Ray zoomed in for a tight close-up, but as soon as he tried for a wider shot, the lens refused to budge.

"This sorry piece of junk!" he growled into his headset as he tried to free the lens by hand.

"What's wrong?" the NBC correspondent asked.

"The damn lens is stuck!"

•   •   •

"Raptor, you are clear to proceed," Luther's voice said.

"Affirmative," Raptor replied, "but the Sponsor is jerking the target all over the place."

"Don't take any chances," Luther said. "Make sure it's clean."

•   •   •

Billy Ray slapped the lens with his fist and it started working perfectly, just as the President began to speak. He zoomed out for the introduction.

"My fellow Americans," President Barnett began. "I have asked you here today to tell you of a matter of utmost urgency. I have spent many hours in fervent prayer as I contemplated how to proceed. I've asked a friend, whose entire life has been devoted to social change through nonviolence, to join with me this morning. I'm proud to introduce the Reverend Jeb Johnson."

Reverend Johnson took the opportunity to shake the President's hand for the photographers and remained standing beside him for several seconds.

.   .   .

"Any time Raptor," Luther said.

Sanders tried to control his frustrations. "I almost had him, but the Sponsor is now focused between Barnett and Jeb."

.   .   .

Where is his speech? Secretary of Defense Norman Trexler felt a wave of panic flow over him. Barnett would often memorize his speeches, but if this one were to fall into the hands of the press, all of this would be for nothing. Raptor had told him to put on the sunglasses only if he had the speech in sight. *It must be in his jacket,* he thought and put them on anyway.

.   .   .

"As many of you know," the President continued, "I'm a firm believer in reading the Holy Scriptures. The Bible says that the truth shall set us free. This morning, while reading my daily passage, I came across a verse which I have deemed most appropriate for this occasion."

The President reached into his coat for his glasses. Reverend Johnson handed the President his Bible.

"I'm reading from Revelation 16:8."

.   .   .

The camera was back on the President, but the scene was so wide that the center of the target was on the President's neck. Instantly Raptor had an idea.

"Do it now," Luther said into Raptor's earphone. "Before he gives the whole damn thing away!"

"Just a second," Sanders growled.

.   .   .

Billy Ray's camera zoomed in so tight that all he could see was the President's necktie.

"Not this shit again!" The curse was just loud enough for the surrounding reporters to take notice. He tried to zoom out, but the lens wouldn't budge. His only choice was to tilt the camera up to the President's face and hope for the best.

.   .   .

The President read the passage with great reverence. "And the fourth angel poured out his vial upon the sun; and power was given unto him to scorch men with fire."

At that moment, Sanders placed his thumb on the head of the pen and squeezed.

•   •   •

Billy Ray's camera lurched and a ringing sound pierced his ears. He raised his head looking for the source, then he spotted something red sprayed across the White House logo. He put his eye to the viewfinder and repositioned the camera back to the lectern where the President's head had been. The lens was still zoomed in tight.

Blood and pieces of flesh and bone covered the formerly pristine logo behind the lectern. He tilted the camera down, the lens working perfectly as he zoomed out. A mass of humanity now surrounded the President. Secret Service agents were spread-eagled over him. Other agents brandished their automatic weapons, searching for a target.

The Reverend Johnson was once again kneeling over his martyred prince of peace, just as he had with Martin Luther King, Jr. on a motel balcony in 1968.

•   •   •

Harold Sanders already had his weapon drawn and pointing toward the crowd of reporters. The sunglasses and pen were safely tucked away in his pocket. The smell of gunpowder hung heavy in the room. Reporters cowered in small groups on the floor. Few of the cameramen were brave enough to still man their equipment.

"Nobody move!" Sanders ordered. "All stations, POTUS is down! I repeat, POTUS is down! Secure all sectors. No one leaves the building!"

•   •   •

Billy Ray kept thinking of Dallas in 1963. He had to keep his camera rolling. He thought of the Zapruder film, the only piece of evidence, which showed Kennedy's fatal head shot. His camera had been focused on the President's head moments before. It must have recorded the best possible image of the moment of impact. The tape could be worth millions and, if so, his name would soon become immortal.

Men were covering the President's body, but the images were powerful. The anguished look painted on Reverend Johnson's face; the bloody logo and the constant screaming. The Secretary of Defense, covered with blood, was holding the President's Bible over him and apparently gathering pages torn from it. The Secret Service agents, with their automatic weapons drawn, were yelling something and pointing their guns towards—

Billy Ray raised his head from the viewfinder . . . *They were aimed at him!*

•   •   •

One camera swiveled towards Sanders and he brought his weapon to bear on its operator.

"I said nobody move!" Sanders repeated.

Everyone seemed to drop closer to the floor, but the camera kept moving, turning its lens toward the agents, its cameraman ignoring the command in an apparent attempt to film the total mayhem. Other agents instinctively followed that movement.

Sanders spotted the evidence he needed; the frayed, burned end of the microphone windsock. "Gun!" he yelled. "His camera is the gun!"

•   •   •

Devrin Crosby and Gerald McMullen stepped out of the booth and shook hands. As they walked towards the checkout counter Gerald gave Devrin the note with the license plate number and a key to the condo so he could begin moving in. Crosby heard a gasp and glanced over at the table where the girls were whispering earlier. Most of them were visibly upset, hands over their mouths and makeup running down their faces. He followed their gaze to the silent television on the far wall. Displayed was a view of the White House Briefing Room with Secret Service agents covering someone on the floor. Other agents had their weapons drawn and were pointing at the camera.

Gerald turned and said, "What's wrong?"

Crosby's cell phone rang. He removed it from his pocket and noted the incoming number. It was the emergency call back number issued from the J. Edgar Hoover Building.

He looked back at the screen, saw the red smear on the logo and knew.

"What is it, Devrin?" Gerald asked again.

"My God, the President has been shot."

I hope that you have enjoyed this preview of
THE SPECTRUM CONSPIRACY.

The Spectrum Conspiracy has won 8 literary awards including the Beverly Hills Book Award's Best Suspense Novel, The Readers Favorite Gold Metal for Best Suspense Novel, and was a Shortlist finalist in the 2010 and 2012 William Faulkner/Wisdom Pirates Alley Competition and a semifinalist in 2011. In 2014 it was one of seven finalist in the Killer Nashville Silver Falchion Awards, and it's book trailer won 2nd place in the MARSocial International Book trailer Competition.

You can purchase the 357 page novel as a Trade Paperback and E-Book. It is available at Amazon.com, BarnesandNoble.com, and BooksAMillion.com. Also at www.bellarosabooks.com, www.CraigFaris.com, or at your local independent booksellers.

AFTERWORD

Thank you for reading *A Den of Rhyme* - a collection of short stories and one-act plays. I hope you enjoyed this collection, and if so, please show your support by writing a review on Amazon.com at www.amazon.com/A-Den-Of-Rhyme-Short-Story-Collection-Craig-Faris/9781622681716.

While reviews might seem unimportant, they really are the glue that parks a writer's butt in their computer chairs for hours on end. I really enjoy writing, but our lives are always getting in the way of completing all of those stories in my head. I especially like writing short stories, mostly because they usually only take about three days to complete, as opposed to three years for a standard size novel.

I would also like to acknowledge the book cover designers included in this collection. Many of the designs were created by my graphic design students at York Technical College in Rock Hill, SC. They are all excellent designers and their names are listed on the acknowledgement page in this book. I would like to thank all of them for allowing us to use their work within these pages.

Many of the stories herein are based on real events and tales that I have heard throughout my 67 years. As of this writing, we are in the middle of the worst pandemic since the 1918 Spanish flue took the lives of between 21 million, and more likely 100 million humans worldwide. I really hope that all of us will survive this terrible time, as I still have so many more stories that I would love to tell before it's my turn to leave this earth. I pray that each of you will continue to stay safe and healthy until that time comes.

For more information on my novel, The Spectrum Conspiracy, including reviews, book trailers, and video blogs, please visit my website at www.CraigFaris.com.

You can also reach me anytime at CraigFaris3@Gmail.com.

About The Author

Craig Faris is a forty-five-time award-winning author of fiction and plays, thirteen of which were First Place or Best of Issue. He has been published twenty times. Five of his short stories have won the South Carolina Carrie McCray Literary Award for Best Short Fiction, and his début novel, THE SPECTRUM CONSPIRACY, published in 2013, has won eight awards including the 2016 Gold Metal for Best Suspense Novel in the Readers Favorite International Book Awards, and Best Suspense Novel in the 2016 Beverly Hill's International Book Awards.

Craig served on the Board of Directors of the South Carolina Writers Workshop from 2000 until 2006. He was Vice-President of the Southeast chapter of the Mystery Writers of America from 2000 until 2005. He works professionally as an adjunct professor of digital design at York Technical College. He lives in Rock Hill, SC with his wife, Deena and they have two grown children, Katie and Charlie.

Published Credits

Echoes from the Ether, Best of Issue, 1999 *Horizons*, Anthology Collection, (juried regional competition)

Dawn's Last Gleaming, Best of Issue, 2000 *Horizons*, Anthology Collection

Last Run to Broad River, Honorable Mention, 2001 *Horizons*, Anthology Collection

Chaney's Gold, Best of Issue, 2002 *Horizons*, Anthology Collection

Through a Perilous Plight, Honorable Mention, 2002 *Horizons*, Anthology Collection

Broken Anvil, Best of Issue/Plays, 2003 *Catfish Stew*, Anthology Collection (juried regional competition)

Cinders in the Attic, Honorable Mention, 2003 *Catfish Stew*, Anthology Collection

Guatemala, Third Place, 2004 *Catfish Stew*, Anthology Collection

A Catfish Stew, Third Place/Plays, 2004 *Catfish Stew*, Anthology Collection

Drowning the Agent, Article, April 2002, *The Quill*, Published by the South Carolina Writers Workshop

Drowning the Agent, Reprinted June 2002, *The Scarlett Letter*, Mystery Writers of America

Drowning the Agent, Reprinted Oct. 2003, *The Midwest Chapter*, Mystery Writers of America

The First Book, Article, June 2003, *The Quill*, Published by the South Carolina Writers Workshop

The Wrong Way to Get Published, Article, April 2003, *The Scarlett Letter*, Mystery Writers of America

Silent Assault, 2005 *Catfish Stew*, Anthology Collection

Big Daze, 2005 *Catfish Stew*, Anthology Collection

The Spectrum Conspiracy novel, 2013 Bella Rosa Books

Den of Rhyme, 2020 SCWA *Catfish Stew*, Anthology Collection, 2021 *Cotton Alley Writers' Review*

The Ground Before Zero, 2020 *Cotton Alley Writers' Review*

A Den of Rhyme Short Story Collection, 2022 Bella Rosa Books

Additional Literary Awards

Silent Assault, 1999 Carrie McCray Literary Award for Best Short Fiction (State-wide juried competition)

Souls of the Abyss, 2000 Carrie McCray Literary Award for Best Short Fiction

A Pretty Good Year, 2000 Carrie McCray Literary Award for Best Nonfiction/Essay

Chaney's Gold, 2001 Carrie McCray Literary Award for Best Short Fiction

A Special Place in Hell, 2011 Carrie McCray Literary Award, 3rd Place Nonfiction

Den of Rhyme, 2014 Finalist, William Faulkner/William Wisdom Short Story Competition, 2012 Semifinalist, William Faulkner/William Wisdom Short Story Competition

House of Ruth, 2005 Carrie McCray Literary Award for Best Short Story

    2011 Fourth Place, (out of 11,800 entries) 80th Annual Writers Digest International Writers Competition

    2007 Honorable Mention, (28th place out of 19,500 entries) 76th Annual Writers Digest International Competition

    2010, 2011, 2012, 2014 Shortlist Finalist, William Faulkner/William Wisdom Pirates Alley Competition

    2014 Second Place, York County Arts Council's Literary Competition

The Ground Before Zero, 2020 York County Arts Council's Literary Competition

The Spectrum Conspiracy, 2010 Carrie McCray Literary Award for Best First Chapter in a Novel

    2010 Shortlist Finalist, William Faulkner/William Wisdom Pirates Alley Competition

    2011 Semifinalist, William Faulkner/William Wisdom Pirates Alley Competition

    2012 Shortlist Finalist, William Faulkner/William Wisdom Pirates Alley Competition

    2012 Semifinalist, Killer Nashville Claymore Thriller Competition (11th place)

    2012 Book trailer, 2nd Place, MARSocial International book trailer competition.

2014 Finalist (1 of 7), Killer Nashville Silver Falchion Awards, a contest with over 1,000 entries from major authors
2016 Best Suspense Novel, 4th annual Beverly Hills International Book Awards
2016 Gold Metal for Best Suspense Novel, Readers Favorite International Book Awards

CPSIA information can be obtained
at www.ICGtesting.com
Printed in the USA
JSHW051357120323
38820JS00002B/66